THE ACCIDENTAL
DATING EXPERIMENT

LAUREN BLAKELY

Lauren Blakely Books

COPYRIGHT

ABOUT THE BOOK

I've spent the better part of eight years resisting my best friend's little sister. What's one more week?

The hardest week ever when it includes a proposition to be her dating coach.

Eight years ago I fell into a secret summer fling with the bright, big-hearted Juliet before our lives went in different directions. Now, I'm the grumpy to her sunshine on a popular dating podcast we host, and when a wealthy fan gives us a charming coastal cottage as the biggest thank you ever, we head to the town where I grew up to give it a makeover.

And find the house has only one bed.

Located under a mirrored ceiling.

To make matters even harder, the woman I've been pining for tells me she wants to try to find *the one* and *would I please be her dating coach for the week*?

Like hell I'll let her date other men. I'll coach her on three dates *with me*.

But the second I take her out, I don't feel like her teacher. I feel like she's mine, especially when the first night ends with us tangled up together in that bed.

Each night we grow closer, but this dating experiment forces me to face my greatest fear – whether a man like me is worthy of her love.

Even though I'm already head over heels for her.

DID YOU KNOW?

To be the first to find out when all of my upcoming books go live click here!

PRO TIP: Add lauren@laurenblakely.com to your contacts before signing up to make sure the emails go to your inbox!

Did you know this book is also available in audio and paperback on all major retailers? Go to my website for links!

For content warnings for this title, go to my site.

PROLOGUE: THINGS I DIDN'T KNOW

Monroe

We don't agree on when this thing started.

We never agreed on anything. Not when we were younger. Not when we worked together. Not even in bed most of the time, but that only made it more fun.

But I'm telling the story of our so-called dating experiment, and *someone* has to pick a starting point, so it looks like that's me.

Maybe it began the day we walked into the house we were gifted. She'd disagree, of course, rolling those feisty green eyes and insisting it started with the suit I wore a few nights later.

You know. That suit, she'd say.

Well, I do look damn good in a three-piece.

But, with the advantage of hindsight, I'd say it began with the bet.

My intentions weren't entirely friendly when I made that impulsive wager that afternoon in the studio.

Not that I realized that at the time. For a smart guy, I didn't know much at all.

It took a cheese date, all sorts of mirrors, a can of paint, and a whole lot of role-playing in a small town to show me what had been right in front of me the whole time.

I should never have let her get away.

1

DATING IS MY SUPERPOWER

Juliet

A few months earlier...

He's so wrong. Monroe thinks he can analyze my prospective date for tonight, but my co-host is wronger than wrong. He issues his prediction from his podcast throne, jaw set, blue eyes steely, expression a little unnerving.

"I'm calling it now. There won't be a second date with this guy," he declares into the mic.

"Yes, there will. And not just because I'm overdue for a second date." I give it right back to the infuriating man across the sleek, metal table in the podcast studio. "Want to know why?"

"Enlighten me," Monroe says with too much amusement. "Tell all the Heartbreakers and Matchmakers listeners how well you think this date will go with...Who's the guy tonight? A gym bro? An art critic? A get-in-touch-with-your-chakras guru? A hot suit? You love the hot suits."

"I am a sucker for a suit," I admit. "But he's not a suit."

"A mysterious, inscrutable dark knight, then?"

I square my shoulders. "None of the above."

Ha. Not even close.

"Is he a hot nerd? You love the hot nerds." Monroe fake coughs as he mutters, "Slang for a tech bro bad boy."

Narrowing my eyes, I grip the edge of the table for a second, but nope, I don't give in. I let it go. I am calm. I am peaceful. I won't let him wind me up, not even for the "Predict Juliet's Date" segment of our podcast, where he always tries to push my buttons. Listeners love it when he does.

Besides, my recent string of bad dates is a relatable problem for single women. It's part of modern dating in your thirties. When you first join an app, you're a hot new release. But if you're not paired up and happily ordering monogrammed hand towels with your new love interest a few weeks later, the algorithm drops you to the bottom of the sea of single despair.

That's why I took extra time, did extra research before swiping in the lead-up to tonight's match. It's one I feel pretty good about, so I counter the know-it-all across from me with, "Tonight's date is with an artist, and we've been having a great exchange on the app about—"

"—poetry and wine?"

Grrr. "Song lyrics," I grumble.

"So, poetry then."

"But not wine." Details matter, after all.

"Don't worry. I'm sure he knows everything about every vintage. But the song lyrics? Yeah, that's a sign."

"Of what?" I ask, a little indignant.

"That you won't be headed on a second date together."

"Are you saying I'm undateable?" That irks me. It's not my fault the algorithm is evil.

Monroe folds his arms across his chest. "I'm saying he is."

Wait. What? How could Monroe say that? "You don't even know him!"

He gives me a look like, *Sweetheart, I know him.* Then, with a thoughtful hum, he strokes his lightly stubbled jaw.

That's a little distracting, because...stubble. Nice, golden-brown stubble, a little lighter than his thick brown hair. Also, the pose displays those tattoos on his left forearm. He lowers his hand, making life a little easier for me. "Actually," he says, "You might even cut out early."

Blasphemy. Utter blasphemy. "As if I'd do such a thing. I give all my dates a fair chance."

"I know you're not the problem. But why don't we take a listener on Mister Song-lyrics-and-wine's prospects for a second date?"

"Bring it on," I say. I love hearing what listeners think. They're always more hopeful than Monroe, but that's what I'd expect for a relationship call-in advice show.

Monroe turns to our wunderkind producer at the other end of the table. Sadie's in the studio with us for every episode, occasionally piping in with a sidekick comment but mostly running all the gadgets and doodads. "Sadie, want to work your magic?"

"I'm on it," she says with a crisp nod. Pink streaks of once-blonde hair poke out from under her rainbow-striped beanie. She hits a button on her keyboard, opening up the polls for pre-date voting while I take over the talking.

"And feel free, friends, to weigh in on whether I'll make it to a third date or even a fourth one. But I'm telling everyone, and especially you," I say, pointing at Monroe with a firm stare, "that I'm breaking my string of bad dates tonight. Want to know why?"

Monroe leans back in the chair, linking his hands behind his head, his eyes twinkling. Even the scar on his chin looks amused. "I really do."

I sit up straight with determination, visualizing the date unfolding wonderfully. "Because the guy and I planned this evening *together*. We've picked something we both want to do. We're already vibing. In fact, I bet we have so much fun tonight that the date lasts longer than planned." Ha, take that, Monroe. "Like a first date and a second date all in one. It's the extend-a-date plan."

"Wait. Wait. You're claiming this *combo date* is a thing."

"Yes," I say, chin up, bravado on.

Monroe shakes his head, his gaze calling bullshit. "You don't count a longer-than-expected first date as a second date. There's no such thing as a two-in-one combo date."

Sadie chuckles, winking at me. "Tell that to my girlfriend and me."

I smile at her. "See, it *is* a thing," I tell Monroe. Then I switch to an exaggeratedly gentle voice. "I know it's been a while since you've been out there, Monroe, but try to stay with me here. It's called... ExtraDate."

There's a curious pause from him. Brief. Then he says, "An ExtraDate, then. Okay. Fine." Monroe's smile is even more challenging than usual. "Care to bet on it, Juliet?"

From her producer's chair, Sadie whistles. "Oh, he went there."

A bet on how long my date will last? This is new. I won't back down from a dating challenge though.

"Sure. Bring it on," I say, wiggling my fingers his way.

"Fine. If it lasts more than an hour, you can ask me any personal question you want on air."

Sadie's jaw drops.

Me? I just blink. Monroe *is* serious. Those are real stakes. He hates personal questions. Ironic for a guy known as the Love Doctor, who started this advice call-in podcast meant to hit every stage of a relationship, from the matching to the dispatching. There has to be a catch. "And you'll really answer *any* question?"

Without hesitation, he says, "Yes. I will." Then, in a

voice peppered with innuendo, he adds, "I never leave a woman hanging."

My brain whirs with questions I could volley at him in our next episode. Like, *what do you really think when you walk into a date? Or what are you hoping for when you swipe? Or maybe do you ever think about that night we spent together years ago? The night you definitely didn't leave me hanging?*

But I probably won't ask that one. Because *I* certainly don't think about that night with my brother's best friend. I've moved on. I'll just ask one of the other questions. No big deal.

"I'm in," I say, accepting the challenge. Not only do I want to win, but I do want this date to work, dammit.

"And what do I get if I'm right?"

"You won't be," I answer.

"But what if he is?" Sadie puts in, the college-age producer herding two unruly cats.

"Fair question," I concede, then turn my gaze back to Monroe, ready to make my own offer. "Fine, then *you* can ask *me* anything."

I make it sound like a generous offer when, truthfully, I'm an open book. If Monroe takes this bet, he's a fool.

But that gleam in his eyes turns a little mischievous, and he reaches a hand across the table. "Let's do it."

After we shake, Sadie handles the phones, taking a few calls from listeners. "And we've got Eleanor Longswallow on line one," Sadie announces. "She says she has a very important question for the Heart-breakers and Matchmakers."

I brighten as Sadie gives us the signal that our self-proclaimed superfan is on air. "Hey, cuties," she says in a familiar, gravelly voice that feels like your grandma's hug.

"Hi, bestie!" I say. "Please tell me you're working on your tan."

"And drinking mai tais," Monroe adds.

"Only piña coladas for this old dame. Which brings me to my question—what should I pack for my...wait for it...honeymoon?"

I squeal. "He popped the question?" I'm giddy with excitement. We helped coach her through her burgeoning romance with the younger tennis instructor at her club. Guess it's burgeoned.

"Please," Eleanor chides. "I did. I don't have time to waste waiting around for anyone. I asked my honey, and he said yes, and now we're cruising around the world."

"Congratulations!" I clap my hands together. "And as for what you should take on your honeymoon, I believe they say 'less is more.'"

"Exactly what I was thinking." Eleanor cackles. "What about you, Monroe? Would you have bet on that first date of mine going the distance?"

"Absolutely. I had a feeling way back when that you'd be glad you went for it with him," Monroe says with a warm smile that's different from the smirks he slings my way. But that's fine. I don't expect him to needle listeners like he needles me. "Now, be sure to have a good time. And that's the doctor's orders."

"I will," Eleanor says. "And you two should be sure to enjoy yourselves."

She must mean on the show, so I add, "We always do."

We take a few more calls from listeners who mostly say encouraging things about my ExtraDate prospect, and then it's a wrap. Once we're no longer recording, I push back from the table and gather my things. Sadie tells Monroe she has some listener emails to review with him. That's his area, whereas I focus more on social media marketing, which means I'm free to go.

"I don't have any clients till four, so I've got some time," Monroe tells Sadie.

"Great." Then she turns to me. "Good luck tonight. I'm rooting for you. But I hope he doesn't talk about wine because that sounds snooze-inducing."

Time to play my ace. "Elijah and I will have no wine talk! It's going to be so fun. We're going to Zelda and Nico's Cheese Experience. It's reserved seating and ours is at eight, so yeah. The date is totally going to last more than an hour."

No one leaves the cheese experience early. It's legendary. Maybe I played dirty, holding this Gouda and cheddar intel back. But I don't care. Let Monroe eat his words when my date goes ExtraDate. Combo date. Extend-a-date.

But the cocky man just scoffs. "Doesn't matter. It's not going anywhere. You only do first dates these days."

I fume, my brow pinching. "It's not my fault! I keep getting bad matches."

Monroe holds my gaze for a good, long beat, his

bedroom eyes taking me in, roaming up and down until I wonder if Sadie should even be in the room. "Or maybe you don't pick the right guys," he says.

Nope. Not true. But I let him have the last word because I have something better coming.

A great date. I just know it.

I leave on a cloud of hope.

That's the only way to move through this prickly, harrowing modern dating world. Otherwise, it'll eat your soul for breakfast and barf it out like a cat yakking up a hairball.

2

IT'S A CUTTHROAT WORLD

Juliet

Is there anything better than cheese? Okay, fine. There are dogs, cats, orgasms, chocolate, good music, a steaming cup of tea, a soft scarf, and nights with friends.

But cheese is up there in life's top ten things. So tonight will be great because it's a cheese date.

I'm getting ready for it on FaceTime with my older sister from my cute little apartment in Hayes Valley. Mustache perches on the bathroom sink, tail twitching, eyes following my movements as I slick on some lipstick.

He's kind of into me.

"I have a good feeling about this one," I tell Rachel as I set down the tube then blot my lips on a tissue.

"Because you're the world's most optimistic breakup-party planner." Rachel is puttering around, watering plants in the home she shares with her husband.

"Just because I plan parties that celebrate a relationship's end doesn't mean I can't find love myself." I fluff out my brown waves and strike a pose to show off my red top and jeans, accessorized with platform sandals and a necklace with a ladybug charm Rachel gave me for my birthday last year. I went through a major ladybug phase when I was a kid. I still like them, which is lucky because family never lets you forget your childhood obsession.

"How do I look?" I ask.

"Younger than me, dammit," she faux grumbles as she looks me over.

I roll my eyes. "Like you're old."

"Older than you."

"Which you've wielded to your advantage every day of my life."

She waves me off. "Go. Have fun. I can't wait for the date report. But send me your location. Do you want me to call you in thirty minutes for an SOS?"

"Nope." I shake my head, certain I won't need a lifeline tonight.

We say goodbye, and I give Mustache a well-deserved scratch on the chin—one of only two acceptable cat quadrants for petting, even for a cat who's into me—then take off for the Thursday evening cheese-tasting extravaganza at the wine bar a few blocks away.

Zelda and Nico's Cheese Experience takes place behind the heavy brushed-metal doors of an industrial-style establishment, with exposed pipes and brick walls, servers in leather aprons, and some kind of music with ukuleles in it playing softly overhead.

Of course.

I scan the place, looking for Elijah from the app. Doesn't take long to find the graffiti artist waiting by the bar, wearing a black scarf and horn-rimmed glasses. He looks almost like his photo but a few years older. Okay, maybe ten. Or possibly a dozen.

But age is just a number, right? I'm not bothered by a slight photo mismatch. Or a not-so-slight one.

As I approach, he stares past me without recognition, like he's waiting for someone else. Hmm. Maybe I got him wrong? He did say he'd wear a black scarf, and he's the only one since it's, you know, summer. Still, he really seems to be expecting someone different.

Nerves swoop through me, but I soldier on. Maybe the prescription on those glasses is as out of date as his profile picture. Besides, what's the worst that could happen when he sees me? He'll pretend to be someone else? I'll deal.

When I reach him, I give my best, most cheerful smile. "I'm Juliet. You must be Elijah."

He surveys me quizzically for a few seconds before he breaks the silence with a strained, "Yes. I am."

Oh god. He hates my hair. My face. My nose. My... everything?

But then he seems to dismiss whatever is concerning him, and he pastes on a smile. "Good to meet you at last, Juliet."

He stares at me with a burning intensity. Not once, not for a freaking second, does he break eye contact.

It's a little much, but I'm not going to toss him out this early for a little eye contact. If I did, I'd lose the bet.

And, more importantly, the eight p.m. seating.

* * *

A folk singer croons about love and luck while Elijah and I discuss types of cheese. It's been a solid-ish date so far, aside from the extreme eye contact.

"Cheese-making is an art form, don't you think?" Elijah plucks a slice of Camembert from the charcuterie board, holding it up to consider intently.

"I imagine so," I say. "I would think it requires passion, craft, and commitment." That's just a guess. I don't have a clue what it takes to make this delicacy.

"And each bite builds on the next," he says. "A true progression in flavors. A good cheese tasting, then, has to be treated like a blank canvas."

As he waxes on, he continues to study my face. Like, lab-experiment-under-a-microscope type study. His eyes tour my forehead and down my neck as if he's cataloging my appearance for a scientific journal.

I don't know what to make of his level of interest, so I try to keep the mood light. "You'd need a cheese creator and a cheese curator. Are they the same though?" I ask playfully, spearing a small piece of Gouda and popping it into my mouth with a bright smile.

You can do this. He might stop sounding like a cheese douche any second now. If I don't give him the opportunity, how will I know?

A year ago, I would have cut my losses early. I ended romances that were going nowhere. Now I wondered if I should have given some of those "maybe" guys a chance while there were still a few non-wackadoodle men left in the dating pool.

But Elijah's not a wackadoodle. He's just intense. I focus on his good qualities like, for instance, he's clean. A recent shower is a nice change from my last date, who believed that daily showers were a symptom of the consumerist chokehold on the working class. Me, I like rebellions that start with soap.

Moving away from the danger of cheese elitism is the perfect chance to flex my dating muscles. I'm naturally curious, so it's easy to ask a question about his work. "Speaking of art, here's something I've always wanted to know about graffiti art. Do you sketch out your work in advance? Do you have to sketch it on a huge canvas, or can you scale it down?"

Elijah goes starkly silent for several seconds. Then several more. Funny, I didn't think that question was a stumper. Maybe my graffiti insight has struck him speechless.

"Everything okay?" I ask, just in case he's *not* thinking, *Graffiti questions and cheese, and she doesn't care that I'm a dozen years older than my picture? The algo loves me.*

Finally, he shakes his head like he's shaking off a daze and blurts: "I'm so sorry. But I thought you were twenty-five."

Wait. Why would he think that? "You...did?"

"In your pictures. On the app. You looked younger."

I blink, trying to orient myself to this next-level

"Weird Shit I've Heard on Dates." I've heard *I only date models*, *I just got out of jail*, and *Would you give me a bath tonight?*

But did he really just accuse me of lying?

No. He accused me of a worse dating sin in his book —looking old.

"They're literally photos from this year," I say, irked. "My profile says I'm thirty. Which I am. And all those pics were from the spring." Breezily, I add, "I'm a big believer in using recent pics."

Translation: I'm giving you the benefit of the doubt, but we both know I'M NOT THE LIAR HERE.

The message is lost on Elijah, who points a finger and eyes me skeptically. "In this one pic, you were outside on the ferry just before sunset. The wind was blowing."

"Yes, that's one of my profile shots. From May," I say pointedly.

"There was another at the same time of day, maybe at a rooftop cocktail party." He groans and drops his face into his hand. "I'm such a fool. I know what happened, and you're right. They are recent...but you took them at the golden hour. That's what tricked me into thinking you were twenty-five." He shakes his head, offering a weak smile. "I should have known better. I really can't continue this date."

"You're rejecting me based on good lighting?" I ask, struggling to process the absurdity of his reason.

"I feel terrible, but I do have an age limit. It's the only way I can survive online dating. My sincerest apologies." He holds up his hands in surrender. "Please know that I truly did try to look past the age issue because of our mutual interest in cheese. But I can't, and this is all my fault." He sounds genuinely remorseful now, so remorseful I almost feel bad.

Almost, but not quite. "How considerate of you," I deadpan.

His chair scrapes against the wood floor as he pushes back, readying to take off. "I only date women who are under twenty-six. You're such a nice lady. I'm sure you understand."

He says it like I couldn't possibly find this unreasonable, when, in fact, I find his rejection the height of dating bullshit. I'm about to say as much when a hand lands on the back of my chair, and I catch the scent of cedar and old books.

"She does understand," says a familiar masculine voice. "She also understands that you owe her an apology."

Is that really Monroe? Here at my date? I glance up at him, then back at Elijah, who looks genuinely perplexed.

"But I already apologized. Many times."

"Not for being a douche," Monroe corrects. "Say 'I'm sorry for being a judgy jackass.'"

Holy smokes. Monroe is stern. And bossy. And not at all off-base.

Elijah's jaw comes unhinged. He gulps. "I...didn't... Are you her boyfriend? Because I was just leaving anyway. Sorry, man."

"That's not what this is about. Say you're sorry."

I'm tempted to say this masculine show isn't necessary, but it's too delightful to watch Monroe school this ageist, cheese-ist prick.

"I-I'm sorry I was a judgy jackass," Elijah stammers. "Can I go now?"

Monroe scoffs. "Pay first."

Elijah squeaks—actually squeaks. "Of course, of course." He opens his phone, swallows, and meets Monroe's steady gaze with watery eyes. "What's your Venmo?"

Seriously? I wave off Elijah, ready to be done with him. "It's not necessary. I've got this."

"No. It is necessary." Monroe tips his head toward the bar. "Also, pay the damn bar, not me. I'll escort you."

Monroe guides my former date to the bartender. Alone for a minute, I contemplate my life choices. My bad dating streak remains unbroken, despite all my efforts. I brought my most positive mindset. I tried so hard to speak his language, to find common interests, and to look past his cheese snobbery.

Where did that get me? Feeling foolish and no closer to finding the one.

Maybe I should just admit dating is my kryptonite.

The man in the obnoxious hipster scarf rushes out of the bar, free to find a woman young enough to ride his ride. My prickly podcast partner returns to the table and parks himself in the abandoned chair across from me, flashing me a smug smile as he rolls up the cuffs on his shirtsleeves like he's just finished a hard day at work.

Great. Just great. Now I have to deal with Monroe

when he's not dispensing advice and saving women from bad dates. When he's just prickly, prodding Monroe with the inked forearms and the grin like he knows all my secrets.

I swallow my embarrassment and put on my armor. "Did you show up to rub it in?"

His smile widens, turns a little wicked. "Nope."

"To gloat? To collect your winnings early? Fine. You were right. He didn't even last through a special reserve cheese-tasting seating. You win."

Another shake of his head. "I'm not here about the bet. I showed up to make your day."

I'm not in the mood to wander lost down this road. "What are you talking about?" I ask, exhausted by these dating shenanigans.

He slides open his phone, swivels it around, and shows me a document. It looks like the title to a home in Darling Springs.

His hometown, where eight years ago I spent a summer that included one week of perfect dates and one fantastic night with this man.

A night we've never acknowledged since.

3

THAT'S A THANK-YOU GIFT

Monroe

She stares slack-jawed at the document on my phone. "Is this for real?"

Like I'd show up here without doing the research. "Fun fact—you can gift a house to someone," I say.

"Without them knowing?" Her eyes are wide.

"Yes. I googled it this afternoon. It's what's known as a gift deed."

The crease in her forehead deepens. "Eleanor gift-deeded us her house? In Darling Springs? Your hometown?"

Juliet's shock is understandable. I've had a few hours to process the magnitude of the gift. Sadie and I had grabbed a cup of coffee in the dingy café next to the bare-bones studio, where we reviewed the recent *Heartbreakers and Matchmakers* emails. Today's included this one from an attorney letting us know that Eleanor had sent us—in her words—*a little something.*

"Apparently, it's a thank-you gift," I explain, trying to keep my cool about this unexpected generosity. "She'll also pay the gift tax on it. I gave her attorney a quick call to confirm all the details. And I spoke to Sawyer since he's done some business in Darling Springs recently and knows the property value there."

Her brother isn't an attorney, but he is my college friend and was scoping out real estate there for his growing business.

"What did he say?"

"What I suspected—it's *the* hot small town."

After he confirmed the red-hot potential, he remarked curiously, "You and Juliet scoring a house from a listener? That's something I never thought would happen."

"You and me both, buddy," I said.

"Will you live in it? With her?"

I nearly choked.

"I live in San Francisco," I said, stating the obvious. I didn't want to tread anywhere near the thought of living with Juliet in any capacity. Sawyer doesn't know about our week-long fling all those summers ago. Nothing came of it, so there was no need to mention it, then or now.

Juliet still looks gobsmacked, running her fingers through her thick chestnut waves while she sorts through the words on the screen. When she raises her face, she studies me skeptically with those bright green eyes. "So you're really not here to mock me. To laugh, not with me, but at me?"

She's so doubtful it's kind of adorable. "That's your concern? I show you this, and you still think I came to tease?"

She gives me a *Why would I think otherwise* look. "That's kind of your thing."

"On air," I point out. I mean, it's a persona, all that poking. *Mostly.* But I don't want to talk about us. I want to focus on the *holy shit* gift that's landed in our lap. "It's not every day someone gives you a house. I wanted to tell you as soon as I had the details. So I was waiting outside—"

"Waiting for my date to flop," she says.

Now's not the time to hurt her when she's down. No need to tell her I was pacing as the clock struck nine, confident there would not be an ExtraDate, a combo date, or an extend-a-date.

"I came here *only* to discuss this house," I say and that's mostly true. Fine, the jerk in me likes the fact that her date went as I'd suspected. The jerk in me is also the reason I'm divorced, but I can't resist adding, "It just so happened your date was a douche."

She has the worst taste in men. She's also too nice to people. I'm not sure which is the bigger issue in her dating life. All I know is I wanted to stab that guy with an olive toothpick.

Fortunately, Mister Cheese Douche is gone, and I won't be arrested for attempted murder.

"And now we've got...a vacation home?" she asks, reading the screen to verify for a second or third time.

As she does, I steal a glance at her date attire, taking in the details of Evening Juliet.

That red top sloping slightly off one shoulder, offering just a hint of her pale skin, so tempting to touch.

Her eye makeup, a little smoky and seductive.

And that tempting lipstick she applied for someone who doesn't fucking deserve her. As her friend—okay, frenemy—and her co-worker, I definitely care who deserves her. So far, the answer is no one.

I reorient my thoughts to her question. "A vacation home but really an investment."

Over the last few hours, I've plotted a path, and I lead her down it now. If we sell this bad boy, I can finally pay off the never-ending medical school loans that I put on hold during my divorce a few years ago. Loans that are extra painful reminders that I only practiced psychiatric medicine for a few years before I admitted I hated it and switched to clinical therapy. It's an expensive way to learn your dad's goals for you are not your own goals.

We could also use some of the proceeds to grow the podcast. Maybe market it in new ways. I started Heartbreakers and Matchmakers a couple of years ago with a married couple. They provided the *real person* viewpoint, I brought the clinical therapy POV, and when Juliet joined she shared her fresh approach to ending relationships with grace and class. But when our married co-hosts moved on, Juliet and I took over the show ourselves, along with the expenses. It makes a little money, but mostly it runs close to the bottom line.

If we marketed it properly, I'm confident it could become a cash cow.

Juliet arches a skeptical brow. "I don't get it though. It's so generous. She always seemed like a gifty person, but this? This is big. Why did she give us a house?"

"I asked myself the same thing. Besides the obvious —she has excellent taste in recipients of expensive gifts," I say, which earns me a small smile, "Eleanor said we were the people she wanted to thank for helping her find love after she lost her first husband."

I pick up the phone and read out loud the letter that came with the deed. "Dear Monroe and Juliet, As I plan for my cruise, it occurs to me that I wouldn't be stepping onto this ship with Sandeep if not for the two of you. You encouraged me to pursue my heart's desire with, in your words, honesty, authenticity, and humor, and I can't thank you enough. So please accept this house as a token of my appreciation for the fine work you do. Perhaps you can even use it for recording the podcast. The show must go on, and I know it can't be easy putting out a labor of love every week."

Juliet furrows her brow. It's too cute the way it crinkles. "She's trying to pay it forward?"

"It's her thing. You're right—she is a gifty person. My quick research showed that she donated a new wing to a dog rescue in the city, and decades ago, a portion of the proceeds from her Christmas album went to a music school."

"She's a singer?" Juliet seems both flummoxed and delighted. "I mean, she did have a kind of sexy, smoky voice."

"I had no idea, either, because...why research a listener? But yeah, she is. I dug enough to get the basics. She's a very pay-it-forward person. I guess the goal is for us to keep the podcast going for as long as we want. The house money would help." I've got a feeling Juliet might not be as keen about this situation as I am. For all her optimism about romance and love, she's plenty skeptical about people and their intentions. She's like an onion. So many layers.

"But it's too much. It's so much," she says, full of the doubt I expected.

"You *can* turn it down," I begin, knowing she'll want all the details. "But you said the podcast has been helping your party business."

She blows out a thoughtful breath. "True. It does."

"And it definitely helps my business and the seminars I'm developing." Thanks to a partnership with a university, I've started teaching an online class on improving your relationship skills. I'd really like the class to *not* fail. I'd really like that a lot.

She's quiet for a moment, lost in thought. "It's a big thank-you, Monroe. Can we really accept it?"

I recognize the *want* in her voice. Time for a closing pitch. "We could go check out the house. See what it needs."

"Right. True. Maybe we were gifted a hideous pile of wood and tile that's only good for demolishing," she says.

"Or maybe it's a gleaming mansion," I say. "But we won't know till we kick the tires. I did look it up, and from the pics I saw on Zillow, I don't think the place needs much work. When that's done, we can sell it. Use the money for the next phase of marketing for the show. Zillow and I think the house could net us a decent amount," I tell her, then give her a number.

She mouths a *whoa*, like she's afraid to say out loud how juicy that number tastes on her tongue.

"And you could use some of it to expand your breakup party business," I say, sweetening the deal.

"True, true. Business has been good, but I want to go bigger. Reach new clients, work in new cities, plus expand into some new areas. Sawyer's been looking at my business plan, and he thinks the expansion is a good idea too. *If* I can pull it off."

"What sort of expansion?" I ask.

"Maybe it's silly, but my friend Aubrey had this idea to make a line of fun breakup champagne with names like *You're Better Off Without Him* and *I Never Liked Him That Much Anyway*. She's a hairstylist, so it's not something she wants to take on, but I really love the idea of a branded champagne. My brother does too."

I hum, mulling it over. "Breakup gifts. I like it."

"Yeah?" She sounds skeptical but hopeful.

"I do," I confirm.

She nibbles on the corner of her lips, clearly thinking. "And you could finish paying off your loans."

She gets it. Nice.

"And look..." I've been dreading this part of the pitch, but I have to power through it. "I need to go to Darling Springs, anyway. My dad's retiring, and his colleagues are throwing him a retirement party next week."

Her voice pitches up in surprise as she asks, "He's retiring?"

"I know, right? Figured he'd work forever."

"Same here. And you're going to his party?" She sounds wary. Maybe even a little protective of me. That's sweet but unnecessary. I can handle Dad on my own. I've been doing it since I was thirteen.

"I have to," I grit out. But there's a silver lining to returning home. "Maybe we can do any necessary work on the house ourselves before we sell it. I truly don't think it needs much, but I'm pretty handy."

"Which is weird. You know that, right? Shrinks shouldn't be handy."

I raise my arms, the evidence. "I'm a man of many talents. I know how to use my hands. I can fix things."

Her eyes pop, and for a second, I think she will make a naughty comment about being good with my hands, especially when her lips twitch in a smile. Instead, she says, "You just want the distraction from having to see your father." But her teasing is full of sympathy and understanding.

"Exactly. I usually take a few weeks off from my practice during the summer, anyway, so the timing should be good," I say.

What better place to spend one of those off weeks than the town where I acquired all my old wounds in the first place? Of course, mine are already healed, but it could be a good refresher, nonetheless. One I could use to help others.

"So, you and I would go? And what? Push each other's buttons the whole time?" Juliet asks, but she sounds like she's saying *keep convincing me, I'm almost there.*

"It's our favorite pastime," I say.

She snorts. "Speak for yourself."

"You know you like pushing buttons, Juliet," I say, goading her toward a yes, surprised at how much I want her to say that word, maybe because I want her to get out of the city with me for a week.

"Are you willing to bet on that?" she retorts.

"As if you didn't love the bet."

She rolls her eyes, then lets out a sigh. "Fine. I admit the idea of checking out this house is intriguing."

I pump a fist.

"Try not to be too excited," she says.

"What? I like money. So sue me."

"I like it too. Plus, my mom is nearby. I haven't seen her since the split," she says.

I give her a sympathetic smile. Having supported adults with older divorcing parents, I know that's not an easy situation to deal with.

She picks up a piece of cheese, pops it between those pretty lips, chews. Then she nods. "I have clients to meet with tomorrow, but nothing in town this upcoming week."

C'mon. We're almost there.

Aloud, I say nothing and patiently wait for her to get to "*yes.*"

She gives a decisive nod. "I have a party to host on Saturday afternoon. Let's leave on Sunday."

Yes. Fucking yes!

"I'll be at your door with the top down." I taste a

chunk of Comté and aim a derisive scoff after the long-gone Elijah. "He missed out," I say, and a beat later, I realize the double meaning in my words. "The cheese," I clarify.

She's silent for a few seconds. "Yes, of course. The cheese." She sounds defeated, maybe a little hurt. Well, that guy was a dick. It's a good thing I arrived in the nick of time. Because fuck men like him.

At least I know I'm bad news for a woman, and I've never pretended to be dating material. But guys who act like they'll be there for you and then aren't? Those guys need to learn their lesson.

And Juliet sure looks like she needs a break from all these city men. "A week out of town will do you some good," I say.

"Are you saying you know what's best for me?"

Ah, there she is. "That's my sparring partner."

"Yep. Ready to spar and push buttons. And now I should pay my bill."

She rises, grabbing her purse, but I wave her off. "Cheese Douche paid it."

"Oh." She stops in her tracks. "I'd have thought he'd protest."

"He did. He tried to convince me splitting the bill was feminist and that you'd appreciate his respect for women." She snort-laughs, and I add, "I told him insulting his date was anti-feminist, so he could damn well part ways with his cash. But if he hadn't forked it over, I'd have paid."

"You would have?"

I lock eyes with her. "I made it pretty clear that a

man pays for a woman on the first date, no matter how it ends."

Her lips part, and a breath of surprise coasts past them. "That was...nice of you," she says with softness around her mouth.

"Don't mention it," I say.

And I won't mention that I like the way she said that —*that was nice of you.*

Instead, we make our way out of the bar and finalize our plans to get out of town.

There are worse ways to spend a week than fixing up a house with a beautiful woman, even if that beautiful woman is a friend you should never have dated, even when you were young and foolish.

4

THE SLIPPERY DIPPER

Juliet

Last night while I was packing and repeating my mantra—*I'm regrouping while moving forward into my best self*—I had a fun little vision of this trip. I pictured myself looking all movie-star glamourous with cherry-red lips, big sunglasses, and a laugh like bells as the souped-up convertible flew along the Pacific coast, my hair blowing in the breeze.

That's how you road trip. You do it right, all dolled up, as your best self. So, for a hot hour, that was my plan.

Until it hit me—I didn't want to look like I was trying too hard, dressing up like I might for a date, especially after the other night's dating fiasco. So last night's me deserves a big thank-you for my travel outfit —jeans, a crop top, and a freaking hoodie because Monroe's electric car is like a freezer.

After we left the city, Monroe put the roof up and the temp of the air con down to somewhere between frigid and Arctic. He's not even cold. Of course not. The man's impervious to temperature. But if I ask him to raise it, he'll tease me relentlessly.

At the moment, though, my biggest problem isn't the subzero temp. It's connecting my phone to the car speakers so I don't have to subject my ears to any more news. I'm careful, though, as I try to get the Bluetooth working. I don't want the car to develop a mind of its own and start broadcasting my plethora of self-improvement podcasts. From *You 2.0*, to *Happier Now*, but especially to shows like *Up Your Dating Game*, I do not want Monroe to know what's in my ears on the reg. It's deeply personal, my devotion to bettering myself at love, dating, and being human.

"And in breaking news in politics today, Congress once again—"

I stab the dashboard. "I can't. I just can't. The news is the devil. I need show tunes, and I need them now."

Why does this Bluetooth connection require an advanced engineering degree?

"Show tunes," he groans as I fiddle with the buttons. "Are you trying to kill me, Juliet?"

"If I were trying to kill you, I would not give you any advance warning, trust me."

"You just did though."

I shoot him a look as he drives. "Show tunes won't kill you, buddy."

"It's been known to happen."

"Only among the weak."

He scoffs, shaking his head, but a damn smile teases those lips. Behind aviator shades, his eyes stay fixed on the road. "Then play the brassiest, most can-can show-stopping number you want."

I pat his arm. "I knew you'd see it my way," I say, when the phone finally connects to the dashboard, displaying a text from my brother.

Sawyer: Hey, knucklehead. Can you grab some of that citrus beach lotion from The Slippery Dipper? Katya is asking for some more.

I reply, *Yes, since it's for your girlfriend and not you*, adding a winky face, of course, because I'm not a dick. Then, the dashboard switches to the album art from *Moulin Rouge.* "Yes! I am victorious!"

"I see you've passed the car's entrance exam."

"I feel like I just built a rocket. Also, who doesn't have music on their phone?"

He points a thumb at himself. "This guy."

"Why? How? Are you even human?"

"Flesh and blood, baby."

"So why don't you have music?"

"Too hard to keep up on it," he says as the car hugs the curves on the road toward Darling Springs. "The musicians, the names, who they are, and so on."

"Let me get this straight. You don't listen to music because you don't want to have to research who sings it?"

He nods. "Yup."

"You don't have to know everything, Doctor." I usually only call him that when he's being obsessive about information. Which he often is. "Especially since you're missing out. Music is one of life's great pleasures. Right up there with good food, chocolate, and dogs." Then, in a whisper, I add, "and sex."

His lips twitch in a grin. "Sex and music on the same level?"

"Sometimes," I say.

He scoffs. "Sex should be better than music."

I shrug, doubtful. "It isn't always."

"You're having the wrong sex then."

I stare sharply at him. "Remember when I said you don't have to know everything? You also don't have to be a know-it-all."

He laughs lightly. "Fine, then tell me what music I should listen to. What's the musical equivalent of sex?"

Ooh, this will be fun. I rub my palms together and start at the beginning. "So many. You've got Bryan Ferry and Roxy Music. They'll put you in the mood. Then there are the stalwarts. Marvin Gaye doesn't hold back. Ella Fitzgerald is seriously sensual. You can go old school with Usher. It's hard not to feel sexy when you're listening to Bradley Cooper and Lady Gaga. Don't even get me started on Beyoncé or The Weeknd or Drake. Or Frank Ocean. Or Halsey or Janelle Monáe." I rattle off the names, not sure I can stop. There are so many. I may need to listen to some of my faves tonight. "Need I go on?"

Monroe swallows, a little roughly. "I believe you've made your point."

I shimmy my shoulders, preening a little. "Good. Want me to play some now?"

I kind of hope he says no. I don't need to get in a sexy mood in the car.

"No. Let's continue with the show tunes torture," he says.

Thank god. I hit my playlist, and the big, opening number to the jukebox musical fills the car. "There you go."

He grits his teeth. "I can handle it. I can handle anything."

"It'll make you stronger," I say. "Build your immunity."

"Excellent," he grumbles.

As the catchy music plays, I get down to business. "All right. What do you think we'll walk into in this house? I looked up the link you sent me, but do you think the interior is still the same as in the pictures?"

"As in shag carpet seventies? Neon eighties? And grunge nineties?"

"Yup."

"The decor might have changed since she bought the home. The pics were pre-sale to Eleanor," he says, always the measured one.

"Did she even live in it?"

"The attorney didn't say. He just said everything inside it was ours—the furnishings and whatever else is there. And Eleanor's at sea, and she didn't mention any more details in her note. Maybe it was an investment property of hers all along? And she felt it was time to offload it?"

"Perhaps." I clap my hands together. "Oh, I wonder what the beds will be like. I packed my pillow in case hers is uncomfy."

"I'm not sure we should stay in the house, Juliet. The inn still has plenty of rooms. I checked before we left," he says, and he sounds tense. He likes to know what he's getting into.

"Of course you did," I say. But I'm not concerned yet. There's plenty of time to make that call. "Let's see what we're dealing with, and then we can decide. We were just gifted a house. It honestly seems wasteful to book a room too."

He sighs heavily. He's probably picturing army-green shag rugs, old curtains, and musty closets. I should let him stew on those images. But I'm not *that* cruel to Mister Likes His Routine. "It'll be fine. Whatever's in the home, I know we can handle it. It'll be like when someone calls into the show for advice. We deal with it on the fly."

A laugh seems to burst from his chest.

"What's that for?" I ask.

"You. You prep for dates but not for life."

"Because I can't control what's in a house."

"But you *can* control a date?"

"Yes. Absolutely. You talk to someone. Get to know them. Figure out what they like. And, obviously, you carefully plan your outfit," I say.

As we near the small tourist town where he grew

up, we pass a wooden sign rising up in the hills, declaring, *You're Entering Darling Springs.*

Just like that, I'm thinking of our first date.

Eight years ago, I spent the summer working at the local bookshop in Darling Springs. I'd just graduated from college, and Sawyer had hooked me up with the job since he knew the owner. While there, I used the time to trek along the beach, and try to figure out what I wanted to do with my life and my marketing degree.

One day in August, I bumped into Monroe, Sawyer's best friend from college. Monroe had just finished medical school and had returned to town to see his father in the few weeks before he left for his residency in New York.

I'd met Monroe once or twice when he'd stopped by the house to pick up Sawyer for nights out during college breaks. But I'd been in high school then and hadn't paid much heed to my brother's friends.

We met again by chance one afternoon at The Slippery Dipper, a handmade soap shop on the main drag. I was reaching for the last of the heart-shaped vanilla and honey soap, and he was grabbing the shea butter and rosemary right next to it. I didn't see him at first, but when our fingers brushed, I jumped back.

Maybe I was startled to meet skin instead of soap, but *definitely* my fingers buzzed when they touched his. I met his gaze and drank in those blue eyes, the light stubble, the thick brown hair, a little messy on the top, and the playful smile.

Most of all, I noticed his devotion to soap.

He held up the shea butter and rosemary bar. "You can have the last one, Juliet," he said, offering it to me.

"Oh, I actually wanted the vanilla and honey. I must have reached for the wrong one," I said, thinking, *Chivalry is not dead*.

"That's a good choice too."

"Thanks. I'll let the vanilla and honey know."

"I'd appreciate that."

We bought our soaps from the friendly and delight-fully loud store manager and left together, pausing outside the shop under the awning with its cheeky logo of a woman enjoying a sudsy shower in a claw-foot tub.

I had a hunch he'd felt the same spark I did, but I wasn't sure what to do next. Was I too young for my brother's friend? I was twenty-two to his twenty-seven.

But the man didn't leave me wondering. "Want to get a drink, ice cream, soda, coffee, bowl, anything, everything, whatever you like?"

It was already the best ask-out ever, then he added, "Tonight."

Clearly, being his friend's little sister wasn't an issue —to him, or to me. That date at the local arcade turned into a fantastic week ending in an unforgettable night. The way he kissed me, touched me, talked to me, both dirty and tender...It was thrilling and arousing all at once.

But as we roll into his hometown eight years later, I *have* to shove away those memories. I don't want to linger on that summer, given its inevitable end and the hurt I swallowed and shoved into a corner where no one—not Monroe, not Sawyer, not anyone—would ever see it.

Besides, it only lasted a week, and I'm over it, one hundred percent and then some.

Monroe turns down the AC at last, and I steal a glance at him. He looks stoic as he drives along the main drag. He's probably not thinking of that time we shared. Like his dad, he's probably thinking of...work. Monroe's good at his job, and he helps people, so it's not the worst thing.

But it's for the best, then, that nothing came of our brief summer fling. We'd have been terrible for each other long-term. We want different things.

I want it all. He doesn't.

I roll down my window and breathe in the fresh seaside air, letting go of the bittersweet memory as we cruise down Main Street. It smells like warm days and breezy nights as we pass The Slippery Dipper, its awning freshly laundered, its sketch of the woman just as cheeky as it was that day eight years ago.

I half expect to see the store manager outside, sweeping the sidewalk like she did back then, offering boisterous hellos and pieces of life advice to everyone passing by.

If she saw us, what would she say?

I whip my gaze away, just in case. But as the shop fades in the rearview mirror, there's a tinge of something else in my chest.

Not sure what though. A bittersweet feeling? Maybe regret? Or is that a hint of longing?

Whatever it is, I'm not going to think about it too much. We have too much to do in the next week.

Like get a house ready to sell.

Soon, we're driving down a winding road into the golden California afternoon, the sunlight reflecting off the water as the GPS announces we're two hundred feet from our destination.

I'm antsy and excited, especially when the home comes into view. It's stinking adorable.

Thank god. I sigh in happy relief. This will be the perfect place for my dating regroup. I bet while I straighten up the house, I'll figure out the best path forward when it comes to romance. All that cozy will be good for my soul.

"It looks so much better than the pictures."

"It's a charming California coastal cottage," Monroe says, shoulders relaxing, white-knuckle grip on the wheel loosening slightly.

He slows the car on the gravel driveway. As soon as he turns it off, I fling open the door, then dart up the wooden steps to the quaint wraparound porch before propriety gets the better of me.

I really should wait for my...*co-owner*. "C'mon. Let's check out *our home*," I say, giddy now that it's real. I've only ever rented. I don't own a single square foot of space in the city. San Francisco real estate is far too expensive for me. And this cottage is Pinterest perfection with its freshly painted exterior, its picturesque wraparound porch, and its bright white door with the gleaming brass knocker.

When I turn back to urge Monroe to hurry, he's

right behind me, trotting up the steps. Seems he's eager too. He swipes open the screen on his phone, taking a moment to find what he's looking for. As he reads, I study the knocker. Is that a couple twisted around each other in an embrace? Aww, that's sweet.

"Here's the code," he says. "Six-nine-six-nine."

My fingers hover, poised over the keypad, and I look up, arching a brow at the naughty combo. "Sixty-nine, sixty-nine?"

"Yes," he says, completely deadpan.

"Okay," I say, then punch in the number, bouncing in my Converse as I swing open the door.

5

MIRROR, MIRROR ON THE CEILING

Monroe

In the doorway of the main bedroom, I stand scratching my jaw, trying to understand why anyone over the age of twelve would want bunk beds at all, let alone two king-size ones stacked on top of each other. I hunt for words and come up blank except for the obvious. The *only* thing to say, actually: "Why?"

Next to me, Juliet gawks at the double serving of bed. She must be wondering the same damn thing.

Except...nope.

She's not gawking. She's grinning, then running past me into the room and diving onto the lower mattress. "This is the best," she says, flopping face down, then moving around like she's making snow angels on the bed.

I'm still no closer to an answer. "Do you really want

to sleep staring at another bed three or four feet from your face?"

"One, I don't stare while I sleep."

I roll my eyes. "You know what I mean. Don't we outgrow the desire for bunk beds?"

"You're such an only child," she says into the mattress. "And no. Bunk beds are like birthday cards with money in them. You never outgrow that."

Damn. She's not wrong about that.

"Besides," she continues, "haven't you ever heard of fun? Kitsch? Nostalgia?"

"Sure. But that doesn't mean I want to sleep in a bunk bed."

She rolls over, propping up on her elbows to face me, but then she tips her head back. "Oh." The word comes out a little sensual. She points upward, a mischievous smile on her face. "Right there, Love Doctor. That's your why."

As I step into the room, I look where she's pointing. Wow.

The underside of the top bunk is a mirror. I'm intrigued, and I sit on the foot of the mattress next to Juliet, looking up.

But hold on. There's more of *us*.

I pop off the bed and crane my neck to see the ceiling, where there's a mirror above the top bunk too. I let out a low whistle of...approval.

I didn't see either mirror when I was standing in the doorway, but now I see both clearly. Now, I'm not considering the *why* of bunk beds. I'm contemplating the *why* of mirrored ceilings.

As if I needed an incentive to think after-dark thoughts of Juliet. Now I've got all these reasons reflecting back at me.

I take a few moments then clear my throat, trying to clear away the dirty thoughts. "I stand corrected. I get it now," I say.

"Then get back here and enjoy the full mirror experience."

I don't need the temptation of being next to her in bed. I've reached a nice, even Zen in our working relationship. No need to rock it. "I'm all good."

"C'mon Doctor Stuffypants," she taunts. "Remember? Birthday card with money. You just need to try it once."

"Twist my arm," I say, and I definitely don't hate being near her in bed. But that's sort of the problem.

I park my ass on the edge of the bottom bed again. That should be enough.

She grabs my shoulder, her tone excited. "C'mon. All the way. You have to see it."

Not helpful.

I lie back on the bed, keeping several inches between us. It'd be rude to lie too close to my co-worker. Also, I don't need the temptation when her eyes distract me every damn day.

They're pretty. Really pretty.

And, yeah, that's not helpful at all, seeing her and me, reflected back. Seeing her inviting smile, her bright eyes, her exuberance.

She sighs in contentment. "I'm totally breaking this

in tonight. Apparently, I get to mark something off my to-do list that I didn't even know was on it."

Don't think of her breaking in a bed, I tell my brain. *Don't you dare think of that.*

"Sleep in an adult-size bunk bed with mirrored ceilings. Yeehaw!"

Her excitement is infectious but far too distracting. I push up. I really shouldn't be in bed with her. Working with her on the podcast is manageable, partly because neither of us talk about that summer long ago. Why would we? It was just one week, and we both moved on. Partly, too, because I was fresh off my divorce when I joined the podcast crew, and I was far too prickly to wander down memory lane.

Then, we found a new normal—working together, goading each other, and now, evidently, testing mirrored bunk beds together.

Ducking my head, I get out of the bed. "Then, the main bedroom is yours," I say. Such a generous soul I am. "I'll sleep in the guest room."

Wherever that is.

"But let's check out the closet before we see the rest of the home," I say, recentering on our kick-the-tires-on-this-house mission. We need to see what we're dealing with in terms of furnishings and stuff.

As she pops up from the bed, I turn toward the door that must lead to the walk-in closet and yank it open. "Holy shit."

"What is it?" Juliet asks, joining me with a gasp. "Wow. It's like a costume shop. This must be the singer side of her. I bet she sang cabaret before she did that Christmas album."

"I bet you're right."

"Look at all the gowns and dresses and glittery things."

She strides right in like she owns the place. Well, she does. But damn, her go-getter-ness makes blood rush faster to all parts of my body. I take in the plethora of satin and sequins, feathers and beads.

In a corner, there's a hat rack that holds dozens of feather boas in precious jewel colors. Juliet snatches a ruby-red one and tosses it around her neck.

She spins around, juts out a hip, and says, "Why don't you come up and see me sometime?"

Then, with her lips tilting up in a sensual smile, she simply waits for my answer—waits and lets her hand graze down her chest.

Is she aware of how enticing that move is?

I answer her with a husky, "Yes."

Yes, she's sexy. Yes, she's sunshine. She's funny and witty, and she takes zero shit from me. And, yes, once upon a brief time, she was mine.

I've handled that in the city, even working with her. Now that we're out of town, I need to do a much better job of managing this...lust.

Yes, that's it.

It's basic, simple lust. I can handle lust.

"All right," I say. "We've got mirrored bunk beds, feather boas, and costumes, and we haven't even gotten past the main bedroom. What else do you suppose we have?"

At least finding out gives me an excuse to get the hell out of the danger zone without looking like I'm running away.

* * *

Twenty minutes later, my head is spinning. I didn't know a house could be this sultry. But this one vibrates and hums with pheromones. From the sitting room with the satin chaise lounges and wet bar to the den with the vintage oak desk and black-and-white photos of Hollywood legends in their sexiest poses, everything about this home whispers, *Let's go to bed.*

It's like the home is a goddamn aphrodisiac. I tug on my shirt as I go from room to room, getting hot under the collar. I tap notes into my cell phone—Things to Take Care Of. A few of the rooms need a new coat of paint. You can't sell a home with burgundy, cherry, and fuchsia walls. The kitchen's in good shape, but it's next-level cluttered.

We've been through almost the whole home. All that's left is the second bedroom, at the end of a hall-way, and I stalk forward to claim it. I'm going to need some serious distance from Juliet in those mirrored bunk beds, looking sleepy and sexy as she drifts off.

I tug the door open and groan.

Fuck me. It's unfurnished. Not a single thing is in the room.

Juliet comes up right behind me. "Oh. That's odd. There's so much stuff everywhere else."

"Yeah," I say hoarsely. She's so fucking close to me, I can smell her vanilla-honey scent.

She shrugs cheerily. "See, aren't you glad adult-size bunk beds exist? We can share a bed, and it won't be weird. Do you want to be on the top or the bottom?"

I stare at her, trying to form an answer that won't give away all my resurrected dirty thoughts. *Top, bottom, it's all good.*

I grunt something unintelligible, and she furrows her brow. "What did you say?"

Fuck. Shit. "Hungry," I say roughly, sounding like a caveman instead of just thinking like one.

She snort-laughs. "Or maybe hangry. You always do get cranky when you're peckish. Anyway, I'll take the bottom. You take the top." Then she tilts her head, tapping her chin. "Come to think of it, I might be headed toward hangry too. But I really want to look through those sequined dresses."

She breezes off, and I catch her scent as she goes.

I tug on my shirt collar again. Yeah, this won't be weird at all.

Think fast, Monroe.

"I'm going to grab some dinner for us, okay? I can bring it back here and we can work on a to-do list."

"Sounds good," she calls, and I fly out the door.

6

SPICE TOLERANCE

Monroe

My phone trills as soon as I put the car in drive. Yes! A distraction. If it's a spam call peddling new self-employed insurance, I'll take it. I might even listen because, hello, healthcare is a buzzkill, and I'll do anything to murder this buzz right now.

I answer without looking to see who's calling.

"Blackstone here," I bark as I head toward the road, the gravel crunching under the tires.

"Oh, I thought I was calling *Doctor Blackstone*. I'll hang up and try again."

It's Carter, my good friend and next-door neighbor, and he'll serve as a perfect distraction. "I don't often answer the phone with *Doctor*."

"Yeah, you do," he says.

"I don't," I insist.

"You do. Don't argue with me, I have recordings."

I peel out of the driveway and onto the road. "You don't."

"Always keep the receipts, man," he answers, making me chuckle as I cruise the winding road away from the unexpected resurgence of annoying desire.

"Anyhoo," Carter says. "I'm at your place, and what the hell? How many deliveries do you get?"

I'd asked him to bring in any packages I receive, so they won't pile up in the lobby while I'm gone. "Not that many," I say defensively.

"You've been gone less than a day, and there's already a ton of boxes."

"Wait. It's Sunday," I realize with a wince. The pre-season just started and I feel bad for missing a game. "Didn't you play today?"

"I did. Kicked the New York Leopards ass and thank you very much for not listening on your drive. It *is* on the radio as well as TV. We are Big Game winners." He can brag—he has the two rings to back it up.

"Yeah, well, I had to suffer through show tunes all the way to Darling Springs, so this is information that would have been helpful a few hours ago."

"Someone is prickly," Carter observes as I near Main Street. "What crawled into your coffee this morning?"

"Good question," I grumble, then I sigh as I brake at a stop sign, trying to breathe out some of my irritation.

There's a long pause, then Carter says, like a light bulb has clicked on, "Oh, shit. You just realized you're hot for Juliet."

"What? No." Is he a mind reader?

"Yeah. You did. And it's making you mad." He laughs, a deep, rich sound. I can hear him flop down on a couch. "The drive to your hometown was like a trip back in time, and you realized you haven't forgotten that week long ago."

"Why did I ever tell you about that?" I mutter as I take a right onto Main Street.

"Why don't you ask yourself that, Doctor?" he says.

But I know the answer. After my residency in New York City, I met Elizabeth, another psychiatrist. We went into practice together, fell in love while working late nights, bonding over the field we both loved, then got married. Trouble was, a year into our marriage, I grew disillusioned with psychiatry and the limited medical solutions it offered and became interested in the complexities of the human heart and mind. I wanted to change to clinical work, instead.

She said she felt abandoned.

I said I was leaving psychiatry, not her.

Then she said I already worked too much, invested too much time in patients, and that it was only going to get worse as a therapist.

And, oh, also, she wasn't in love with me anymore.

So yeah, that didn't work out.

"Anyway," I say, now with a sigh. "It's all fine. It's just fine. I can handle it like I handle everything."

"Yeah?" Carter asks.

"Yeah." I'm grateful he doesn't press. "So, what's going on?" I ask as I pull over near Clementine's, a new tapas bar in town. I looked it up in advance, betting Juliet would like it.

"Mostly I just wanted to know where you want me to leave all your Well-Groomed Man of the Month supplies."

I groan. I'd forgotten that was arriving today.

"Like, should I unpack them and set them up on the vanity so they're ready for you? Looks like"—he pauses, gearing up to mock me—"shaving cream, cologne, and fancy soap in here."

"Kitchen is fine," I mutter.

"You sure? I want to provide excellent service as your building concierge during your trip."

"Fuck off," I say.

"But wait. Should I sign up for this too? I mean, this shit is cool. It's all cruelty-free and plant-based, the box says."

"Yes, try it sometime." Why did I ask him to pick up my things? Oh, right. Because the building management hates it when shit piles up.

"I think I will. Also, good luck with your crush, man. That can't be easy."

I appreciate the acknowledgement. But it's not a crush. Nope. "It's just nostalgia, that's all. I'll be fine."

He chuckles. "Whatever you say."

We end the call, and I get out of the car, grateful that I've gotten some breathing room from the house. I roll my shoulders, loosening my muscles before I head inside, where I grab a brushed metal stool at the bar. The counter looks like it's made of reclaimed wood. The walls are warm, exposed brick. I like the vibe, and it's a new spot, so the proprietor probably won't know me. Perfect. I'll order some food, bring it back to Juliet, and it'll be a fresh start. And while I wait, I'll read my book on how to help clients who over-research every-thing on the Internet.

That'll be all I'll need to unwind.

The woman behind the bar strides my way. She has a pierced lip and a closely shaved head. Bracelets jangle up and down the deep brown skin of her arms. With a confident tilt of her head, she says, "I'm Clem, and you look like you need a drink."

I laugh mirthlessly. "That obvious?"

She holds up a thumb and forefinger. "Only a little."

"And I was hoping I appeared less tense."

"If you want to be less tense, I highly recommend the spicy olive mix. Locally grown olives with farm-to-table chili peppers. A little olive oil and salt takes your mind off the day."

"I'm sold. But no drink. I'm driving. I'll place an order for takeout."

"Sounds good," she says and taps the placard with the QR code to start an order. "I'll get those olives fired up."

As she heads to the open kitchen to give the order, I pick a meal for myself then a salad and a risotto dish I think Juliet will like.

Juliet, my friend.

Juliet, my co-worker.

Juliet, the woman I was gifted a house with.

I take a deep breath, finally, *finally* feeling like my momentary bout of lust has burned off. I am all good.

After Clem brings the olive and pepper mix, I

munch on a few Castelvetranos as I return to my book. A few minutes later, a throat clears behind me.

"Monroe?"

Shit. I turn toward the familiar voice. Yup. That's my dad alright, shrewd blue eyes crinkled at the corner, gray hair thick like a lucky motherfucker, and questions—always questions—in his tone.

"Hello, Doctor Blackstone," I say.

"Hello, son." His head is tilted as if he can't believe I'm here. I RSVPed to his party, but I didn't tell him I was coming early. "You're back in town already?"

I square my shoulders. "Yes, I am."

"The party's not for a week."

"I'm aware. I'll be here for the week." I don't share the details.

He blinks like he can't make sense of me, which is standard for us. Then, he seems to remember that fathers hug sons, and he comes in for an uncomfortable embrace, punctuated with staccato back claps. It has to be as awkward for him as it is for me.

He steps back, glancing at the stool next to mine. "I'm meeting a friend here in a few minutes, but I'll join you till she arrives."

"Great," I say, pasting on a smile.

There's an uncomfortable silence for a few moments. "I was surprised to see you. I wouldn't have thought you could take a random week off. I suppose your new line of work allows you more free time."

My jaw ticks.

Here we go again.

Down *Therapy Isn't as Tough as Medicine* Road and then onto *Should Have Been a Practicing Medical Doctor* Lane. The street he always travels.

"I do have appointments."

"Right, right," he says, amiable at first, then sliding back to critical. "I just mean it's different, having a session versus a—"

"Surgery?"

He smiles, sort of self-deprecating, but there's nothing truly unpretentious about the surgeon who practices at the prestigious university on the outskirts of town.

A guy whose reputation is sterling. Whose colleagues adore him. Whose protégés think he walks on water. A man who put his entire heart and soul into medicine after his wife—my mother—died unexpectedly when I was thirteen.

"I'm taking a week off to—" I stop. Don't want to mention the class I'm developing, the house we were given, or any of the things I'm doing that aren't good enough. He has a way of making me feel like an ant under a magnifying glass on a sunny day, insignificant and scrutinized at the same time.

"—to work on some online studies," I finally say.

He nods a few times like he's giving it some thought. "Good. Good. Education is good."

We have *so much* to say to each other. "Yup."

More silence as my dad fiddles with a napkin. Then, he clears his throat awkwardly. "We should have lunch while you're here. Better yet, dinner. Or play a round of golf. Did you ever learn to play golf?"

Yes. But I learned because my friends play golf—Carter, Sawyer, and our bar-owning buddy Gage. We play because it's fun. My dad wanted me to learn because *doctors need an outlet to relieve stress.*

But therapists? I don't even want to hear how low stress he thinks that job is.

"Lunch works," I say.

"Or golf. I've got a standing tee time on Wednesday."

I'm saved from any more invites when Clem returns, giving him a bright smile. "Doctor Blackstone. Good to see you." Her tone is playful. "Here I was thinking you'd left me for another tapas bar."

"It's only been a few days," he says, amiable once more. "And I'd never leave."

"Whew. Thank god," she says.

I'm pissed now that this place isn't mine. It's his. Like this whole damn town.

Then, Clem turns to me and plunks a brown paper to-go bag on the bar. "Here you go. If you love it like I know you will, be sure to leave a review."

She flashes a warm smile, and I can't be pissed at her. She's just a good businesswoman. "I will. The olives were great."

She looks down at the small bowl in front of me. "Want me to pack up the rest of those for you to go?"

Dad looks at the dish with skepticism. "You like peppers now? You always hated spicy things as a kid. I didn't think you'd ever develop a spice tolerance."

He says it like "develop a spice tolerance" is code for "grow the fuck up."

"I did," I say. "And yes, I'll take them, thanks."

But before Clem picks up the dish, I fish around for a little red pepper, pop it in my mouth, and let that spicy vegetable burn my tongue. It's a little five-alarm fire, but I don't let on. I just smile and eat, then say goodbye.

7

THE HORNY HOUSE

Juliet

The stars flicker brightly in the beautiful night sky, visible through the kitchen window as I scrub the last bowl to a shine. Nope. There's a remnant of dinner still on it. I attack the risotto speck, and then, victorious at last, I set it on the drying rack.

"That's done." I hang up the towel next to a white wooden cupboard. "Is the kitchen the *only* room in The Horny House that doesn't feel like a retro brothel?"

Monroe is sorting the takeout containers into compostable and recyclable.

"That's your name for it?" he asks as he folds up the paper bag.

He seems ultra-focused too. The dinner he brought back—a mouthwatering asparagus risotto and a delish arugula salad for this vegetarian, and chickpea cakes and seared salmon for him—took care of the *hangry* in both of us. While we ate, we tackled his preliminary notes from earlier, and he mentioned that he ran into his dad. He didn't share details, but I figured that was why he needed to zero in on tasks.

By the time we'd finished eating, we had the start of a plan for the house and a list of everything we needed to accomplish. I contacted a realtor who we'll meet with at the end of the week. While we're here, we'll paint some of the rooms, and there's *so much* sorting to do. Monroe was out hunting and gathering when I found another room at the end of the hallway, sort of a small storage room full of mirrors—mirrors with scalloped edges, with gilt frames, with exposed light bulbs.

I sweep a hand toward the rest of the home. "I'm honestly surprised there's not a stripper pole somewhere in here."

He smiles at that and drops the cardboard into the blue plastic bin. "Me too. I figured there'd be one on the garden level for sure."

"Just a few tables and a wet bar for your average Darling Springs underground poker game," I say, amused with the decor, then I shake my head, chuckling softly. "But good for her. Eleanor seems like—well, if the house is any indication—like someone who enjoys life. The gifting fits too. I think generous people are often the happiest."

Monroe cocks his head like he's considering that. "You're probably right. And she definitely seemed to be enjoying her new tennis instructor whenever she called about him."

"Definitely." I smile as I think of our favorite fan. It's

easier than thinking of the long text exchange I had with my mother while Monroe was out. But I can't keep putting off the topic, especially since Mom's partly why I've been winding myself up with worry.

"Hey," I say, in a vulnerable tone, opening up.

"Yeah?" he asks, leaning against the counter.

"My mom's coming to town tomorrow." She only lives twenty minutes away, so it's an easy drive. As soon as I mentioned I'd be nearby, she jumped at the opportunity to get together, which concerns me a little.

"Oh." He scratches his jaw. "That's good?"

I nod a few times, nerves winging through me. "I hope so. I'm worried about her. We're having breakfast in the morning at the café at The Ladybug Inn."

"I know that place. Good pancakes, but why are you worried?"

That's a good question, which I've been chewing on, not for a few hours, but a few months. "Their divorce was only final two months ago. I had to travel a lot for business, so I haven't seen Mom since they split. We've talked plenty, but I should have seen her sooner. Same with my dad, but he always seemed so steady, so certain. I'm more scared of how she's doing." It's a relief to give voice to that fear.

"That's understandable, especially when we think we might have to take care of our parents in some way."

I knew he was the right person to share with, that he'd get it immediately. "She was always so secure. So even-keeled. I'm genuinely nervous about the effect that divorce might be having on her."

"Your dad was always her rock of support, right?"

"Yes. I just hope she's doing okay. There wasn't even a big reason for the split, you know? They both said, repeatedly, it was amicable. They realized they just weren't right for each other." I'm still a little shocked when I repeat those words. "I mean, how does *that* happen? After thirty-five years?"

He's quiet for a moment. "Maybe that's why you didn't see her for a few months. Maybe you weren't ready." This side of him calms me at times, soothes me when I need it. He's masterful at getting under my skin, but he's also surprisingly good at saying the right thing.

Well, I suppose it's not surprising. It's literally his job. But I haven't told him the kicker.

"She said she had some things to talk to me about," I blurt out, twisting my fingers.

He tenses, eyes flickering with concern that he quickly seems to let go of, maybe for my sake. "Is she okay?"

"She assured me it was a—quote—*good thing*." I sketch air quotes as I imitate her. "But I'm still nervous." I lock gazes with the man I'm sharing a bunk bed with tonight, and his eyes are kind and caring. I'll need that tomorrow. "Would you come with me?"

His smile is as instant as his answer. "I will."

"Thanks. I'll text her and let her know. She'll be excited," I say, then I yawn. "I should get ready for bed. I'll see you in the bunk."

* * *

Hmm. I realize quickly that I didn't think this through. The whole bra-free lifestyle I practice at night, I mean. And really, what woman *doesn't* go braless as often as she possibly can?

I frown at my softly lit reflection in the bathroom mirror, plucking at the loose neckline of my sleep T-shirt. Yes, it goes down to my thighs. Yes, I'm wearing sleep shorts.

But...

The girls are jiggling and wiggling around.

They're not huge, though they aren't small either. Am I going to just sashay out that door, say *sleep tight*, then slide into bed all free-range?

It's not anything he hasn't seen before, one voice says.

I know, but we don't talk about that, the other voice whispers.

He knows you have boobs, the first voice says.

I roll my eyes at my reflection. Whatever. It's fine. We're not technically sleeping in the same bed, anyway.

I yank open the door of the en suite bathroom walking into the bedroom, then I have to grab onto the freaking wall.

Because...gray sweatpants, so help me god.

Monroe's bent over his suitcase, riffling around for something. He's wearing a T-shirt from his alma mater and sweats that make me sweat.

Dressed in a T-shirt, all his ink is visible. A half sleeve covers his left forearm, with a sturdy tree in the center. Maybe it's a maple tree? It's surrounded by flowers, a rich red rose, a deep sapphire dahlia, a tiny white calla lily. Sunbursts hug the flowers, coasting down his fair skin, and they're such a contrast to his by-the-book personality. It's rare to find a doctor with visible ink. I've certainly never had one. I associate tattoos more with artists, athletes, and bartenders, not with someone who's guarded, who keeps his emotions close to the vest.

It's not the first time I've seen Monroe's ink, of course. But it makes my pulse speed up just the same.

I swallow once. Then again as he stands, a blue shirt in his right hand. "Just making sure I had something nice to wear when we see your mom," he says.

The man plans for everything. My planner heart is doing a jig. "That's a nice shirt," I say, and I offer a smile that I hope is friendly. A nice friendly reminder that we're friends and colleagues. That I'm his friend's sister. That his sexy ink and low-slung sweats aren't affecting me.

Just like my shirt probably isn't affecting him.

Except when his eyes take a quick tour of my attire, stopping, no, lingering on my chest, I'm pretty sure my shirt is doing something.

But then he shakes his head and mutters, "excuse me" before he heads off to the bathroom.

That wasn't too awkward. I get into the bottom bunk, then stare up at my reflection.

This is an odd view. You don't normally look at yourself in this pose. My hair's fanned out on the pillow. My boobs are flattened now. Is this how I'd look if he fucked me in this bed? And do I really want this view?

Or maybe, the first voice says, *he'd want you on top so he could watch you.*

The second voice chides the first one with a *stop, just stop.*

"You weirdo," I say, then I grab my phone and click open my book, a workplace memoir about human-centered design that's really about how to be a better, kinder human. Perfect reading for tonight. I should aspire to be my best self here with Monroe, with my mom tomorrow. In general.

And a better human won't linger too long on gray sweats, sexy ink, or mirrored beds.

A few minutes later, the bathroom door creaks open, and Monroe returns to the bed, appraising it once more, shaking his head in amusement. "All right. Let's see what the bunk bed hype is about," he says, then heads to the foot of the bed and climbs the wooden ladder, giving me a perfect view of his gray sweats as he ascends.

He stops, though, before he reaches the top, his calves in my line of view. How are they toned even through his sweatpants?

"Why are you a weirdo?" he asks.

I groan privately. "You heard that?"

"Well, you said it out loud. I was curious."

Of course he was. And really, I don't need to hide the truth. Just to obfuscate it a tidge. "It's just that mirrors on the ceiling are weird. I'm not sure I want to look at myself as I'm reading in bed."

He laughs softly. "Pretty sure they're not for reading, Juliet."

I groan out loud this time. "Yes, I know."

Then he climbs up the rest of the way and out of view, settling into the big bunk bed above me.

He's sliding under the covers, then patting the pillow from the sound of it. He lets out a long sigh, then says, "Yeah, it's a little weird to look at yourself."

"Ha. See? I'm right."

There's a pause and I have no idea if the conversation is over. But a few seconds later, he says, "But I suppose if I was in here with someone else, that's not who I'd be looking at. Goodnight, Juliet."

My skin is hot as I manage a goodnight.

8

THE GOOD THING

Juliet

New day. New chance to be my best self. Just like Badass Babe would say in her podcast. Every day you can be a better version of you.

Today I am the good daughter version as I head to the back door to find Monroe. He woke up early—of course he did—and left a note saying that he'd be in the shed checking out *tools and stuff*.

I'm jittery, but at least I'm dressed, made up, and ready now, so I wander through the house texting my sister as I go.

> Juliet: Wish me luck. I'm going to see Mom in a bit. She said she has news for me. Anything I need to know?

> Rachel: Um…is this a trick question?

> Juliet: She said it was a good thing.
> Shit, is she preggers?

Rachel responds with a *Home Alone* gif of Kevin's shocked face.

> Juliet: Okay, not that :). But what do we think it is?

> Rachel: I don't know, but you'd better tell me after! I demand it. Also, how's the house?

> Juliet: It's sexy. Yes, that's apparently a thing.

> Rachel: And is it a good thing?

I smile, feeling a little less jittery as I reply with a simple *It's just a thing.* Because that is really all it is.

Then, I drop my phone in my pocket, and swing open the back door into the bright summer sunshine of a Monday morning. Across the emerald-green yard teeming with pink and purple wildflowers sits a work shed painted a deep red, like a farmhouse. The wooden barn door is wide open. I can just catch the outline of Monroe's silhouette, the cut of his shoulders, the muscles in his arms.

"Did you find tools and other manly stuff?" I call out.

Monroe emerges, holding a wrench. Not a bad look at all, especially in those trim jeans and a San Francisco Cougars T-shirt.

"Told you I was handy, and I'm going to prove it to you."

"Of course you are," I say, though I'm grateful for the morning distraction of chitchat. I'm still frazzled thinking about Mom. I want to make everything right for her. If only I could. I worry about her more than Dad because she's always seemed to need him more. "And what is this proof, Mister Handy?"

"I fixed the chain on the bikes." Monroe waggles the wrench.

"Bikes?"

"Those things that have two wheels that you pedal."

I huff. "I know what a bike is."

"Want to ride into town?"

"I thought we were going to drive?" Riding a bike feels like a project, and I'm not sure how many projects I have in me this morning.

"You're such a city girl," he says dryly.

"You're a city boy! You lived in New York and now San Francisco."

"But bikes are fun, city girl," he goads.

Maybe. But not when you're dressed and already nervous. I'm wearing jeans, platform sandals, and a crop top. My hair is blown dry, and I've traded out my ladybug necklace for my heart pendant today. Rachel has a matching heart one. Seems fitting for today's mission, a sign of sisterly support and all, though Rachel's the better daughter and has already seen Mom post-divorce.

"I'm not really in bike riding clothes," I say, then I

pat my hair, piling on the excuses. "And I did my hair and everything. And I'd have to wear a helmet."

Ugh. I sound like I'm terrified of riding a bike. But the truth is I'm not one of those girls who looks good after a workout. Pretty sure the women Monroe usually dates *do* though.

Not that I've looked them *all* up. But if I had looked up a few on Instagram, I could have said with confidence his dates are the kind of women who can cruise along the boardwalk on a mint green bike, singing folk songs in a perfect soprano pitch, and still look fabulous even without a stitch of makeup on.

Me? I don't leave the gym dewy and rose-cheeked. I leave sweaty and panting. I'm already nervous. I don't need to add to that.

But Monroe's in a teasing mood it seems, since he advances toward me, saying, "You can tell me the truth." He's striding across the lawn with a sly smile curving his lips, mirth in his eyes.

"What truth?" I counter.

"That you don't know how to ride a bike."

I scoff. "Shut up. I do."

"It's okay, Juliet. I can teach you. I like to teach."

No kidding. His entire online persona centers on teaching listeners about emotions. "I'm aware, Love Doctor. But I didn't think *your emotional fluency* includes how to bike," I say, sassing him right back.

"Bikes can be very emotional, Juliet. They take us back to childhood," he says, and he's not dropping the routine, but the playful spark in his eyes reminds me he's having fun.

"Then tell me your deep emotional scars from childhood caused by a bike," I tease.

But the spark in his blue eyes shifts. Turns to something more vulnerable. That's rare in Monroe, who stops a foot away from me now. "Well, I do have this scar." He points to the faded scar on his chin, a pinkish white against his fair skin. "Courtesy of a Christmas gift ten-speed when I was five. I flew over the handlebars when I was riding on New Year's Day. Landed face-first on the sidewalk when my mom was teaching me. Sliced my chin open. Needed to go to the ER for stitches. My dad stitched me up."

Oh. Wow. He hardly ever talks about his mom. "How long did it take for you to get back on?"

"The next day. Thanks to my mom."

I'm hungry for this story. "What did she say?"

"She said we could stop riding or keep trying. It was up to me."

That's kind of a nice story, and it's also good advice —the *up to you* part. Sometimes we don't truly make decisions for ourselves. Maybe even most of the time. "And you kept going?"

"Yes. And biking turned out to be my favorite thing to do in town," he says, then stage whispers, "even if it ruined my blow-dried hair."

I swat his very firm chest. Way for him to end an unexpectedly sweet story. "I just want to look good for my mom," I admit.

"I'm just giving you a hard time. Let me change and we can drive."

He wedges past me into the house. I catch a whiff of

his scent. He smells like the shea butter and rosemary soap he bought that summer. My mind starts to meander back into the summer memories, but then I latch onto the words he's just said.

Biking is his favorite thing to do when he's in town.

Monroe isn't an overly indulgent man. Yes, he likes his espressos. He enjoys his expensive scotch. And he likes his electric car. But he's not demanding or needy. He doesn't require a lot of watering.

Being here in Darling Springs can't be easy for him with the memories of his mother and the reality of his father.

What's a little sweat between co-workers? I turn around and call out, "If the helmet is pink, I'm in."

* * *

The helmet is not pink. It's fire engine red, and probably doing a number on my hair. But it turns out, The Ladybug Inn is only a mile away and the roads are flat, and my city girl mind was somehow—ridiculous, I know—imagining I'd have to crest hills and battle traffic on two wheels.

Instead, I'm enjoying the curving country road along the water, the sunshine warming my shoulders, and the sea breeze kicking up the ends of my hair. Soon, we're pedaling up to the inn, remarkably undrenched. That wasn't so bad after all.

After we lock the bikes on a rack painted with lady-bugs, I unclip my helmet. Monroe side-eyes me. Oh shit. Am I wrong? Do I look like I'm a leading candidate for slots one through five in a top-five BuzzFeed Bad Hair Days list?

"What is it?"

He steps closer, lifts a hand, then says, "Your hair."

I'm right. It *is* bad.

"Just a touch out of place," he says, then smooths out an errant strand near my shoulder. A tingle spreads down my chest. Now I suddenly want every strand knocked wildly around my face so he can fix them.

One more stroke of his fingers. One more brush of his hand, then he lets go. "There."

I catch my breath. My heart's beating faster, especially when his eyes take a quick, furtive tour of me, then land on my neck. "No ladybug necklace?"

I half expect him to fiddle with the blingy heart one. I wholly want him to. "Not today. It felt too matchy-matchy. I'm pretty sure Mom picked this place anyway because of my ladybug phase."

His smile is devilish. "You had a ladybug phase?"

I roll my eyes but *at myself*. "Yes," I admit.

"Did you wear red with black polka dots all the time?"

"For a while," I grumble. "I was in second grade... and third grade."

His smile is infinite. "That's—"

"Silly. I know."

He holds my gaze. "I was going to say...*adorable*."

The word comes out more sensual than its meaning. Adorable isn't just for children when he looks at me. "Thanks," I say, feeling unsteady in the stomach-flippy way.

But I can't linger in this fluttery little interlude. Time to set these shudders aside and face that weird place in every child's life when they become the comforters of their parents. I hope Mom's not in a bad place. I hope I can give her the support she needs.

We head into the café at The Ladybug Inn, where a silver-haired woman greets us wearing striped glasses and an apron that says, "I'm Pear-Shaped and Pears are Awesome."

"Welcome to the café at The Ladybug Inn. We have the best ladybug pancakes below the arctic circle—" She breaks off and her eyes pop out. "Monroe Jameson Blackstone! Am I seeing things, or is it the good doctor's son?"

His lips twitch like he's fighting off a cringe before he manages a smile. "That's me."

"Why don't you ever come back and see us?" She wags a finger, punctuating her playful demand, then scurries out from the hostess stand to throw her arms around him.

Monroe doesn't look as uncomfortable as I bet he feels. "Just busy in the city, that's all. But good to see you, Agatha."

"Ridiculous. You're never too busy to come back home more," she chides, keeping that hug going on and on.

Finally, Agatha releases him but not without a last reprimand. "Get that doctor butt home again soon. You hear me now? You should be seeing your dad more often."

Before Monroe can answer, I cut in, smiling

brightly. "It's just so hard for him to get away," I say as I clasp his arm like a proud friend. "His clients adore him and depend on him. He can hardly leave."

Agatha whips her gaze to me. "Where are my manners?" She quickly introduces herself, then says, "And of course his clients love him. He's a Blackstone. Now, were you after a table for two?"

"Three," I reply. She grabs some menus and gestures to a booth at the back. We follow, weaving through the charming café, where everything's decked out thematically with red tablecloths and little bug illustrations as well as ladybug art on the walls—photographs alternating with illustrations.

"Here you go. And you be sure to come back for Christmas. With your dad retiring, he'll have all this free time, and he'll need you."

On that do-more-for-your-dad note, she returns to her post. Monroe inhales deeply, then blows out a big breath. My heart aches a little for him.

"Ironic, right?"

With his jaw set hard, he meets my eyes. "When I was a kid and needed him, he was too busy for me. But no one knows that because..."

"Because they see him as this brilliant surgeon from Darling Springs," I supply.

"Exactly. He barely spared a second for me after my mom died," Monroe rage-whispers, "but somehow I'm not here enough for him?" Then he quickly shakes his head, like he needs to eradicate those notions or perhaps just gain some distance from them. "But enough about me. You ready to see your mom?"

He'd almost always rather talk about someone else. I smooth a hand over my shirt. "To give her a pep talk after a *breakup*? As ready as I'll ever be."

"Talk about irony," he says.

A laugh catches my attention, and I snap my gaze to the doorway. There is my mom, smiling brightly, laughing with Agatha, looking nothing like *Mom*.

Agatha gestures to us, and Mom breezes in wearing not-mom jeans.

A not-mom shirt too. And not-mom shoes. It's like she stopped shopping for clothes at the same store where she buys her groceries and went to the boutique where the cool kids shop. She's dressed in high-waisted flare jeans, a wine-colored scoop-neck top, and platform Converse sneakers.

Her bangs have grown out, and they're swept into beach waves.

"Hello, sweetheart," she says, reaching the table. I pop up, and she draws me into a hug. "You look amazing. Radiant. Glowy. Thank you for meeting me."

"Anytime and thank you. Also, what's with the fashion makeover?" I blurt out when she lets go. Because this whole glow-up is throwing me off.

"Oh, this?" she asks, plucking at the jeans like she's just noticed what she's wearing. "Thanks. I hired a stylist." Before she can say more, she turns to my companion. "I'm so glad you could make it, Monroe. When Juliet told me you'd be coming, all I could think is *that makes a good thing even better*."

What is this good thing? I need to know, and I need to know, stat.

"You're looking great, Harriet," Monroe says. "It's a pleasure to see you again." They've met a few times through Sawyer, but she also knows him from the podcast. "And it looks like divorce is treating you well."

I love that he doesn't say *I'm sorry you split.* He doesn't offer a sympathetic frown. Instead, he embraces the changes in people's lives. It's the therapist in him. But I'm having a hard time embracing this new fashionable mom who's dangling a good thing in front of me.

"What's the good thing, Mom?"

With a serene smile that would make the Mona Lisa jealous, she whips out her phone. "This is the good thing. I need your help selecting which of my many online dating matches I should go out with first. I've started dating, and it's so much fun."

Up is down, right is left, and my off-the-market-for-thirty-five-years mother likes dating so much more than I do.

"Who are you, and what have you done with Harriet?"

9

I'M NO GOOD AT TENNIS EITHER

Monroe

The problem with being a shrink is you can often, unfortunately, spot the emotions in yourself you'd rather not see. Like jealousy.

I'm actually envious of Juliet. I wish I had this kind of problem with my dad. Sorting matches, rather than dodging insults.

Instead of wallowing in envy, I give all my attention to studying the matches.

Juliet's mother swipes the phone screen once more with enthusiasm and natural skill. She's been showing us man after man.

"Just a few more." She swipes to a photo of a balding Black man with crinkled eyes and an easy smile. "Josiah owns a hardware store, likes to play Scrabble, and believes in being the best parent to his adult children and, get this, *his cat*." Harriet beams like that detail makes her day. "I like cats."

She flicks to the next candidate—a white guy with a full beard. "Darren here is a short-order cook who believes the best of life is ahead." Next, she swipes to a ginger-haired guy with a pale complexion. "Patrick is a professional photographer, but he's never been married, so even though he's very funny, he might be a player." She screws up the corner of her lips, seeming delightfully concerned about the playboy potential as she scrolls to a guy who looks to be Indian. "Then, there's Raj. He's a divorced dentist who plays pickleball, and, well, I play pickleball." She says it like that's even more wonderful than the guy in the cat fan club. "I always wanted someone to play pickleball with."

"Mom, how many matches do you have?" Juliet asks, gawking at the screen.

With a crease in her brow, Harriet hums. "Well, let's see." She clicks on her notes, where she's listed each man with a checkmark for Monroe, Juliet, and Harriet to rate his potential. She mutters numbers under her breath, counting.

"And the answer is—she can't count that high," I say.

Juliet's mom chuckles, then pats my arm. "I always liked when Sawyer brought you home." She shifts her attention back to her daughter. "Can you help? You two are the dating experts, and I just don't know where to start. How do I even winnow them down? There are so many." She wrings her hands at the quandary.

"Yes, it is a problem," Juliet says flatly, as if she can't wrap her head around her mom's entrance into the dating pool from a ten-meter diving board.

"With only an online bio, how can you tell what someone's really like?" Harriet asks.

Without her saying a word, I know what Juliet's thinking. She's a dating veteran, and even she can't quite tell. "It's hard to work that out," she admits sadly.

Harriet pats Juliet's hand. "Oh right, sweetheart. Whatever happened with the artist? Did you have your *ExtraDate*?" She sounds hopeful as she sketches air quotes. "But of course you did. You always had such good people skills. You're a great judge of character. When is the third date?"

There's so much genuine hope in Harriet's voice. It's fun to see the tree that Juliet and her sunny disposition fell from.

But Juliet winces, and my heart hurts for her as she says, "It didn't. We weren't a good fit."

She's too nice. Too kind. "He was a jerk," I bite out with a ferocity that surprises me. But the intensity fuels me too. "A cheese douche who didn't deserve your daughter, Harriet. He was a narcissistic, self-centered bad boy whose emotional growth was stunted at the age of two and whose self-improvement ended at potty training."

Harriet growls, going full mama bear as she whips her gaze to Juliet. "Where is this man-child? I'll give him a piece of my mind."

Juliet pushes her hands down toward the table, a

sign to let it go. "It's okay. Let's move on. Let's look at your guys."

But Harriet won't relinquish the post-mortem. "Don't let a bad date get you down, Juliet. And do *not* settle for someone who doesn't deserve you. You deserve the world."

Juliet sighs. "Mom."

Harriet turns to me, determination in her eyes. "Doesn't she, Monroe?"

There's no doubt in my mind. "She does."

But Juliet's had enough, shaking her head and pointing to the phone. "I'm on a dating break anyway. Let's focus on you."

Harriet's not quite convinced. "Are you sure you don't mind?"

"I've had a million bad dates," Juliet says. "I'm over it."

A million man-children. A million bad boys. A million guys who don't deserve her. That's part of her problem, too, I'm just realizing. She deserves someone who gives his whole heart. Who's open and open-minded. Who's funny and hopeful and kind. Someone who's capable of a big, bold love. Someone who agrees to ride a bike because she knows you want to.

That's why she said yes to the ride into town. Then, she stepped into the uncomfortable conversation with Agatha to prop me up in front of one of my dad's fans. And now, she's not even throwing shade on Mister Cheese Douche, who I sincerely hope slices jalapeños one night then forgets to wash his hands before he jacks off.

No wonder she hasn't met a decent guy. There's hardly anyone worthy of her. The odds are not in her favor.

Because she deserves the best. She *is* the best. As I watch her from the other side of the booth, a part of me wishes I could be that guy for her.

Just the small, emotional part of me though. The intellectual part knows I can't be that guy and is fine with that. With my dad uninterested in parenting after my mom's death, I learned to raise myself by only relying on myself. Now, I make sure other people have the tools they need for connection, love, and intimacy so they don't have to feel the way I did growing up. Love isn't my thing, personally. I've tried it, have the scars to prove it, but I also have the wisdom I gained. I'm not good at big love, as evidenced by my failed marriage to Elizabeth. But I'm no good at tennis, either, and I'm fine with that too.

"The right guy is out there for you. I just know it," her mom says.

"And for you too," Juliet says gamely, shucking off her earlier surprise. She grabs her mom's phone and waggles it. "Let's do this."

No wonder no one deserves her. It took only ten minutes for Juliet to turn her mood around.

When the ladybug pancakes arrive—chocolate chip, of course—we eat and select Harriet's dates.

She seems tickled pink with the choices. "That's three this week. Who knew online dating could be so fun?" She spears a piece of her pancake and eats it glee-fully, like she didn't just emerge from a merely okay marriage. Or maybe it's just that she believes the future is brighter on the other side.

When she finishes chewing, she clicks her tongue, her brow scrunching as she turns to Juliet. "Now, sweetheart. I know you haven't had the best of luck with online dating in the city. Why don't you try it here in a small town where you might meet a nice man instead of one of those workaholic city guys?"

Wait.

What?

She wants Juliet to date a Darling Springs dude *this week*? While she's living in Eleanor's house *with me?* While *we're* working on the cottage together? No. Just no. That can't happen.

Because...fuck.

Because it fucking can't. It can't. That is all.

Juliet offers a *thanks but no thanks* smile. "I'm fine, Mom. I just need to regroup."

But her mom tuts. "With a love doctor as your co-worker? Please. I bet together we can get you the best matches. Right, Monroe?"

I'm speechless. Because if I speak, I'll spew fire.

Harriet races on down the track. "Let *us* help you like the two of you just helped me. Monroe and I can find you some matches here and pick the best ones for you."

"I'll be fine, Mom," Juliet insists.

"But if this artist guy turned out to be a jerk, and you aren't getting to that second date, maybe it's time for a new strategy."

Yes. Yes! It is. Thank fuck someone else said it.

Harriet's eyes twinkle. "Just think. You can be my dating wingwoman. We can do it together!"

Juliet stares at her mother like she's gone mad. But as Harriet presses, my mind is whirring with a new idea to solve Juliet's date-picking problem.

10

DATING WITH MOM

Juliet

I stab Rachel's name on my phone and slam it against my ear. It rings once. "Answer, please," I mutter as I tromp toward Pick Me Up, the nearest coffee shop. I need caffeine, and I need sister time, and I need an answer ASAP.

I pass a tattoo shop dubbed Blue Roses, bustling with customers and displaying art with fine linework of vines, foxes, skulls, and blue roses. I'm wondering which came first—the art or the name—when Rachel answers.

"Hey! What's going on?"

I cut to the chase. "We need to talk. Now."

I'm still worked up. When breakfast ended, I told Monroe I needed to talk to a client and I'd get the bike later. I told my mom I'd call her tonight, and I marched downtown.

"Okay, talk," Rachel says. "I'm at the store, though, so if a customer comes in I have to go." I near the next block. A consignment shop called Second Time Around boasts vintage blouses in the window, but I refuse to look at the pretties right now.

"*Your mom* wants me to be her new dating bestie!"

Rachel scoff-laughs. "My mom?"

"Yes. *Your* mom."

"She's always my mom when you're worked up."

"Because she is," I sputter, building up a new head of steam, dodging a pair of older men power walking. "This is such a thing *your mom* would do. And I'm left to deal with it because you went out and got yourself married. You met a perfect man in Carter, and Sawyer's dating Katya, and I'm left to be Mom's dating buddy. She was like, *let's do it together.*" I pass a small-batch ice cream shop with delectable flavors like tequila and lime, and I'm pretty sure that's a need. A *tonight* need. Maybe it will help me make sense of New Mom. "And she wears Converse now. She doesn't wear mom shoes. Help me, Rachel!"

Rachel's just laughing. Or maybe chortling. Whatever it is, she's definitely doing it at me, not with me. "But you're the dating expert. So now you have to help Mom figure out how to date!"

Across the street, a pack of yogis floods out of a studio and into the Pick Me Up coffee shop. With an aggrieved groan, I turn at the corner, then stop and lean against the bright green wall of the town library, where the scent of lavender wafts through the air. It smells so nice, it almost relaxes me. *Almost.* I'm still completely baffled.

"I don't know who she is," I say quietly to Rachel.

She pauses briefly, then asks, "Is that really what's shocking you? Or is it that Mom's enjoying dating and you're not?"

Way to see inside my soul. I slump down against the wooden wall. "What am I doing, Rach? I'm in Darling Springs with this va-va-voom house and the guy I dated once upon a time and my mom asking us both for advice, and meanwhile, my dating life sucks. The last guy I went out with told me I was too old to ride his ride, and he was easily forty. And this is becoming my norm. It's embarrassing. I have the worst luck with men. No wonder I'm a breakup-party planner."

Rachel sighs sympathetically. "Is it really such a bad idea, then, to date with Mom?"

I don't even know anymore. "But what about Dad? I don't want to be disloyal to him. *Hey, Pops. Your ex-wife is DTF, and I'm gonna help her get some.*"

"I'm pretty sure Dad is doing just fine post-divorce," Rachel reassures me. "He's going to stop by later today. He told me he's coming to the city to do some shopping, and he sounded great. But let's talk about you, J. You haven't had much luck dating in the city. Maybe this Darling Springs dating experiment is a good idea. Maybe you need a small-town guy to, I dunno, reset things."

I shake my head, adamant. "I like the city. I like the hustle and bustle. I like my business. It's a city business. I like all the people, and the opportunities, and the chances. I don't want to find a guy here. This place is cute and adorable, but..."

"But what?" She's gentle but insistent.

My gaze strays to Main Street. To the arcade. To the single-screen movie theater where Monroe and I went one night, laughing our way through the 1990s comedies of the retro movie marathon before we kissed as the credits rolled.

It was a kiss that melted me. A kiss I was sure was better than any silver-screen kiss.

A kiss that still makes my skin tingle.

I drag my gaze from the theater, but it lands on The Slippery Dipper just beyond. This town reminds me too much of one stupid week. One stupid, wonderful week I can't forget. How can a one-week fling eight years ago stay with me like this?

Oh, right. Because it was with my co-worker.

Great decision, doing a podcast with him.

Darling Springs is a seductress. Its hip, modern, small-town energy will not seduce me again. "It'll be fine. I don't need a dating reset after all. I'll just come up with a new dating plan in San Francisco. Join a new app or try a matchmaking service, even. Some of my clients have. I can get some good recs."

"True. But maybe, hear me out, in Darling Springs, you'd get some fresh experience with different men there?"

Except what if nothing changes? What if I'm just bad at love?

The shop bell tinkles in the background, and she says apologetically, "I have to go. Think about it."

"I will," I say, then hang up and drop my head in my hands, downbeat again and hating being that way. Especially when everyone else is so upbeat. Mom has never seemed happier.

But what about Dad? Is he as good as Rachel says he is? As he says he is when I've talked to him? Fine, Mom and Dad said it was amicable. They said it was *conscious uncoupling.* But they're not even supposed to know that term, let alone use it.

And what if it's not? It might be rude for me to wingwoman my mom if my dad is hurting. Sure, he's shopping, but what if he's shopping for gratitude journals because he's sad about his split?

I should help him. He needs me! I hit his name in my contacts, and he picks up immediately. "Hey, sweet pea. How's everything?" He sounds rushed, but kind.

"I'm fantastic," I say, putting on my best cheer. "I just haven't chatted with you much and wanted to say hi." He's probably wandering the streets of San Francisco, hunting for a book of affirmations. I should send him one. Pop into the Darling Springs bookshop and grab one.

"Oh. Well. I always love chatting with you," he says. There's a clink of plates in the background, then a faint voice saying *your avocado toast.*

I startle. "Where are you?"

There's a pause. Then a clearing of his throat. "I'm at Oak and Vine. Why don't we catch up later? I'm, um, just having a bite."

I groan. He's on a date, and he can't even tell me. "You're on a date?"

Another pause, then a sheepish, "Yes."

He says something, but it's muffled, then I hear footsteps for a few seconds before he speaks in a clear but low voice. "And she's great. A very nice woman. I'm taking her shopping at your sister's store after brunch. Let me call you later, sweet pea."

"Of course," I say, then I let him go.

Brunch. My father has a brunch date. He has a shopping date. He's taking a woman to a trendy restaurant in the city.

Both of my aging parents, who haven't dated in over thirty-five years, are rocking the single life. If the two of them can kill it at dating, I should be boss-level by now.

And yet, here I am, slumped against this wall, feeling sorry for myself because I officially suck at dating.

I blow out a frustrated breath, then consider moping and moaning all day long.

I really need to get it together.

When I lift my face, there's a fair-skinned blonde with tattoos curling over one bare shoulder walking toward me. She's clutching several bouquets of lavender and wearing a snug lavender tank top that says *Bees Do It*.

She looks happy enough. I bet I look like a grumpy city girl. That's not me. Why am I in a funk that my mom is dating and my dating life sucks?

A voice in my head says *get it together*.

I snap to it. "That lavender smells amazing," I say, standing too.

"You can't go wrong with lavender. That's just a fact. Especially if you're having a bad day."

I frown. "That obvious?"

Her smile is kind. "Just a guess?"

"A good guess," I admit, a little ashamed it's so apparent. "But I need to get out of this funk."

"Well, I run a lavender farm. It lifts your spirits. So if that helps, come on by," she says, her brown eyes friendly.

"You live here?"

"Yes, I'm Ripley. My farm is that way," she says, pointing behind her. "But I'm bringing these to my friend who runs Downward Dog All Day. It's a combo yoga studio/doggie daycare."

"Shut up. That's too cute," I say, then I give a wave instead of a handshake since her hands are full. "I'm Juliet. From San Francisco." And...screw it. I might as well ask her advice about the prospects here. She'd know better than my mom or I would. "Can I ask you a question? What's the dating scene like here?"

The laughter that falls from her lips is unlike anything I've heard before. It's knowing, resigned, a little reluctant, but totally amused.

I'm too curious to return to my bike. "Now I really need to know."

"How much time do you have?" Ripley's tone is pure deadpan.

Thirty minutes and a latte later, I have a new friend, a bouquet of lavender, and a handful of tales about dating in a small town.

The conclusion? It's full of ups and downs like

anyplace else. Full of duds and bores, frat boys and tech bros, bad boys and good guys. It's full of hope and heartache.

"For someone who specializes in breakups, you're pretty freaking positive," Ripley says as she sets down her emptied London fog. "I say give it a shot. Like you said—every breakup gets you closer to the one. You'll meet some jerks—trust me, I have. But maybe you'll meet someone...fantastic. Maybe I will too. So try it."

It sounds so easy. Almost as easy as making a new friend. So easy I should do it. "Thanks, Ripley. It was great meeting you."

I say goodbye after we exchange numbers, then I return to my bike and set my lavender in the basket and pedal home. When I reach Eleanor's—I mean *our*—cottage, Monroe's pruning the bushes in the front yard.

No time like the present. I hop off the bike and announce: "I'll do it."

As he looks up from the bush, pruning shears in hand, his expression is unreadable. "You want to date here. This week?"

Like he needs to make sure I've really said that.

I nod vigorously. "I'm not backing down. I won't be the girl who slumps against libraries in a dating funk. I will be the woman who tries again."

A line digs into his brow as if he can't make sense of everything I've said.

But I've said it. Now I'm doing it. "If Mom can, I can. I'm making a change. Time to turn over a new leaf. Now, I'm going to tackle the kitchen," I say, grabbing the lavender bouquet and bounding up the steps.

"Okay," he says, sounding a little dazed.

Perhaps I surprised him with my decision. I yank open the door, then shrug happily. "In fact, I'm going to start tonight. And *you* can help me pick the guys to date."

I might be bad at love, but I won't let that get me down.

11

BE MY DATES

Monroe

Like hell I'm going to help her pick another man to date.

I've got a better plan. I've spent the rest of the morning refining it, fine-tuning it, and tonight will be the perfect time to present it.

But if I've learned anything in my years as a therapist, it's that you need to meet people where they are. Talk to them in a way that makes sense to them. And Juliet does well with food.

She likes restaurants, choosing what to order, and finding new vegetarian fare. That's her happy place. Just my luck—a quick Google search told me there's a new vegetarian restaurant that's walking distance from the house.

It's like the universe wants the same damn things I

do. With that in mind and the pruning shears still in my hand, I call out to Juliet before the front door shuts. "Let's do it tonight. Over dinner. At Happy Place."

She smiles. "Ooh, I love dinner. I love all meals."

Like I've got an ace up my sleeve, I say, "I know."

She heads inside, seemingly more centered and upbeat than when she left the inn. The question is—what will her mood be after she hears my idea?

* * *

We don't head over together. I spend the early evening running errands in and out of town, stopping at Josiah's Hardware Store to pick up some paint and brushes, then screws, nails, and hinges to fix a few loose doors and cabinets, then bags to collect donate-able items in.

At ten minutes to eight, I pull up to Happy Place, a few blocks from the water, just close enough to catch the salty scent of the sea. The restaurant is unassuming on the outside, and I go in and give my name to the host. He seats me and tells me the other party hasn't arrived yet.

Perfect.

When the server arrives, I take the liberty of ordering the cheese plate and a bottle of rosé. As I wait, I look around. The decor is cozy and inviting. On every table, there's a vase of freshly cut flowers. Fairy lights adorn the windows. The walls are painted in muted shades of sage and cream and decorated with framed pen-and-ink foxes, raccoons, ducks, and other forest friends by local artists. Pop music—at least, I think it's pop since I hate it—plays softly from a speaker.

But this isn't about me. This is about her.

After a few minutes, the server returns with a plate of creamy brie and cheddar, Gouda and blue cheeses, all topped with honey-roasted walnuts, dried cranberries, and slivers of apricot. "And here's our best rosé. It's light and floral. Want me to open it?"

I shake my head. "Sounds perfect. But I'll wait for my—"

I stop myself before I say *date*. This is simply dinner with a friend I have a proposition for.

"Of course. I'm sure they'll arrive soon," the server says, just as the clicking of heels on the tiled floor catches my attention.

Juliet walks toward me, wearing a pastel-yellow sundress that brings out her eyes and platform sandals that bring out my dirty thoughts.

Just look at those legs. I can't stop staring at them. I rarely get to see them. Does she ever wear a skirt on the show? She usually wears jeans. But last night in bed she wore sleep shorts that sent my mind spinning with thoughts of how those legs would feel under my hands.

Now, I'm admiring them again, and my skin is heating up. Her legs are long, strong, and temptingly touchable. They'd look great wrapped around my hips. They'd look fantastic in a reflection.

As the server leaves, I do my best to wipe away the racy thoughts. I pull out her chair, focused on being the opposite of the guys she usually goes out with. "Glad you could meet me here," I say. But that hardly covers it. I sound clinical. Like she's my patient, and I've invited her for a session over cheese.

"Thank you. I took a Lyft and barely had to wait for it. And you look great." She seems unperturbed by my approach and gives me a quick once-over. I flick an imaginary speck of lint from my short-sleeved Henley, and I swear her eyes linger on my tattoos. I've had them for so long, I don't even notice them. I had most of them when I spent that week with her. Not all though.

But her lingering gaze is probably wishful thinking. Clearing my throat, I try once more. "Thank you again for having dinner with me."

And I still sound like I'm thanking a patient who's rescheduled. What the hell is wrong with me?

You're attracted to her, asshole.

Yeah, no shit, brain. Tell me something I don't know. But I can handle a little attraction.

Surely, I can.

She gestures to the charcuterie board approvingly as I sit. "Look at you. Breaking out the cheese plate. You really are getting into this whole Love Doctor thing." She reaches for a slice of Camembert and pops it past her lips.

Her pretty, glossy lips. Now, I can't stop staring at her as she eats cheese.

This is my life—I talk to her like a client, or I think of her like she's the object of my dirty fantasies. I've got to find the middle ground.

"The cheese good?" I ask, trying to talk normally.

Grunting, "Cheese good," is not an impressive conversational achievement.

"It's better," she says.

The meaning isn't lost on me. She's saying, so far, this evening with me is better than her last date. That's a relief, and it eases my nerves at last. Time to focus solely on her. That's why I developed my plan after all—to help her navigate the wilds of dating. "Then, what do you say we make it past the cheese plate portion? ExtraDate. Combo date. Extend-a-date?"

She rolls her eyes, but a smile teases her lips. "Fine. You win. Let's order the main course and get to the extend-a-date."

"It's a plan." I shouldn't feel so victorious at lasting past the cheese plate.

But I do.

Fuck Mister Cheese Douche. I'm a better date than he is.

After we order, Juliet meets my gaze, all businesslike and eager. "Ready to help me find some small-town men?"

Ha. If she only knew. "First, want some rosé?" It's all part of my plan.

She tilts her head, her lips curving up in welcome curiosity. "That's my favorite. Did you know that?"

"You mentioned it once. A year ago. You were talking about a date with some dude named Grady," I recount, managing to keep the sarcasm out of my voice. What a feat.

"The blacksmith," she says, and I don't roll my eyes

at that either. I'm seriously fucking impressing myself now.

That was the first clue Grady was a bad boy—he claimed he was a blacksmith when he actually worked as a metal collector. But he makes a good lead-in to my pitch.

"His only redeeming quality was his taste in rosé," I say, quoting her back to her.

"You remember what I said." She sounds surprised, maybe even delighted.

"I remember lots of things." I hold her gaze as I pour us both a glass.

She reaches for one and lifts it. "I'll drink to that, then," she says, and I think she's talking about memories, but I can't be sure.

Only, tonight isn't about the memories of us in Darling Springs. It's about new ones she'll make here.

After she takes a sip, she lets out a moan of culinary enjoyment. "Mmm. So good I could kiss the bottle."

A wave of heat rolls down my spine at that unexpectedly filthy image. Juliet kissing a bottle of rosé. I didn't know that was a turn-on till now. But I add it to the long list of things she does that arouse me, then return to my goal. "I've solved your dating dilemma," I announce.

"You have? I thought the dilemma was, um, already solved? I'm going to date with my mom. Try small-town men as my new dating reset."

I suppress the growl that builds in my chest, quieting the slumbering dragon. No need for jealousy again because I've got a better plan. With my chin up and my confidence on, I tell her, "I'm going to be your dating coach."

She tilts her head quizzically. "What does that mean? That you'll help me sort through the matches like we talked about?"

Yes and no. Herein lies the brilliance. "Yes. And then I'll be your dates. All of them."

12

COSPLAYERS

Monroe

If I'd thought she looked confused seconds ago, that was nothing next to her expression now. It's like I've started speaking in differential calculus.

She squints at me as if trying to figure me out. "You're going to be all my dates? Are you a dating superhero?"

"Yes." I square my shoulders. "I can be your dating coach and your dates all in one. I've been working on this idea since breakfast, and I think this can help since you said you've gotten low-tier matches, and you want to choose better ones."

"That's true." She's arching a brow but leaning closer. She's skeptical but intrigued. "But how would you being all my dates help fix that?"

"It'll be like a role-play dating exercise. I'll pretend I'm all the dates you pick. Like that, I'll help you figure out the red flags so you can avoid the bad boys and break your one-date streak."

From her dubious stare, I can tell she's not buying what I'm selling. "Every guy I've one-dated lately has been completely different, and there hasn't been a motorcyclist in the bunch," Juliet protests.

I wave a hand. "Doesn't matter how they dress. They're all bad boys cosplaying as artists and micro-brewers, blacksmiths, and musicians," I continue, on a roll as Juliet reaches for some more rosé. "A bad boy is someone who is emotionally unavailable but pretends to be looking for love and the woman to fix him. Your kind heart makes you want to help these guys, only to be disappointed. No motorcycle necessary."

She groans. Heavily. Deeply. From the center of her soul. "Ugh. That...may be true."

"It is true," I say gently, but firmly. I've been watching her valiantly try romance over and over. But she keeps missing the mark while aiming for what she wants most—the real thing.

All because she picks men who are emotionally unavailable.

I should know. I'm one of those guys. The difference between the average online dating bad boy and me is that I have a modicum of self-awareness. Well, I'd better. The job and all.

"So who picks the matches, then?" she asks, still skeptical.

I nod with certainty. "You do. And since I know people and personalities, I can behave how each of them would on a date."

I brace myself for pushback. The idea does sound unusual now that I say it out loud. *"Hey, let's practice date. And I'll pretend to be a string of different men while I try not to get distracted by your sexy mouth."*

She hums doubtfully. "You really want to do that? You did bet me the other day that my date would fail."

Ouch. Fair point. "But that was for the show," I say, defending that on-air choice. "And that was before I met Elijah and nearly punched him in his full-of-himself face for being such a douche. I never want you to date douches again if I can help it, and I can. I definitely can."

Curiosity flickers in her eyes. "Wait. Let's go back to the *you wanted to punch him* part. You did?"

"Actually, I wanted to stab him with an olive toothpick, but same idea."

She smiles, looking a little more relaxed too, like that detail reassured her. "Okay, okay. I'm seeing this. And, not to be a douche too, but what about your track record?"

The reminder of my failed marriage is a fair one, but it doesn't sting as much as it would have when I was fresh off the split. It's part of who I am now. Part of my history. And part of my toolkit. "Failure is the best teacher. Isn't that what they say?"

"Then I should have an advanced degree," she fires back, then picks up her rosé. She takes another sip and then lets out a thoughtful breath. "You do have the experience and the male perspective I've been lacking. And I suppose I would like to move past my unsuccessful dating years and into a stable relationship. But what's in it for you?"

Answering that question requires one of my least favorite emotions—vulnerability. But she's been putting herself on the line. I have to do the same.

I meet her green eyes, ready to be open.

I don't tell her I'm battling jealousy.

I don't tell her I imagined watching her wrap those legs around my face in the mirror last night.

I don't say that sharing a bunk bed with a mirrored ceiling presents its own challenges.

I do set aside my baser desires and give her the truth. "Look, I know we give each other a hard time on air. I know we have this whole—"

"—Cat and mouse thing?" Her tone is borderline flirty for a moment.

I like that tone. I flash a cocky smile her way. But I still answer from the heart. "Yes. And I want to help because...I think you're great, and I care about you, and I know how much finding a partner means to you."

I don't say no one deserves her though. And I hope she can't hear it in my voice.

She seems to give that some thought before she adds, "Can I sleep on it?"

"Of course," I say, relieved and hopeful.

The server arrives with our dinner, and the conversation shifts. Over the meal, we talk about our marketing plans for the podcast and the things we can do to grow it with the home proceeds. Then we segue to Eleanor's sensual home itself, likely funded by her Christmas album.

"She sent an email this afternoon, asking what we thought of the house," I tell Juliet.

"And did you tell her we already gave it a nickname?"

"I kept *The Horny House* between us. But did tell her it's fantastic and we're so grateful, then I asked how her honeymoon was. She said, and I quote, *so good that I've only come up for air to send this email! Ta ta for now. Enjoy Darling Springs.*"

She laughs. "Have I mentioned I love her?"

"She's pretty great," I say.

"The town's not so bad either," she says, then she gives me a dead-on look. "Is it hard, though, me doing this dating thing with my mom?"

That's a gut punch. But only for a second. "Losing my mom was a long time ago."

"I know, but still. I can tell she was...special."

I nod, memories tugging on my heart. "She was. There aren't many moms who build you a tree house."

Her green eyes sparkle with delight. "She built you a tree house *and* taught you to ride a bike."

"And to read a book," I add.

"All the best things in life," she says.

"Yeah." I don't even try to picture my mom anymore. It was so long ago, more than two decades. But she's all the good things from when I was younger. "Also, you'd have liked her. She liked cats."

"The woman had taste," Juliet says.

"How's your boy doing?" I ask, moving the conversation away from me and onto her.

She shows me a picture Rachel sent of the black-

and-white guy rubbing up against her leg and purring. "This was taken even *after* she fed him, proving I have the best cat," she says.

"Yeah, you do."

She looks at the pic on her phone a little longer, then sets it down. "And I suppose it'd be nice to have more than his company."

I hate how sad she sounds right now, but I hope she'll let me help solve her dilemma. I desperately want her to agree, for all the reasons I shared with her.

And also...maybe because a tiny part of me is hoping for a little romance.

No, that's not the right word. It's just that, unlike those bad boys, I know how to treat a woman.

I'd like to show Juliet what it'd be like to date a real man.

When dinner is done, I pay. That's the very least that a man should do.

13

THE SECRET SAUCE

Juliet

As I lie awake in bed alone on Tuesday morning, I don't even bother tuning in to one of my dating or self-improvement podcasts to learn more about this so-called *role-play dating*. That can't possibly be a thing, can it? It's not fake-dating, or plus-one-ing. It's a whole new dating frontier. Maybe it's reserved for the worst cases?

Ugh. This has got to be one of those last-ditch, we've-tried-everything-already options. I bet there's a school of dating coaches somewhere who say things like *and the last resort for the truly hapless is role-play.*

Monroe's gone. He took off early, judging from the ungodly time stamp on his **out for a bit** text. He's probably off running, or biking, or working on his new course in a coffee shop after having already biked and ran.

I grab my phone and google dating coaches.

Huh.

That's interesting. There are a ton of dating coaches in San Francisco alone, promising to help you write a great bio, give you pointers on what to talk about, analyze your dates, and improve your conversational skills.

Okay, their services aren't too weird or pathetic. Those offerings don't scream, *You suck at love.* Dating coaches just give you some truth and a little boost.

Monroe's role-play offer is basically to just help me analyze my dates. This would be a live, real-time dating analysis, which could be super helpful.

But we do work together. Is it dicey to mix business with pleasure like this?

I flick through my text messages, finding the group chat with my girlfriends. A modern woman can't survive without her besties. I click open my near-daily communiqué with my friend Hazel, a romance writer who lives in New York; my sister, Rachel; and our friends Elodie and Fable, who live in San Francisco. Elodie's a chocolatier who recently married a single dad bartender. And Fable's happily single and working as a merch designer for the city's football team.

> Juliet: You know how happily married and coupled-up friends love hearing the antics of the single?

> Hazel: Ooh, I'll bite. Tell me!

Elodie: Watch out, J. That means Hazel's in full thief mode.

Fable: She sure is. She's going to steal anything good you share for her next book.

Hazel: Of course I am.

Rachel: So shameless.

Hazel: Exactly. So don't make me wait. Tell us everything, J.

I draw a deep breath, then open my optimistic heart that's, admittedly, a little beaten down.

Juliet: To make a long story short, Monroe offered to be my dating coach while we're here in Darling Springs. I'll start fresh and pick a few potential guys to date. But I won't really date them. Instead, he'll help me spot the signs of trouble in the men I choose… by, well, pretending to be the different guys on a series of dates. And I'm considering saying yes to his outrageous proposal even though, as I re-read this note, it sure sounds like the sign of a woman who's hit dating rock bottom. I guess you'll find me on the bottom of the dating pool, sinking in a pair of concrete Louboutins.

Before I lose my nerve, I hit send, wincing as I wait for the bubbles to appear.

They don't. At all. Not for ten, twenty, thirty seconds. Not for a whole minute. Oh god. My friends think I've lost my mind. They're staging an intervention. They're—

Oh! FaceTime is calling. And it's the girlies. All four of them.

I answer, but I fling my hand over my eyes, groaning in embarrassment. "Yes, you can come pick me up and whisk me away for a spa weekend to deprogram me after I've fallen this far."

Hazel laughs, a bright sound with a touch of sarcasm. But that's her natural tone. "Actually, we think it's a good idea—"

"—Potentially," Rachel cuts in as she swipes on powder in front of her mirror while getting ready for work.

"As long as you keep a few things in mind," Elodie adds.

I perk up. I sit up. I stare at them. "You think I should do it?"

Elodie flips the closed sign to open in her chocolate shop in the city, the display shelves a gleaming white and the chocolates making me hungry for treats already. She furrows her brow and peers at the phone screen. "Is that a mirror above you?"

How can they see it? Oh, shit. My camera was flipped. I flip it back. "Yeah. It is. This house has mirrored bunk beds," I say. "Pretty wild."

Fable smirks. "So, is it wild, Juliet?" She asks as she walks along the street near the stadium.

Elodie clears her throat. "Exactly. Since that's sort of the issue."

"Mirrored bunk beds?" I ask, confused.

"No," Hazel says dryly from the red couch in her apartment in Manhattan. It's covered in books, papers, and planning notebooks, and her red hair is twisted in a messy bun. "The issue is your latent, simmering, long-standing attraction to Monroe."

"What?" I ask, flinching in shock.

My sister cracks up. "Don't act surprised."

"That was *real* surprise," I insist.

Rachel scoffs. "That seemed like *Who, me?* surprise."

"I'm going to have to agree with Rachel," Fable puts in.

I sigh. "It was real."

Hazel's bossy mode must be on high today. "Be that as it may," she says, "you're hot for him, and everyone knows it. Just be aware that any form of play dating might lead to temptation."

I roll my eyes like that's so ridiculous. But then my dirty brain pictures Monroe's arms. His heated eyes. His stern attitude. And my skin heats up. "So, I should say no?"

Rachel jumps on the question. "Like Hazel said, we actually think it's a good idea. Just that you should be cautious."

Hold the hell on. "You four decided it was a good idea in the one minute before you called me?"

Fable nods firmly. "Of course we did. We look out for you."

Elodie smiles sagely. "And we don't fuck around with decisions for our girls."

"Okay. Why is it a good idea?" I ask, a little giddy they're truly on board, but I still want to hear their reasons. Validation of the purchase and all.

Rachel brushes on some eyeshadow as she answers. "He's very savvy about relationships, thanks to his job. And I honestly think the guy's viewpoint could be helpful. Like a secret sauce in a recipe."

"Just don't let him give you the secret sauce," Elodie says with a naughty grin as she organizes some boxes of chocolates.

"It's not going to happen," I say, rolling my eyes just to prove how much I believe that. "We've been working together for a while, and if it were going to happen again, it would have. I've moved on. He's moved on."

"And that's why we want you to be careful as you do this," Rachel says. She's evidently the voice of reason on this call. "You two work together, and I know the podcast is important to you."

"And it's not easy to fall for a guy you work with," Hazel says with a knowing look because she would know. It happened to her. She's now married to her writing partner, but it was a long and complicated road to her happily ever after.

"I'll be careful, then," I say, tugging the blanket closer, already picturing how this role-play dating scenario might work.

"Then use that man," Elodie says, like she's calling

out *ride 'em, cowboy* at a rodeo. "Pick his big therapist brain. Ask him a bajillion questions."

"And get all the insider tips you can get. It's rare when we can ask a man what he thinks and know he's telling the truth," Fable adds as she turns into the stadium.

"But don't go all *bang me on the bunk bed* because that could lead to getting your heart hurt," Hazel warns, wagging a finger. "And this time, it might hurt for real."

Last time it hurt, too, but I barely let on. To anyone.

Now though? Monroe's even less available than he was that summer. Back then, I'd dated the man for seven days and had been about to tell my brother I'd fallen for his friend. I'd planned to tell Monroe, too, of course. I'd wanted to tell Monroe I'd wait for him, I'd do long distance, I'd try to make it work. Then he'd said, "This was always supposed to be a summer fling. Like we'd talked about. Right?"

And I'd shut my squishy heart, putting on a cheery face as I'd lied, "Yes, absolutely. Just like we'd talked about."

In the end, it really wasn't. You can't truly fall for someone in a week. The past is the past, and now it's the present.

"I'm honestly not worried," I say to Hazel.

* * *

An hour later, I'm dressed and searching for Monroe. You'd think finding someone in a two-bedroom, two-story home would be easy.

You'd be wrong.

He's not in the work shed. Or the kitchen, or even the mirror room. I keep calling his name, my stomach churning each time. "Monroe? Mister Handy? Love Doctor?"

But there's no answer.

I'm sure he's on the premises, though, since I found a text after I got out of the shower saying simply, **back**.

The man is nothing if not concise.

I fluff out my hair, draw a deep breath, and head down to the garden level of the home where I turn into the poker room, with its late-night vibes even in the morning. The dark wood, the green felt, the wet bar, and the...

I stop in my tracks, adding a new item to the sexy vibes list: the man standing on a ladder screwing in a smoke detector with his back to me, giving me a perfect view of a round ass.

Has he always had such a great butt? It's Butt Hall of Fame level. It's the kind of firm you could bounce a quarter off. The kind you could grab and hold onto all night long.

A memory flashes—pulling him deeper, moving under him, tangling up with him.

I shake it off. "Monroe!"

Nothing.

He's probably got AirPods in. It is ten in the morning on the dot. Is he listening to the top of the hour at full volume? Yeah, that's so Monroe.

I weave around the ladder, giving him a wide berth since I don't want to startle him while he's up high, working a screwdriver and my fantasies. When he spots me, he reaches for his phone in his pocket and hits a button.

"Blasting NPR? Rocking out to Morning Edition?"

With a smug smile, he climbs down and shows me his phone. Oh. He was listening to...Nirvana. He says nothing, just smiles as if he's delighted at surprising me.

This is more than surprise—I'm officially shocked. "But you said you didn't like music?"

His smile widens victoriously. "I said I don't like keeping up on it," he points out.

I hold up a finger, rewinding to our chat in the car two days ago, then replaying it. Dammit. "That's true," I grumble.

"But see," he adds, coming closer, "I don't mind retro music. I don't really have to keep up with anything when it comes to Nirvana."

Is there no point he can't turn to his advantage? His brain is unfairly big and diabolical. "You win."

He holds my gaze for a few moments, his expression shifting slightly from triumphant to...vulnerable. "Also, you were right. It's kind of sexy."

"Is it?" I don't know what else to say. I'm a little thrown. He's listening to music after I compared it to sex. But is Nirvana sexy? I'm not so sure. "Sexy?" I add with a scratch in my voice.

"Well, the song is 'Come As You Are,'" he says.

And what the hell did I come downstairs for? My brain has gone blank. My body has turned hot.

"Cool, cool," I finally manage. But I still don't know

what I'm doing here other than thinking about sex and music.

After a few more beats of awkward silence, he says, "I've got a list of things we need to work on today," he says, but his eyes look almost sad.

Then, he scratches his jaw—something he usually does when he's thrown off too.

Oh. Wait. I've left him hanging. Maybe he's waiting for my answer. Hoping I'll say yes?

He turns away and crosses the room toward an open toolbox on the poker table. "I want to fix these tables. They're a little loose. The legs are a bit wobbly. But I can add some new screws and tighten them. I think we should leave the tables in though. The game room is sort of fun and could be a selling point, right?"

Is he rambling?

Holy shit. He *is*.

Monroe is worried. He's uncomfortable. He's wondering. That warms my heart, and I want to hug him. I also deeply understand discomfort, and I don't want him to feel it.

"Yes."

He turns around, arching a brow in question and maybe in hope too. "Yes, what?"

"Yes," I say, and I'm hopeful as well—for better days, better outcomes. "You can be my dating coach."

His smile spreads quickly and genuinely. Like he truly wants this. "Good."

"But I have a few rules," I say.

He looks ready for any and all.

14

STAND DOWN, DRAGON

Monroe

In hindsight, I should have realized why I rushed out for a run on Dogwood Lane, why I hit the weights with a guest pass at a gym, and why I kept busy with chores at the house.

It wasn't to avoid my father's **Want to play golf Wednesday?** text.

I was wound up waiting for Juliet's answer. Hoping she'd say yes.

Now that she has, I'm not going to kick back. I'm going to make damn sure I can deliver for my friend and colleague.

Who's pretty handy, it turns out. I'm learning all sorts of things about Juliet during our stay in this house.

How much she cares about her parents' happiness.

How open-minded she is to new ideas.

And how well she knows her way around a toolbox. Right now, she's kneeling on the hardwood floor in the poker room, plucking screws from a compartment while she uses a Phillips head to emphasize her points.

"I've got this whole dating coach thing mapped out," she begins, and I'm damn eager to hear her plans. Hell, I'm thrilled she's devised some already. "So, I'll pick three men from Date Night. We'll go on three dates."

Rather than stand here like a sloth, I join her on the hunt for screws. "Sure, that makes sense. Have you used that app before?" I ask as I kneel next to her, looking for the right size in the toolbox to fix this table.

She rolls her eyes. "Yes, only a few thousand times, and I've picked badly. Though, in my defense, the single men of the world are pretty skilled at hiding their toxic traits long enough to lure you in."

Shit. I don't want her to think I was judging or blaming her for her dates not being worthy of her. "Completely understood," I say. I look up from the toolbox, meet her gaze, and speak from the heart. "Honestly, I think what you're doing is totally brave. It takes a lot of guts to put yourself out there."

"You do?" It comes out gentle, curious. Like my opinion matters.

"I truly do."

"Thanks," she says, dipping her face for a few seconds. Then she looks up, her expression soft. "I appreciate you saying that and your encouragement. It is a little scary. But I think I'm excited."

"Me too," I say without any sarcasm either.

She holds my gaze for a beat longer than I'd expect, and the look in her green eyes makes my pulse spike. But that's just how things go when I'm near her. I'm used to my body's reaction when we get close.

She breaks eye contact and pokes around in the toolbox some more. When she finds the screw she's looking for, she brandishes it theatrically. "And to answer your question, yes, I used Date Night when I went out with Ludwig a few weeks ago."

"Was he as douchey as the name implies?"

"If by douchey you mean did he like to quote famous women like Maya Angelou and Ruth Bader Ginsburg and Marie Curie, and choke up while quoting them, then yes. And if you want to know why he cried, it was because he was, quote, *so moved* by the accomplishments of women he had to share."

I cringe. "Like I said, bad boy. But that's the worst kind of bad boy. Because he thinks he's a good guy."

"He was convinced he was an inspiration to women everywhere," Juliet says as she lines up the screw in the joint of the leg where it meets the table.

My palms are itching to do something. I feel a little useless right now, and I hate it. "Can I help?"

She flashes a smile. "Yes, you can help by listening to my rules."

Fair enough. I comply.

"Anyway, I'll use Date Night to find the men I would like to date," she says, and my eye twitches.

My nose crinkles.

My chest burns.

The dragon is disturbed. But I remind myself she

won't really be dating those guys. She won't be dating anyone for real this week.

Except me, for all intents and purposes.

Stand down, dragon.

"That makes sense. But I've got a rule of my own," I say, holding my ground. This matters.

"Okay," she says cautiously.

"No picking for shock value. We want this experiment to work."

Her glossy lips part in an exaggerated O. "You mean don't pick a twenty-two-year-old who lives at home, doesn't vote, and says he only wants a girl who's not like other girls?"

"Well, yeah."

"Though, it *would* be fun to see you try to role-play an apolitical, sexist jerk," she says, returning to her normal voice. I can spot the compliment in there and I like it. But I won't make too much of it.

"I know you're tempted to do that for the pure entertainment value," I say.

"Soooo tempted," she says as she turns the screwdriver. "But I'll behave and select legitimate potential matches only. And then you'll familiarize yourself with the guys...and choose the date activity?"

That all sounds reasonable, like a well thought out dating experiment. I only have one question. "When do you want to start?"

Shit. Did that sound too eager? Nah. I'm good at playing it cool.

But she takes her time fixing the loose table leg. Just

when I'm about to give in and say, *Well, when, Juliet, when?* she sets down the screwdriver.

"Now?" she asks.

The dragon thumps his chest. Yes. I can absolutely take her out tonight.

That's a discovery—I can't wait for this not-date this evening.

To help her of course. That's it. That's all.

I sort of believe my own lie.

That afternoon, Juliet stretches out in the sitting room on a rose-color satin chaise lounge—which is not tempting at all—testing whether she wants to keep it for her San Francisco apartment, while she selects the first dude. His name is Jared, his dark hair is perfectly trimmed, he's in real estate a few towns over, and I hate him on principle.

But I can't let on. Instead, I put on my shrink hat as I review his profile on her phone while she shifts around on the unfairly sexy piece of furniture.

It's unfair, too, that she looks so damn good lounging on her side, dressed in simple leggings and an oversized T-shirt that reveals a collarbone I want to kiss.

I'm careful as I sit next to her on a small patch of satin real estate. Careful not to accidentally touch her, because I'd probably groan. Or growl. I focus on my job as her dating coach, studying this dude in detail even if Jared makes me grind my teeth, especially when he uses those irritatingly trendy terms. But if this is who she likes then this is who she likes. I suck down all the negativity since I need insight into her preferences if I'm going to do this dating coach thing right. "Tell me why you picked him," I say.

She sits up straight, her chestnut hair swishing as she rises, then catching on her lip gloss.

"Oops," she says, swiping at the strands with her free hand and brushing a finger against her pretty lips.

My gaze zeroes in on those lips. Soft, lush, full. The first time I tasted her lips was eight years ago, down by the beach a few miles away after our first date. We'd gone to the retro arcade and hogged the Frogger machine all night, trading off low scores because we were both that bad at the game. When we left, I took her hand in mine, thrilling at how good—how arousing —holding her hand was. We wandered down to the dunes where the waves lapped the shore peacefully and, like when I'd asked her out, I didn't waste a second. I tugged her close, then said, "I have a confession."

"Tell me."

"I can't stop thinking about kissing you. I've wanted to since the second I saw you at the store."

She nibbled on the corner of her red lips, then said in the flirtiest, most inviting tone I'd ever heard, "Then stop thinking."

I cupped her cheeks, dropped my mouth to hers, and kissed her deeply, the kind of kiss that blotted out the world. Or maybe the world narrowed to her and me and the soft lull of the waves under the moonlight.

I got lost in that kiss.

I get a little lost in the memory now too, until I blink at the sound of her shifting around on the satin chaise, mere inches from me. It roots me back to the present. To my reality. To a world where I'm the guy who helps others. That's my specialty—teaching romance, not doing romance.

She's answering my question, telling me why she picked Jared. "He's in real estate, so he's not afraid of commitment," she says.

Huh? "What?" It comes out a little incredulous. Or maybe a lot.

She heaves an amused sigh. "A mortgage is a commitment, Monroe. So if he's in real estate, he's used to mortgages. Hello!"

Oh. Wow. This is harder than I thought. "Okaaaaaay," I say.

"What? You don't agree?"

I mean, maybe. I rent. But that's not the point. I need to get more intel ahead of this date. "What else drew you to him?"

"He goes to the gym, so he cares about his health. That's good. I like to do my functional fitness videos and yoga so I can feel capable and healthy and strong, so that's another thing we both like."

"That's important to you—having those sorts of things in common?"

"Well, yeah. Isn't it to you?"

"Core values are important to me. If health is a core value, then sure," I say.

"And he said lately he's really into *slow dating*," she

adds, lifting her phone and waggling his stupid profile at me. I mean, his profile.

Yeah, I hadn't heard that term before I read it in his bio, but I can figure it out. "And you like to take things slow?"

She shrugs noncommittally. "It's more that slow dating means he's open to the real thing. To slowing things down and getting to know someone. You know, the opposite of swipe thumb."

I nod, taking that all in, developing my plan for this guy. "Got it."

She frowns. "What is it? You think I made a mistake picking him?"

My heart aches for her even though she'll never meet him in real life. And yet, I want to punch Jared through the screen. "I think you picked who you liked," I say, evenly.

"So you'll be Jared?"

"I will definitely, absolutely be Jared."

A sigh of relief comes from her. Then, she goes thoughtful. "But we should have a safe word."

My eyebrows rise in excitement. Another part starts to rise too. "What kind of safe word?" I ask, laying on the gruff tone for fun.

She slugs my arm. That's not the turn-off she thinks it is. "I mean, a safe word if I need you to be you," she says.

"Ah, so like when you want to summon me?"

"Yes, like in a game of Jumanji," she says, dryly.

"Then Jumanji will be our safe word."

"Jumanji it is."

I check the time on my phone. "I need to take off, but I'll text you the date plan," I say, then share a few more details on how I want to meet up with her.

"Sounds like a plan, dating coach," she says, and she sounds excited about tonight.

That makes two of us. I leave the sitting room but stop in the doorway, turning back to look at her one more time as she lounges on the pink satin. "You should keep that chaise. It suits you."

Then, I leave and head to a men's store a few towns away.

Well, I need a suit. Jared would definitely wear a suit on a date. I'm going to look so much better in one than Jared ever would.

15

SLOW DATING

As I read the text from Monroe in the early evening, I'm shaking my head in admiration.

> Monroe: Hey. It's Jared. Want to meet at Prohibition Spirit at seven-thirty? I'll be the guy in the suit at the bar. Coming straight from the office. I was nonstop all day.

Of course there's a whiskey bar in Darling Springs. Of course that's what Jared would pick too. *Well played, Monroe.*

Jared, real estate broker, would also use zero exclamation points, and he'd *schedule drop,* weaving in a mention of how busy he is.

But I don't mind. One, I like suits. Two, I like men who aren't lazy. Three, I prefer when guys take a little initiative. Monroe probably doesn't even realize he just won points with me.

Well, Monroe's Jared did.

As I head to my suitcase on the floor of the bedroom, I tap out a reply.

> Juliet: Sounds great! I'll be there!

I hunt through my bag for something to wear to a whiskey bar, when...fuck. I didn't pack for a date. I only had that yellow sundress I wore last night. I brought it because I figured I'd want one cute little thing. But I don't have two cute things.

I whip my gaze to the cat clock on the wall. The black tail twitches ominously. It's six.

I paw through my bag, just in case I accidentally packed something pretty enough. But nope. I only have jeans, leggings, and casual tops. I don't even have time to hop on a bike and ride into town to find something at Second Time Around. Monroe has the car. He said before he left that he'd meet me at the date location, and that I should take a Lyft there. "We want tonight to be as date-like as possible," he said.

Then, he installed his credit card on my ride-share app, so he could pay for the ride. Which was not at all date-like, but which I loved, nonetheless.

Trouble is, now I'm staring at a suitcase of unsuitable clothes, tapping my toe, trying to figure out what will look good for a whiskey bar date with a guy in a suit.

"Oh well," I say, grabbing a snug, white tank top. "Casual is the new black."

But as I head to the bathroom to take a quick shower, an idea strikes me, and I let a sly smile take over.

Eleanor Longswallow would never let me down.

I thank and tip the Lyft driver, then walk up the stone path that meanders through overgrown gardens to Prohibition Spirit. It's right on the edge of town, not far from the beach. The door is a deep, rich red and the windows are up high, near the ceiling. Too high to see through. It's impressive, this speakeasy vibe from the outside.

I take a deep breath, drawing in warm summer air tinged with a salty sea breeze. But I still feel...jangly, with nerves hopping left and right. I hope this outfit isn't a mistake. I hope this whole dating experiment isn't a mistake.

I smooth a hand over the satin corset I found in Eleanor's closet of sexy wonders. It's black, tight, and hot. No idea how vintage it is, but I'm just grateful Eleanor and I fit in the same clothes. I also sprayed a tiny dab of my vanilla and honey perfume on the corset, and voila. It doesn't smell like a closet. It smells like me.

I glance down at my bare arms, a little glittery thanks to the lotion I rubbed in.

I've got on jeans and a pair of red platform sandals. My hair's swept up in a loose twist with tendrils framing my face.

I really should go in, but my belly swoops once more with nerves. Is this too outlandish, this dating experiment? Is this outfit too sexy? Should I dab off my red lipstick?

Probably. I snap open my purse and hunt around for a tissue when shoes click on the stone path behind me, then deep voices laugh. Two handsome men are heading my way. One has deep brown skin and shiny shoulder-length hair and wears a sharp vest. The other is fair-skinned and freckled and sports a tight paisley shirt.

"Need anything, hun?" the blond asks kindly, stopping a few feet from me.

"Just a little courage for meeting my date?" I ask.

The guy in the vest shoots me a sympathetic smile. "First date?"

I nod.

"You look great, if that helps. And this is a great place for a date too. This is where I met Bowen a year ago," he says, then runs a hand down his date's arm. Bowen looks at the dark-haired man with such affection my own heart skips a beat or two. They seem so happy. That's why I'm facing these nerves. To move closer to finding my own happiness.

"But I met Vikas online first," Bowen points out.

"And we're getting married on the lavender farm here next month," Vikas puts in.

Small world indeed. "The one Ripley runs?" I ask, thinking of my new friend.

"The one and only." Bowen reaches out and squeezes my arm affectionately. "You never know when you're going to meet the one. Now, c'mon, hun. We'll walk you in if you're ready."

I am so very ready. "Let's do it."

Bowen swings open the door, and I head inside, jazz music greeting me. Immediately, I soak in the atmosphere —dark wood walls, mahogany bar tops, leather furniture, and subdued lighting. A long, elegant counter is stocked with a variety of whiskey brands on mirrored shelves.

"Do you see him anywhere?" Bowen asks, looking around. "Please say he's the hunk in the suit at the bar."

Vikas gives a low whistle. "Yesss and please and *sir*."

Bowen chuckles, then drops a possessive kiss onto his soon-to-be husband's cheek as I turn my gaze to the end of the bar, searching for Monroe, playing Jared and—

I gasp. My heart stutters. "Ohhhh."

Vikas laughs. "That's right. We told you the vibes were on point."

And so is my dating coach. He's wearing the hell out of a deep blue suit that hugs his strong body. No tie. Monroe's holding a tumbler of amber liquid, and he hasn't seen me yet. He's sitting at the bar, casual, relaxed, and...powerful.

When I swallow, I realize my throat is dry.

"Go get your happily ever after," Bowen says.

"I will," I say to them, and my voice sounds a little floaty. Hell, I feel a little floaty as I head to the bar.

As I walk, Monroe's gaze swings to me. His eyes darken, smolder, glimmer. He never looks away.

It's thrilling and gives me hope for this *date*.

When I reach him, the butterflies are flapping full speed in my chest. "Hi. You must be Jared. I'm Juliet."

I stick out a hand, and when he takes it, he looks like he's about to whisper a reverent *wow*. But he must switch gears because the words that come out of his mouth, in a slightly deeper tone than usual, are "Looks like it's my lucky night."

What?

That's kind of a trashy opening line.

Immediately, all the sensual vibes slip out the door as Monroe/Jared pats the barstool next to him. "What's your poison, babe?"

Babe?

Seriously? He's playing one of those first date *babe* guys? This is so not fair.

"Anything's fine," I say, irked that Monroe's already tanking the date. Is he doing this deliberately? And do I need to summon Jumanji already?

"You need to get the Woodford Reserve. Only the best," he says in that voice he must have assigned to this character. He licks his lips wolfishly. "And you look like you deserve the best."

I arch a skeptical brow. It's a compliment, but it's also too much. "Sure. Sounds good," I say, keeping my tone even. I don't want to let on how doubtful I am. I truly want to try this experiment.

He lifts a finger toward the bartender, who strides over. "What can I get for you?" the man in the leather apron asks me.

"Your best Woodford Reserve for the gorgeous lady," Monroe says. "And put it on my tab."

"Will do," the man says, then heads off.

The second he's gone, Monroe turns back to me. But right before he tries some new showy tactic, I grab the reins of the date and turn the conversation in a different direction—a more real one. "You said you worked all day. Sounds like you're a busy man. What is it about real estate that excites you?"

There. That's better than his subtle and not so subtle brags.

For a second Monroe blanches, like he didn't expect me to steer the ship. But he adjusts quickly. "What's not to like? I get to wheel and deal all day long."

"And that's your passion?" I ask, trying to have some meaningful get-to-know-you time.

He leans back, smirking. "I have a lot of passions, Juliet."

Then he winks.

He fucking winks.

I slap a palm on the table. "Juma—" slips past my lips, but then I slam my mouth shut. Nope. I'm sticking to the date plan. I'm not backing down. I'm here to practice.

I strap in and play the game as the liquor arrives. We drink and he brags about the size of his properties, the quality of the liquor, and the frequency of his CrossFit workouts.

It's not awful.

About thirty minutes in, I've managed to endure more deal talk than I'd like. But I'm a trooper. "So you've been into the slow-dating thing lately?"

Proudly, he nods. "Definitely. It works for me since there isn't a lot of free time between the gym and my work."

The logic doesn't entirely add up, but I still think his slow-dating penchant has to be a good sign. "It's nice to get to know someone. Just like this. Out and about in real life. Not texting. Not on the app."

"Absolutely. There's nothing like meeting right away for the slow-dating lifestyle."

Something definitely doesn't add up there. "Right away?"

He flashes a cocky grin. "Well, I do like closing deals. I'd like to close some more now."

I hold up my hands like *What gives?* "Jumanji! Jared said he likes slow dating!"

Monroe drops his facade, his expression turning serious. "Jared said in his bio that *lately, he's really into slow dating.*"

Now I'm even more confused. "Right. That's the same thing!"

Monroe shakes his head, sadly. "No. Because what he meant is *he's trying a new tactic to get laid.*"

I jerk my gaze away from him, frustrated, and a little hurt. "Why would you say that?" I mutter.

"*Lately* and *really* are the key words. He's overselling

his dating approach in his bio, and since this new tactic is something he only started recently, that translates into it's his new tactic to get you to sleep with him."

My stomach churns. I feel so stupid. "Are you sure? What about the things Jared and I have in common? I love my job. He loves his job. We both like to exercise."

Monroe is quiet for a moment or two. "Juliet," he says gently. "He's in love with power. He goes to CrossFit to look good naked. He's trying to impress you with the size of his wallet. And he's only into so-called slow dating as a code for getting *you* naked."

When Monroe says that, his gaze travels up and down me, lingering on my corset for longer than I'm used to from him. Like *he* wants to get me naked. I'm not sure if it's a Jared stare or a Monroe gaze, or why I like it so much, especially when I feel so foolish.

Because Monroe isn't wrong. They all add up, those red flags I didn't see.

"I thought Jared would be a good one," I say, horrified and dismayed. "How did I miss everything, and how did you see it all?"

He tucks his fingers under my chin, then lifts my face so I'm forced to look at him. His eyes are kind, caring as he says with sincerity, "I recognize all the bad boys because I've studied them. I can see them coming. And you have a big heart. You want everyone to have the benefit of the doubt. It's one of the best things about you."

My heart warms from the compliment. "I do. I don't want to become cynical. I wanted to believe he had promise," I say. But I still wish I'd done a better job at picking. This dating practice is suddenly much more overwhelming than I'd expected. "I feel like I have to learn a whole new language. Maybe I've been doing everything wrong all along."

I sigh heavily, then turn my glass in an aimless circle.

"We all do," he says, reassuring. "I bet I do lots of things wrong on dates. Feel free to tell me," he says, and it sounds like he just wants me to feel better.

Which I appreciate. But since he's been honest with me, I ought to be with him. "You role-played a little too hard," I say.

He nods crisply. "Noted." That's all. He doesn't protest. He doesn't deny. He simply adds, "I'll do better next time."

Next time.

My hopeful heart reappears. There will be a next time. I'll try again. I'll learn from this. Hell, I'll learn more from tonight than I ever would from a dating podcast. This is in-the-trenches education.

"Thanks," I say, then fidget with the napkin and glance toward the door. Vikas and Bowen are seated in a booth, cuddled up together. Vikas has an arm slung around his fiancé, and they look happy. Vikas glances my way and gives me a furtive thumbs-up in question.

I smile and nod, then return to Monroe. "I should go."

He reaches for my arm. "I'll give you a ride obviously."

As he settles up, I reapply my lipstick, then tuck the tube back into my purse. When he's done, we walk to the door and I wave goodbye to my new friends, then leave. When I head down the stone path, my attention lands on a gleaming black limo, waiting at the curb.

"Someone in there is a big roller," I whisper.

Monroe is quiet, but when I turn his way, he's smiling smugly. "Jared is."

A laugh bursts from me. "You got a limo to take me back to the house?"

Monroe clears his throat, then adopts his Jared voice and persona again. "Like I said, I'm really into slow dating and deal-making."

He's too much. Too committed to the role. And I'm too amused. I slide back into the game as well, playing the part, stepping closer, fiddling with the lapel of his suit. "Is this how you close deals, Mister Real Estate?"

A low rumble escapes his throat as he stares down at my hand on him. He covers it, pressing my palm more tightly against his firm chest.

"Is it going to work?" His smile burns off. In its place is heat and want.

My pulse surges. I glance at the limo, then at Monroe, then I drink in the whole vibe he has going tonight—the suit, the attitude, the red carpet of gifts.

They're coming from Jared, but really, they're from Monroe.

And they're *for* me.

Impulsively, I tug on the lapel, dragging him a touch closer. "Maybe it is."

He runs his thumb down my cheek, making me shiver. Stopping at my chin, he says, "Good. Because I can tell you for sure that there's one thing bad boys do better."

16

THE GOOD STUFF

Monroe

Screw the experiment. I might regret this in a minute. I might regret this in the morning.

If I were a better man, I'd stop right now, but I'm not a better man. I'm the man who wants this woman. *Badly*.

I shut down all the rational thoughts as I run my thumb over Juliet's bottom lip.

I've missed these lips. Missed this mouth. Wondered too much lately if she tastes as tempting as she did years ago.

I need the answer now, but I also want to take all night finding out. Somehow, I resist for another few seconds, letting the want build as I touch her once again.

She feels extraordinary.

Anticipation thrums between us, a buzzing in the air, a charge in my cells.

She looks up at me, waiting, eager. Trembling. Words press against my brain, trying to make landfall on my tongue. Like *I can't stop thinking about you.* And *it drives me crazy that you're dating.* And *is it the same for you at all?*

I can't risk voicing those thoughts, especially when I can't back them up with action. But this action? I can do *this*. I spread my hand across her cheek, hold her face and drop my mouth to hers.

Everything spirals away in the press of her lips, the taste of her mouth, the feel of her soft body melting against me.

She tastes like lipstick and Woodford Reserve. And the biggest-hearted person I've ever known.

I don't want to stop kissing her, so I don't rush. I brush my lips over hers, exploring every inch of her mouth, kissing the corner here, the corner there, then tugging on her bottom lip before I cover her mouth again. I take my time, savoring every sip of this kiss like it's the good stuff I just ordered at the bar. *She* is the good stuff.

And I luxuriate in every detail of Juliet Dumont. The soft gust of her breath. The sweet sound of her sighs. Most of all, the way she grips my jacket.

Like she doesn't want to let go either.

Then, how she moves with me, parting her lips as I kiss her more deeply, more insistently.

My hand roams to her hair, playing with the soft little tendrils framing her face. A pang of longing digs into my chest. It's not even a longing for more kissing, though of course I want that. It's a longing I can't name. One I don't fully understand.

One I just feel.

I kiss her harder, more passionately, memorizing every single second of this kiss as time falls through my fingers and becomes the past all over again.

Maybe that's what I'm longing for—the present not to stop.

I try to imprint the details of this moment. Her scent, like vanilla and honey. Her hair, soft and lush. Her body, warm and inviting.

Most of all, the way she gives. Juliet is the most open person I've known. She opens her heart to people. Right now, she's opening her soul to this kiss.

There's no reticence from her. Just pure, unadulterated want. She responds like a dream, leaning back, roping her arms around my neck, trusting me, giving me all her kisses, all her touches.

I don't deserve her, but I haul her against me anyway, our bodies colliding in a hot spark. Electricity sizzles so brightly up my spine that I break the kiss.

"Wow," I murmur.

Her smile is soft and kind of amazed. "Funny thing. I thought you were going to say that when I arrived at the bar."

"Wow?"

"Yes."

"I almost did," I admit.

"You didn't want to break character," she says, her breath still coming fast.

Mine is too. "He wouldn't have said *wow*."

She plays with the ends of my hair, asking, "But you felt the wow?"

"I felt the fucking wow," I rasp out, my gaze locked with hers. "I still feel the wow. I feel all the fucking wow."

She nibbles on the corner of her lips then tilts her head. "I'd like to feel the fucking wow."

Hot flames burn inside me everywhere. I tug her toward the waiting limo, but before I can open the door, I'm already missing her lips. It's been too long since I touched her. I yank her against me, kissing her once more. Deep, hard, a little possessive.

No. A lot possessive. Enough for the whole damn town of Darling Springs to know the dating experiment is mine and mine alone. Before I know it, I've got a hand on her ass, and I'm hiking up her leg, and kissing her like we're one of *those kisses*.

The kind everyone wants.

The kind that generates...*clapping?*

I break the contact, snapping my gaze toward the sound. Two men are strolling past us on the sidewalk. "Told you so, hun," the man in the paisley shirt says to the woman in my arms.

Juliet laughs. "You sure did, Bowen."

The other man, the one in the vest, gives me an approving once-over then turns to Juliet. "Like I said. Yesss and please and sir."

"I know. Trust me, I know," she says, like they're best friends already.

He's holding the other man's hand when he calls

out, "And save the date, hun. Three weeks from now, come to our wedding at the lavender farm."

He gives a time and a date, then they wave goodbye.

I have a ton of questions, but I don't even have the patience to ask what that was about in this second. Instead, I haul her into the car, then tell the driver to just drive, and when he says yes and raises the partition, I pull Juliet onto my lap.

"I can't stop thinking about you," I blurt out, and I probably will regret saying that. I can't back it up. I can't act on it. But I just can't keep it locked up inside any longer. Maybe I'm intoxicated on one glass of whiskey.

Though I'm not. Maybe I'm intoxicated on her.

"Same here," she says, sinking down on my lap, straddling me, and then grinding against my erection.

My brain scrambles. My chest is a furnace. And one kiss meant to prove bad boys do one thing better is dangerously close to turning into...well, the thing I want most.

As she rocks against me, she takes the wheel. Grabbing my face, thrusting her body, taking her pleasure.

Seeking it like a huntress. Deserving it too. She's all questing determination and hungry desire, rocking her hips, holding me hard, and using me.

It's the hottest thing I've ever seen.

It's a new side of Juliet.

This isn't the Juliet from eight summers ago. It's the new Juliet, and she's full of craving.

I roam my hands up her back, touching the satin of the corset, and her soft bare skin too. Pulling her impossibly closer, kissing her as she rides my hard-on.

She's relentless as she rocks, and thrusts, and then bites the corner of my mouth.

"Fuck yes," I rasp out, loving this newer, wilder side of her.

She just moans then slams her mouth to mine, kissing me sloppily. Moaning against my mouth. Panting.

Oh fuck.

Oh hell.

I know that sound. I'll remember it forever. She's close. So close. "Let me get you there," I command.

"Please..." she says, the word trailing off.

In a heartbeat, I'm on her jeans, unbuttoning, unzipping, then I slide my hand inside her panties.

She's hot and needy. She angles up giving me room, and I take it, coasting my fingers through the paradise of her wet pussy. "Wow," I whisper.

There's a smile, then a soft moan, then a loud, "Oh god."

"So fucking wet. So fucking beautiful," I say as I stroke her, flicking a finger across the swollen nub of her clit.

She lets her head fall back. "Yes. More," she says, practically begging.

I answer the call, following her cues, stroking faster as she rocks, pinching her needy clit then kissing a path up her chest to the hollow of her throat. "Missed this so much," I whisper against her, barely aware of what I'm saying.

Just needing to say it as her soft breathless sounds

fill the back of the limo. As her desire steals all my thoughts.

"Missed hearing you come. Need to hear it now. I have to hear it now, baby," I say, chasing her pleasure with my fingers, and my words, and my kisses.

Then finding it, as she grasps my shoulders hard. Ferociously. Then she shudders against me and cries out. A long, sensual *ohhhhhh* turns into *yes, yes, yes*.

I don't relent. I don't let up as she rides my fingers into her climax in the back of the limo. Then, she's shaking, shuddering, and smiling too.

She opens her eyes, and blinks, sighs. "So that was…"

"Yeah, it was." And I show her how much I liked it by licking each finger.

When I finish, her eyes are big and glossy. And so's her appetite, judging by the way she glances down at the outline of my hard cock.

But before I can even say, "We're not done," the car stops, jerking me out of the deliciously filthy moment and into a very real one.

I peer out the tinted window. I guess when I said, *Just drive,* the driver interpreted that to mean, *Just drive home.*

The partition lowers. "Will this do?" the driver asks.

I don't believe in signs. Never have. But if I did, this would seem like a sign that it's time for the irrational part of the night to end before it goes too far.

I clear my throat, adopting my best professional tone. "Yes. Thank you."

Trying to reset the night, I turn to Juliet. "We're here."

No shit. Tell her something she doesn't know.

She brushes her hair from her cheek, zips her jeans, and smooths a hand over her wildly sexy corset. "Right. Yes. I should...get to bed. Busy day tomorrow." She grabs her purse. "We need to start painting. I think we forgot to get a roller pan?"

Right. Sprucing up the house. The reason we're here. Not to relive the past. Or to tease a future we can't have. "Yeah. Paint. Roller. That."

I can barely form sentences, my mind is so buzzed on her.

I open the door and say goodnight to the driver. We head into The Horny House together.

But also, apart.

17

THE WOW

Juliet

I can't blame the mirrored bed for what we did in the car. I can't even blame the liquor.

One glass didn't make me tipsy. Monroe did, with his limo, and his *wow,* and his stupid, big-hearted willingness to help me out. Ugh. Why can't he be a bad boy for real?

But it's clear tonight was a mistake. A toe-curling one, but a mistake, nonetheless.

I roll my shoulders as I walk across the lawn, shrugging it off, moving on.

It's no big deal. It was just a momentary lapse of reason, and you'll go back to being co-workers.

But another voice says, *let it lapse again, girl.*

That's not helpful, so I ignore both voices as we head up the steps of the house.

The second Monroe punches in six-nine-six-nine, I snap my gaze away from the lock pad. I do not need this sex house's vibe seducing me again.

I take a deep breath, in and out, letting go of the limo ride fully.

Monroe holds the door open for me. Disappointed, I go inside, wincing as I walk through the living room. Our footsteps echo loudly and awkwardly in our silence.

What happens next? Do we brush our teeth, put on jammies, and hop into separate bunks?

Yes. You do. Like responsible adults.

I hate that thought. But it's what we should do, so when we reach the hallway that leads to the main bedroom, I force myself to adult. "Why don't I get ready for bed and—"

"—great. I'm going to..." But he never finishes the thought. Just turns the other way toward the kitchen.

Okay. That's clear. The man is leaving the limo ride in the past, like everything else.

I swallow past the lump in my throat as I trudge into the bedroom, not even bothering to flick on the lights as I fall face-first onto the bed.

"Ugh," I mutter into the pillows. "This sucks."

I do nothing but lie there, sad, a little empty, and all sorts of annoyed. With him, but also with me, and with this whole damn dating experiment.

After a minute or two of feeling sorry for myself, I grab my phone from my purse, skipping my self-improvement podcasts.

I don't need help. I need music, and I need it fast. I toggle over to my show tunes and click on "Popular" from *Wicked*. It has nothing to do with love or romance, and—bonus—Monroe would hate it.

I hit play, and the bright voices of Idina Menzel and Kristen Chenoweth fill the bedroom. It's like an assist from a witch that can deflect Monroe. This song witch will wipe the kiss and the limo ride from my mind. But when I flip over so I can head to the bathroom and wash my face, I flinch.

He's here, standing against the wooden frame of the bunk bed. His forearm rests against the top bed. The other hand holds a glass of...scotch, from the looks of it. His eyes are hard. Determined. I must not have heard him come in over the music.

He lifts the glass, knocks some back, then says in a rough, commanding tone that *is* clear over the song: "There's something I meant to say in the limo."

"What's that?" I ask above the rising notes.

His eyes lock on mine. His jaw is set hard. His gaze, full of fire. "We're not done."

My pulse soars. I hustle to hit stop on the music. "What do you mean?" I ask, full of dirty hope when the Broadway stars are silent.

"I mean, we're not fucking done at all, Juliet. I should have made this more clear in the limo." He points to the mattress I've been wallowing on. "But I'm not letting you get into that bed alone." Then to the wooden ladder. "I'm not climbing that goddamn ladder another night and sleeping six feet above you."

"You're not?" I ask, barely able to hold back a smile.

He's dead serious as he growls, "I can't take it anymore. Being this close to you and not touching. I can't stand another second of not having my hands all over your beautiful body."

He doesn't even wait for me to answer. He heads to the bureau next to the door and sets down his glass before he turns back to me. "Is it the same for you?"

My throat is dry. My cheeks are hot. I nod savagely as I launch myself at him, flying across the room. "Same." In seconds, I'm back in his arms, my hands grabbing the lapels of his jacket. "This suit."

He lifts a brow, a cocky move. "I had a feeling you'd like it."

"Yeah?"

"You've always said you like suits," he says, grabbing my hips, and manhandling me a little. I don't mind the rough play at all.

"Have I said that?" I tap-dance my fingers up his crisp dress shirt.

"Yes. I believe your words on air the other day were, and I quote, *I am a sucker for a suit.*"

I fiddle with the collar, having too much fun with him again. "So you wanted me to be a sucker?"

He just grins, saying nothing, just dragging me closer. What is he holding back? More words? There are parts of Monroe I'll never truly understand. But when he crushes his lips to mine once more, I stop thinking about the unknowableness of this man. I stop thinking entirely.

We kiss, and we grab, and we grope. Hands travel into hair, around waists, across stomachs. I kiss his neck, sighing happily when I get an up-close-and-personal hit of his soap. Shea butter and rosemary. It makes me a little woozy, and it's not just the scent. It's that he still uses it. Or did he start again? I'm dying to unearth hidden meanings, but what if there aren't any?

Best to leave that alone and focus on how good it feels to touch him again. He plays with the corset, undoing one eye hook as he kisses me madly, the kind of kiss that leads straight to bed.

We're at the door, so I flick on the lights at last. "How do you feel about lights on?"

He flashes a smile. "You don't know."

It's a statement. One he sounds delighted to make. "I don't know," I confirm, and then I swallow and find the guts to acknowledge the thing we don't speak of. *That week.* "We only slept together that one night."

In a tent. At a nearby campground. I had roommates. He was staying with his father. We wanted to be alone, so we made our alone time happen in a tent.

His blue eyes are fiery as they travel up and down my body. "Only once. Such a shame," he says, regretful, wistful, but aroused too. "And now, I want lights on with you. Want you to ride my cock. Want to watch you in front of me and above me. Want to see you fucking everywhere."

I can't breathe. My heart's beating too fast. He's not holding back in the bedroom department. Not one bit. Every single cell inside me is humming. I have no idea what will happen in the morning. But for once in my life, I'm not interested in planning the next date.

I want the here and now.

"We're doing this all wrong," I tease as I tug off his jacket.

"How do you figure?" he asks, working open my corset.

"Well, we're supposed to be in that bed at night and accidentally touch under the covers in the dark, and then one thing would lead to another."

He scoffs. "Fuck accidental touching. There's nothing accidental about the way I'm going to have you. Touch you. Fuck you."

I tremble everywhere, growing wetter with each of his plans.

He dives in for another kiss, stripping me free of my corset at last, letting it fall to the floor right as I undo the final button on his shirt then shove it off.

For a long, luscious moment we stare at each other. Half-naked. His eyes are lasered in on my tits, and mine are keyed in on his firm chest, then his trim abs, then the grooves between them, and finally, the happy trail that I want to play with.

I reach for his pants to undo them, but he's faster, lifting me up over his shoulder and carrying me the rest of the way to the bed. When he sets me down, he's careful not to bump my head and focused on his mission. He slides me onto the lower bunk, then removes my shoes and undoes my jeans, tugging them off. His moves are fast, deliberate, determined. I'm down to just a pair of pink panties, and he's gazing at them with hunger in his eyes.

"Did you wear these for Jared?" He doesn't mask the jealousy.

I shake my head. "I don't sleep with anyone on the first date."

He looks up with hooded eyes. "Not anyone?"

"It's a rule," I whisper, my chest heaving, my core aching.

"You're breaking it." It's not a question, but it's clear he wants to know *why*.

I give him the best answer I can with a hopeless shrug. "*With you*. I'm breaking it with you."

Then, he shudders. All over. It's the sexiest and most vulnerable thing I've ever seen. It's like he can't believe he's here with me. Like he can't believe I said that.

Or maybe I'm reading something into nothing.

I don't even know anymore. I just want this man. My eyes stray to my panties, and I say, "Take them off. They're for you."

He breathes out reverently then slides my undies down, taking his sweet-ass time now, coasting them off inch by seductive inch.

I'm naked and he's still in pants. I pout, then demand, "That's not fair. Get naked now. You wanted to watch me ride your cock, didn't you?"

"Correction: I want to watch you the whole fucking time."

There's something about the way he puts it, the focus on me...but I'll analyze it another time.

He hops off the bed, undoing the zipper as I reach for my purse, finding a condom as he drops his pants to the floor.

My memory breathes a happy sigh of relief. The front of his black boxer briefs are tented. "Off. Now," I demand, pointing.

With a sexy smirk, he sheds them in seconds, revealing a hungry cock pointing right at me. I'm so worked up, so aroused, driven only by this intense need deep within me to touch him, have him, feel him. I reach for his cock right as he climbs on the bed, climbing over me, then batting my hand away.

"Hey," he says in a caring tone, meeting my gaze. "You good with this?"

It's the first admission we've made of what's happening. To all the things that bind us. The past, but also the podcast and our work together, the plans we discussed last night at dinner even. But most of all, to our vastly different wants.

There's an unspoken question in there, but it's not hidden. It's the "you're okay with this just being sex" question.

My throat tightens for a second or two, but then I push past the rush of emotions, zeroing in on the flood of sensations instead. "Very good with it," I answer breathily, then shove the condom at him to prove just how fine I am with fucking him.

With a filthy smile, he looks down at me, then comes in for one more kiss. This one's a full-body kiss. He covers me, his chest on top of mine, his cock nestled against my center, our skin touching everywhere. Sparks shoot through me, radiating to my fingertips.

Monroe kisses me deeply as our bodies say hello again. When he finally sits up, careful not to hit his head on the bunk above us, he smacks me on my outer thigh. "Get on my dick, baby. Need to watch you."

Gladly.

We do the position dance, shifting around, bumping a little awkwardly, but I don't feel weird or uncomfortable with him. I just feel eager as he rolls the condom on, then grabs my hips, guides me over him. He slides one hand up my stomach to my breasts while he offers me his dick.

My mind is popping as I take it, rubbing the head against my wetness.

The sound I make is so feral I'm not even sure it comes from me. It's so wild, so heated. But he feels so good. He's groaning, too, rumbles of encouragement, words too like *yes* and *just like that* as I position myself over him. He nudges his cock against me, opening me more.

I sink down. My moan bounces off the walls as he fills me all the way up.

"Yes, baby," he murmurs, and it sounds almost unbidden. Like he can't help himself. Like he can't help it, either, when he says, "Look at you. Just fucking look at you."

I set my hands on his pecs then gaze down at the man who's sometimes my nemesis, who's often my foil, but who's always, first and foremost, my biggest fan.

That's both a terrifying and thrilling thing to realize in the heat of the moment.

I try to shake off those weightier thoughts. Try to dismiss them as I begin to move, slow and languid at first, adjusting, discovering.

Finding our pace.

This isn't how we fucked that one time. This is all new. It's more frenzied. It's needier. It's somehow even hotter.

He's looking at me with wild desire in his eyes. But I swear there's something more. Something like reverence. Something like that *wow*.

Maybe I just want to see that as I ride his fantastic cock, as my nerves ripple with excitement, as his muscles flex and his hands curl tightly around me.

"You," he bites out, studying me, then looking above, staring wantonly in the mirror. "You've never looked sexier."

"Same," I say. It's all I can manage. It's all I want to chance saying.

His hands clamp my hips tighter; his thrusts grow faster. More frenzied.

And his dick grows harder inside me.

He's so turned on watching me that my belly coils. Pleasure doesn't just build. It races. It rushes. It speeds up everywhere.

I don't even need to play with my clit. He's hitting a spot deep inside me, making sure I feel every inch of him. "Fuck, baby. Need you to come," he grunts out.

But I'm already there, bliss taking me hostage,

pulling me under as I fall apart, crying out as pleasure tears through me, spreading to every cell.

I'm still coming down from it as I collapse onto him, then he grabs my ass and pumps up hard, ferociously, till he tenses for a long time, then stills.

Groans.

Sighs.

Wraps his arms around me.

Pulls me close.

I don't know where we go from here but right now, I just don't care.

18

MASTERPIECE

Monroe

As sunlight streams through the window, I glance at the time on the cat clock. *Again.* It's seven-thirty. I'm never still in bed at seven-thirty.

But I've been awake for thirty-four minutes, and my body's itching to get up. To work on my course. To putter around the house. To exercise.

And yet...Juliet's hair, and Juliet's skin, and Juliet's Juliet-ness is like a magnet, keeping me here. She's not even in my arms. She's curled up, facing the other way, snoozing quietly. I haven't quite gone full Edward Cullen, staring at her while she sleeps, but I'm too damn close for my own taste.

Yeah, that's enough lingering in bed.

Abruptly, I swing my legs out of bed and head to the bathroom. A few minutes later, I've brushed my teeth, I'm pulling on boxer briefs, and she's still asleep.

I gather my clothes from last night, then fold them and set them on my suitcase. Then I pull on a pair of gray sweatpants, grab my phone, and make my way to the kitchen, where I attempt to make coffee that does not suck.

But that's a feat I haven't mastered. Because this cup of joe blows big time. After one more swallow of the disgusting mud, I snap a pic of my caffeine failure and open my messages so I can fire off a text to Carter, who is an espresso maestro. Ah, shit. There's a text from Sawyer winking up at me like it knows what I did last night.

Sawyer: First football game of the season is in a few weeks. Wanna go?

I'll just ignore that. Instead, I tap out a new text to Carter. I'm not lying by omission to him. Attaching the photo, I hit send.

Monroe: This coffee sucks. My barista better be ready with the espressos when I return to the city.

Carter's the morning-est person I know, so I'm confident he'll be up. He doesn't disappoint. A few seconds later, he responds.

Carter: Aww. That's the nicest thing you've ever said to me.

Monroe: Your bar is low.

Carter: Dude, it's you. Have you ever met you? Your emotional range is measured in micro-millimeters. So I translated your text to mean *I miss you and your life-affirming espressos.*

Monroe: Whatever you need to tell yourself.

Carter: My point exactly. So, how's spending every day and night with your crush?

I growl, annoyed at the blunt question. First, she doesn't seem like a crush. Second, because spending time with her in this house is challenging, complicated, and absolutely too wonderful for me to handle well.

I heave a sigh, wishing I knew what to do about last night. How to understand it. What box to put it in. I was so sure I had my thoughts and actions under control when we entered the house post-limo ride, but once she walked into the bedroom by herself, it took all of two minutes for my desire for her to consume me.

Now, in the light of the day, what am I going to do with this desire? It hasn't dampened. It's grown bigger.

But we're still co-workers. And we still live on opposite sides of the romance fence. Not to mention, she's Sawyer's sister. While he'd never pull that *don't touch my sister* bullshit, I still have to contend with the fact that I never told him about our fling eight years ago. Like I'm going to tell him now that I *flung* with her again.

When soft feet shuffle on hardwood, I push all thoughts of Sawyer aside. Juliet appears in the kitchen, wearing a long T-shirt that hits at her thighs. She's yawning and making my heart thump harder from a goddamn yawn.

Fuck, she's cute in the morning. I toss the phone on the counter, not giving a shit that it slides to the corner.

"Hey," she says, a little morning gravelly.

I didn't know she sounded like that in the morning. I tuck that into the ever-expanding Juliet file.

"Hey."

She tips her chin toward the coffee maker. "You made coffee. You are a hero."

"It's awful. I should be outlawed from making coffee again."

"That bad?"

"So bad I should go out and get you coffee right now if you want some," I offer, and I'm ready to go. All she has to do is say the word.

But she shakes her head. "I can do tea instead. I bet Eleanor has tea." Juliet heads to the cupboards and hunts around for a box. I can't stop watching her. The way she lifts her arm. How her heart necklace catches the light of the sun. How her T-shirt rides up to reveal she's not wearing any undies.

"You're naked," I grunt, stating the obvious.

She gives me a look like I've earned a cookie. "Yes, and the sky is blue."

But her tone doesn't deter me. I close the distance between us, crowding her from behind, pushing her hair off her shoulder, and dropping a morning kiss to her inviting neck—a slow, lingering one I don't want to ever end.

She murmurs, then leans back against me, her ass pressed to my groin, her back to my chest. "Monroe," she says.

"Yes?" I ask, utterly distracted by her neck.

"What are we doing?"

It's an icy dose of reality. I let go as she spins around, facing me. We didn't have *the talk* last night. We just crashed post-sex. This conversation was inevitable, though, and necessary. I run a hand through my hair, figuring out what to say. *Let's do it again* sounds crass. *Let's fuck for the week* even crasser. But the truth? *You're under my skin*—that's even worse.

I can't tell this bold, brave woman who's ready to find *the one* that I'm a little obsessed with her.

"What do *you* want to do?" If I had a shrink, they'd smack me. Well, no. My fictional shrink would give me the *you took the coward's way out* look, which is even worse.

Juliet's unreadable for a moment. That's rare for a woman who wears her heart on her sleeve. Then, her lips curve up. "I mean, I'd really like to summon Jumanji again."

I laugh, and it feels like it comes from the center of my soul. I reach for her, tug her against me, then cup her cheeks. "So what you're saying is sex with me *is* better than music."

She shrugs. "Some music."

"Woman," I say sternly.

"Well, I haven't heard *all* your songs," she says, then wiggles an eyebrow.

"Then, let me introduce you to my favorite one." I scoop her up, carry her out of the kitchen, and bring her straight to the rose chaise lounge in the den. I set her down on it, then move to the end of it. "This is what I wanted to do when you were picking through potential dates yesterday."

I don't give her a second to respond. I just push up her T-shirt to her waist and spread those beautiful thighs apart, groaning at the glistening reward of her pussy.

"You're already wet," I rasp out.

"And what are you going to do about it?" she counters.

"Enjoy my favorite breakfast," I say, then I dip my face to her sweet, hot center, kissing my Juliet in the morning.

Her taste goes to my head. So do her sounds, soft and greedy. Little *yeses* and *mores*. I take those words, and I heed them, lapping up her wetness, flicking my tongue across her swollen clit, bringing her closer to my hungry mouth.

Soon, she's moaning, and I'm moaning, too, as I devour this beauty who parts her legs wide for me, who rakes her hands through my hair, who rocks her hips against my face. Who gives herself completely to me as she cries out then orgasms on my mouth.

I kiss her slowly as she comes down from her climax, then stop when she opens her eyes and meets my gaze. "Better than coffee," she announces.

"But better than music?"

"Like I said, *some songs.*"

She reaches for me and pulls me close, offering me her mouth. That's just...hot. She doesn't hesitate. She kisses me while I taste like her, and for some stupid fucking reason, that makes my chest warm up even more.

When she lets go, she says, "We work together."

She's answering the question for me. She's always been braver than I am.

I rein in a wince. "I know."

"You're not looking for a girlfriend," she says.

Talk about cutting to the chase. I could give a simple *that's true*. But she deserves more. "It's not that I'm not looking. It's that I'm not any good at romance," I say, a little embarrassed. I'm the intimacy expert who's no good at love. But is it any surprise, given how I grew up? My father detached from the world when my mom died.

"Did Elizabeth tell you that?"

"The evidence tells me that. My track record tells me that. And you," I say, running a hand through her hair. "You deserve the best."

She smiles brightly. "That's true. I do."

I fucking love that she knows that. And there's no need to keep that to myself. I run my knuckles down her cheek. "Good. I'm glad you know you're a masterpiece."

"Feel free to tell me anytime."

I press another soft, tender kiss to her lips, whispering, "Masterpiece."

When I break the kiss, she slides her hand down my chest, and it feels so good I close my eyes. I have to. I can barely handle how her touch lights up some part of my soul. Especially when she snuggles closer to my neck, sniffing me.

I laugh. "Are you smelling me?"

"Yes. I sniffed you last night too. And you smelled like rosemary and shea butter. Like you got that day."

I freeze. She remembers. I swallow, a little uncomfortably, but it's a good discomfort, like after a workout. "You like that?"

"I always have."

That's not helping my fight. I don't open my eyes, not sure I can handle looking at her right now. I'd probably melt. "I always use it," I mutter.

She's quiet again, then she asks, "Ever since...?"

Here we are again. Revisiting the past, like she dared to do last night. I open my eyes and look into hers, giving her the truth. "Always."

She gasps, then says, "I like it."

My heart thunders, annoyingly. I want to spend the day here like this, wrapped up in her. But there's work to do, and walls to paint, and a tee time with my father late in the afternoon. "Good," I say. That's all I can manage, or else I will say too much.

I sit up, extricating myself from her. "Forget about the tea. Let me go get you a coffee."

"Okay," she says, but there's a crease in her brow. She's concerned.

"What's wrong?"

She inhales deep, like she needs to fortify herself. "Are we still doing the experiment?"

My throat burns hotter than it did when I ate that chili pepper to spite my father. Jealousy thrashes through me, stomping in my chest like an ogre. But I swallow it down and say yes.

I can't stand in the way of her goals. I can get her coffee, though, so I do that.

19

TINY POUNDY PART

Juliet

Fool me once, shame on me. Fool me twice, and damn straight, I grab a fuchsia feather boa and a pair of pink heart-shaped glasses from Eleanor's closet of wonders.

I put them on before I leave for the hardware store. With the feathers tickling my neck, I hop into Monroe's car, leaving him behind to start all the *painting stuff*. There's just that roller pan issue. After I turn the car on, I plug in my phone and blast the speakers off, rocking out to my girl Taylor as I cruise along, singing at the top of my lungs and then some.

My toxic trait is that I think I sound amazing, and I just can't stop.

Or maybe I'm crooning because I got some this morning. By the time I arrive at the shop on the outskirts of Darling Springs, I'm fueled by caffeine, morning sex, and music. The sex didn't end on the chaise. I'm a giver, so I gave him an *O*, too, when he returned with my coffee. Translation: I let him bang me on the poker table, and the flush I felt was definitely of the royal variety.

When I reach Josiah's, I park but don't get out right away. I take a beat to look around his car. I'm a little curious. Maybe I'll discover something new about Monroe. The interior is so clean, though, that there are hardly any signs of him in it. There isn't an air freshener hanging from the mirror. He wouldn't need it since he keeps the vehicle pristine. There aren't wrappers from energy bars eaten hastily on the way to meetings he's running late to. He doesn't run late. There isn't a sweatshirt on the back seat in case he gets cold. He doesn't get cold.

My heart sinks a little. He really is impervious to everything. My throat tightens, and my high vanishes.

I'd been hoping to find some little detail. A candy wrapper, or a packet of ibuprofen. Something to tell me that sometimes, he's vulnerable. A sign that would tell me he might be open to romance even in spite of the fact that if it went up in smoke, it could torpedo the podcast we've both put so much into building. And we're both planning to put so much more into it when we sell this gift of a house and reinvest it.

But nope. He's still strong, sturdy, unflappable, and unknowable Monroe.

I can't even be annoyed about his inaccessibility since he's been honest with me every step of the way. He was truthful eight years ago. He never led me on. He always had said it could only be a brief summer fling. He didn't ask me to wait for him after residency.

I would have said yes if he'd asked. Instead, I sucked down all my silly feelings, and said breezily *it's no big deal*.

He was honest with me this morning too. He's not interested in big love. My throat tightens once more, then my eyes sting with the threat of tears. I hunt around for a tissue. Would it kill him to have a tissue in the car? I slide open the console in case there's one.

But there's just...a photo.

My gut twists with guilt. I'm not even snooping, but this feels like real snooping as I stare at a sepia-tinted photo of a tree from years ago.

Maybe even decades.

It's a maple, standing tall and proud in a backyard. He mentioned a tree house at dinner the other night when I asked about his mom. Is this the tree she built the tree house in? It reminds me so much of the ink on his forearm. Emotion grips me harder and faster. I don't even touch the photo. It's private and personal and so not for me that I slam the console shut, draw a deep breath, and suck in my tears. I dab at my eyes with a pink feather, drying them. Then I rush out of the car, understanding he's not so impervious after all.

And somehow feeling like I know him just a little bit better.

I go inside, blinking off the final remnants of tears that I have no right to feel, and head to the paint aisle. After I snag the remaining items, I make my way to the checkout, but an endcap of hammers catches my attention.

I turn down the aisle next to it. Is there truly an entire aisle devoted to pounding? Why on earth does humankind need so many different hammers? Claw hammers and ball peens and sledgehammers. There are hammers from drop-forged alloy steel, and then this hammer that boasts that it's ultra-comfortable, and this one that brags about its durability. The variety is so staggering that I need to take a picture for my girlies. I grab my phone and snap a shot when a man reaches past me for a hammer with a tiny poundy part.

"Oh, excuse me," I say, even though he kind of got in my way. But it can't hurt to be polite.

When I step back, I nearly lose my footing.

It's the real Jared. He looks exactly like his photo—dark hair, perfectly coiffed. A straight nose. And he's wearing, you guessed it, a suit.

He's looking right at me. Or maybe at my feather boa? Nope. He's staring at my tits. Well, they are fantastic.

"Hey there," he says, and do I detect a bit of wolfish-ness in the *hey there*?

I'm not sure. Maybe I'm just leaning into Monroe's interpretation of him. "Who knew the world needed so many hammers," I say, keeping my reply friendly rather than flirty.

His lips quirk up on one side, a little smirky smirk. "Well, hammering is fun."

Oh no, he didn't say that. But yes, he did. "I guess

humanity has a hammering fetish," I say because really? *Really?*

Now I have to know if he's truly the guy Monroe played him to be.

"Well, yeah. Pounding and nailing are fun," he says.

And it's looking like Monroe was righter than right. To be sure, I reach for a little hammer and then improvise. "I like this one. I have some...deals to work on today. Some hammering deals. I think I can use this one to...nail them."

His grin spreads up, up, and away. "Speaking of deals, would you want to grab a drink? And maybe see how things go? No pressure. Just so you know I'm totally into slow dating lately," he says.

It takes all my self-control not to burst into laughter. "Thanks, but I have another deal to nail down."

I spin around, snickering over how the real Jared is a dick in exactly the ways Monroe predicted. This is both awful and reassuring.

My phone buzzes as I leave the store, and my heart does the tiny poundy thing, hoping that it's Monroe. But it's Mom, and she wants to know if I can meet her at Second Time Around to help find the right outfit for her date.

20

THINGS I WISH I KNEW

Juliet

In the corner of the store, Mom picks a pretty dark purple blouse and holds it up. "Perfect for an art gallery date?"

"It is," I say.

"Good. Now I need something for mini golf." Because of course she's going on a mini golf date. As she hunts through a rack, she asks, "How are your dates going?"

Heat creeps up my cheeks. "Great."

I mean, it's not really a lie. I did have a great date last night.

One well-groomed brow rises. "Oh? Will you see him again?"

Yes, in about twenty minutes, and I can't wait. "I will."

Her smile widens. "I had a good feeling a change of scenery would go a long way. So what's he like?"

I don't want to lie. I don't want to lead her on. But I am *not* going to tell her the truth about Monroe and me. "He's smart and funny. A little reserved, but not afraid to poke fun at me either," I say as she flicks through some short-sleeve blouses.

"He sounds great." She lets go of the clothing hunt, then lets out a mom sigh and squeezes my arm. "I've been worried about you."

I tilt my head. "Why?" I ask.

"Because I worry that your father and I are the example that you and Rachel and Sawyer saw for more than thirty years. And look what happened to Rachel."

Well, she's madly in love with her best friend who adores her, but it took a marriage to a man who lied to her about his secret family, then divorcing him to get there.

"Sure. But how does that relate to you and Dad?"

"We were never very affectionate when you were growing up. We were good friends. We still are. But when we were together, we held each other at arm's length." Mom smiles wistfully and places a blouse back on the rack. "It took me a while to see that, and I just hope it doesn't take you all those years," she says, and someone has definitely been to therapy. Someone is moving quickly through all that self-reflection too.

But my mind whirs with questions that hook into me, that make me think twice about how my parents behaved growing up. Come to think of it, they weren't very affectionate. They were always nice and kind. But they never danced in the kitchen, or kissed in the hallway, or held hands while walking down the street. "You were never in love with him?"

Mom smiles ruefully. "Once upon a time we both were. Then, we became companions more than lovers. Sometimes that works for some. Sometimes it doesn't. But for you and your sister and your brother—I don't want you to just accept the comfort of a relationship. I want you to have sparks and butterflies."

As she heads to another rack, I noodle on that. I like comfort, but Mustache is comforting. I deserve sparks and butterflies.

But something nags at me. What if I'm not picking well for some subconscious reason? What if it's not the algorithm? What if it's me approaching relationships the wrong way?

* * *

We're an hour into redoing the walls in the guest room. The windows are wide open, and we're painting to the tunes of Pearl Jam.

His choice. Not mine.

"How much older than me are you?" I tease as Eddie Vedder croons something beautiful but incoherent while I roll dove-gray paint up one wall.

As he spreads paint in a corner with a small brush, Monroe shoots me a look. "Old enough to know you deserve this for that remark," he says, then closes the distance between us and drops a dollop on my nose.

My jaw falls open in mock indignation. "You asked for it, buddy," I say, then grab a brush from the roller pan like we're sword fighters. I slash it down his arm. "A new tattoo. From me."

He grabs my hip, hauls me close, and slides the brush right above my breasts, slow and sensual in a way I didn't know paint could be. After he drops the brush into the pan, he drags his finger through the paint on my cleavage.

I shiver. Then murmur something unintelligible. Maybe I do understand Pearl Jam.

Monroe's eyes are blazing, but he's quiet as he studies me. My eyes, my lips, my chest. I don't mind his gaze on my breasts at all. I don't mind it so much, I shiver again.

"What is it?" I eventually ask, breaking the silence.

"You," he says. "You're so responsive."

My eyes float closed for a moment, and I feel a little lost in him. When I open them, I shrug in a sort of helpless admission. "I just like the way you touch me." Impulsively, I add, "I always have."

I'm tired of never acknowledging that time we had together. We only started to mention it last night, and it's been such a welcome relief.

Monroe takes my brush and sets it down in the pan, then drags me against him, our paint-stained clothes between us. "I've always liked touching you, Juliet. I did then. I do now."

I flash back on the conversation with my mom. *Sparks and butterflies.* I feel too much of them with him. And since he's willing to talk about the past, I press him more. "Do you ever think about that week?"

He nods, solemnly. "I do. More than I should."

"Me too," I admit.

"I think about how medical school was a mistake for so many reasons. But also because that stupid residency took me away from you."

My heart slams against my rib cage, but then it aches too. Even if circumstances hadn't separated us, what would we truly have become? He's a man who doesn't allow sparks and butterflies outside of the bedroom.

"But wasn't it for the best then? Given everything you said this morning?" I ask, facing that harsh reality rather than avoiding it.

He stares at me with such genuine vulnerability that my throat catches once again. But he doesn't answer me right away. He lets go, grabs a rag from the floor, and drags it down my nose, cleaning up paint, then swipes it across my chest, removing it from there too.

His smile is sad, the scar too. "I wish I knew."

Yeah, me too. "We should get back to painting."

"We should."

But we don't. He kisses me for a good, long time, so long that I stop thinking about painting, and the past, and all the things I wish I knew too.

We take a break from the fumes—even with the bedroom windows open, they're a little strong. In cozy outdoor deck furniture on the back porch, he works on his course, and I answer emails from clients about upcoming parties. Then, we brainstorm new marketing ideas for Heartbreakers and Matchmakers—collaborations we want to pursue with dating experts on social media, guests we might want to bring on, as well as dating trends to discuss. "When Rachel and Carter did that series of five first dates for Date Night, we talked about it on the show," he says.

"I remember that," I say, referring to both the dates they did for Carter's dating app sponsor, as well as the episode. I listened to it during a morning workout since I wasn't one of the hosts yet. "I heard that one and pretty much demanded to be on the podcast."

He laughs. "Yes, you were adorable marching into that board game night at Carter's place and pitching me."

I shrug proudly, owning my gumption then and now. "What can I say? I knew you needed me." I quickly add, "On the show," so there's no mistaking my meaning.

"Yes. I did," he says, fondly, then he stares out at the wildflowers in the yard, maybe at the shed across the grass, his expression turning thoughtful. "We've covered some interesting trends for the podcast, haven't we? I think that's the key. Keep pushing forward in the *dating frontier.*"

Does he mean *this* and *us*? And do I even want to talk about it on the show? But as soon as the thought lands, I catch it and hold it close, knowing the answer instantly. I wouldn't mind talking about the experiment. I've mostly been an open book on air. Why stop now? That's my shtick—sharing. "Monroe, would you want to talk about this whole dating coach thing on the show?"

He shifts his focus to me, but it still looks like the cogs are turning in that big brain of his. "I suppose it was inevitable that it'd feel like podcast fodder," he says and I'm pretty sure he's going to say yes. "It's definitely the dating frontier."

"Especially if I ride you reverse cowgirl," I offer since I'm helpful like that.

"What were we even talking about?"

"Exactly."

"We should definitely experiment with that. *Tonight*."

"Count me in."

"As for the experiment itself..." He blows out a breath and I'm sure the *why not* is coming. But then he locks eyes with me. "Maybe when we're done with it, we can revisit this. For now, I'd rather this be between us. What do you think?"

My heart stutters. I think I love that the experiment isn't about the show. "Works for me."

"Good. That's very good," he says, then shuts down his laptop. I set my tablet on the table and face up to another inevitable aspect of the experiment.

"You were right about Jared."

"In what way?"

"I ran into him," I say, then tell him the whole story, ending it with, "So I guess we really do need to keep going since you were right. You know men."

He cups his ear. "Say that again."

I narrow my eyes then grumble. "You were right."

He lets out a satisfied sigh. "That's sexy. Now come sit on my lap and say it."

"You're relentless."

"And you like relentless," he taunts, then pats his thighs. "Over here."

"And voracious."

"I'm not seeing the problem. C'mon."

"And bossy," I say.

"You like bossy."

I really do. I scoot over on the outdoor sofa and sit on his lap, grabbing my tablet to show him my new picks. But a funny thing happens as I scroll through Date Night options. Monroe wraps his arms more tightly around me. He growls into my neck a little more. He kisses my shoulders more intensely.

He's marking me even as I pick the next man.

His name is Dashiell; he's thirty-four and he's a brewer. "Even you need to be okay with that," I say to him, doing my best to be undeterred by his possessive affection. "Plus he plays softball in a recreational league. That's giving me Elodie and Gage vibes."

He cracks up. "Yes, he'll be just like our friends."

I nudge him with my elbow. "What do you think about him?"

"Tell me what you like about him," he says, putting on his shrink hat as he turns the question around.

I've given it some thought. And I've considered the lesson I learned from the Jared date, which was not to overlook douche vibes in the name of giving someone a chance. No douche vibes allowed from here on out.

With this in mind, I believe this new guy has real promise.

"Brewers must know a little something about chemistry, so there's that. Plus, men not having enough male friends is like an epidemic we address on the podcast a lot, but this guy clearly has plenty, since he plays softball in a rec league. Also, his arms are probably real muscly."

"You like muscles," he says, a little amused, but perhaps a little envious at the same time.

I squeeze his biceps. "Yes."

"Good."

But I want more than a *good*. I want to know his actual take on this guy. "Okay, serve it up. He doesn't have douche vibes like Jared, so what's your problem with him?"

"That would ruin the integrity of the experiment."

A laugh bursts from me. "You ruined the integrity of the experiment last night when you fucked me."

His arms band around me even more tightly. "Fine," he says, begrudgingly. "If you must know, here's my take. Beer and ball games, really? What would this guy even talk to you about?"

"I like baseball," I insist.

"Do you?"

I huff. "I like going to games with friends, okay? But that's close."

"Sure, in the way cars are close to bikes. You use them to get around. My point is you can put a hipster veneer on it, but it seems this guy still wants to live like he did in college."

I gasp. "No! You're looking at him through your...your...your shrink lens."

"Yes. Yes, I am," he says, laughing, but then the laughter fades and he shoots me an earnest look. "But you said not to role-play too hard, so I'll be more subtle in my character acting when you go out with Dashiell tomorrow."

I suppose that's all I can ask for.

He leans in to kiss me, but before he can destroy my panties even more, his phone chimes with an alarm. With a groan, he says, "I need to go play golf with my dad."

It sounds like he'd rather spend time hanging out with Real Jared than see his father. "Sorry you don't get along with him," I say, my heart hurting for the man.

"Yeah, me too."

We untangle from each other, and he heads into the house. I go inside, too, and resume painting. Fifteen minutes later, he returns, freshly showered and dressed in khakis and a trim polo, looking too hot for words.

Wait. I do have words, after all. "Can you ruin the integrity of the experiment again tonight?"

His eyes flash with dirty thoughts. "I can, and I will." He nods to the room, shifting gears quickly. "I'll finish painting this tomorrow. You should stop and...relax. Enjoy Darling Springs. Or take a nap. Maybe a bath."

I study him curiously. "Why are you saying that? So I'll be rested for you to ruin my integrity?"

"Yes. Also, I feel bad for leaving you to do all this. I'd rather do it tomorrow, so you don't have to."

"Aww, you do have feelings," I tease.

He brings a finger to his lips. "Don't tell a soul. Also, send me dirty pictures of you naked in the tub or something?"

I snort. "I'll take things that'll never happen for five hundred dollars."

He shrugs happily. "It was worth a try."

When he leaves, I dip the roller in the pan and work on the next wall. I'm determined to finish before he returns—a surprise for the man who's maybe not so impervious after all.

I slide the paint up the wall, returning to the conversation with my mother from earlier today. She said she wasn't in love with my dad most of the time, nor was he with her. And yet they *seemed* happy enough. They were good parents, they showed up for us, and they supported us. I never sensed they weren't each other's big love.

I stop mid-roll. As a kid, would I have even known what a big love looks like?

I finish rolling to the ceiling, dip the brush in the paint, and then stroke against the wall again, answering in my head. No, I don't suppose I would have known that then. Now, though, I wonder—did their arm's length, friendly love inform how I approach romance?

I furrow my brow, trying to make sense of the past and my present as I paint and paint, until my head starts to spin from the fumes and I stagger from the room.

21

UNDER PAR

Monroe

With an effortless flick of the club, my dad sinks the golf ball, plink, right in the hole. "Huh. Would you look at that?" he says as if it's been ages since he birdied and not just three holes ago.

"Impressive," I say, trying not to sound begrudging. Of course he's beating me. He always beat me at Scrabble too.

He scoops the ball out of the hole, tossing it proudly like it's a pair of keys to a Rolls. Only two more holes, and we're done. Two more holes till I can peel out of here and hit the gas pedal.

The image of Juliet naked in the tub, luxuriating in bubbles, keeps me going. Shame she hasn't sent a selfie, but there's still time. Don't even know if there's bubble bath stuff at the house. But my dirty mind has decided there is.

"Good game so far. Your golf game is better than I expected," Dad says.

Hello, backhanded compliment.

I bite back all the comebacks forming. Like, *because you thought I'd fail at that too?* If I were my own shrink, I'd give me a slow clap for saying evenly, "I play in the city."

Ha. How's that for a placid response?

"Nice. You get out to the links often, I imagine?" he asks as we stroll up the hill to the second-to-last hole.

The implication. Dear god, the implication. "Just enough," I say tightly.

Don't take the bait.

I peer ahead, then behind, hoping someone will spot him again, and hoist the conversational burden from me. Everyone here at the Duck Falls Golf Course knows him since this place is frequented by co-workers from the university where he teaches and the hospital where he's performed life-saving surgeries.

We've played the back nine as the afternoon melts into evening, and he's been stopped a few times along the way, by friends and colleagues in golf carts or walking the course, wishing him well. He's made sure they all know about his retirement party this weekend, and that they're all coming.

No surprise, they all are.

But would it kill someone, *anyone*—a shop owner, a nurse, the barista who serves him his green tea every day since tea is better for the brain—to magically appear right now?

I peer around. No such luck.

Dad clucks his tongue as we walk. That's his thinking sound. We're heading past a copse of trees. Some are maple, and instinctively, I glance down at the tree on my forearm. Dad wasn't like this when she was alive. He wasn't so arrogant, so obsessed, so disappointed. Back then, he joined us in the tree house she built. He went out for bike rides after she taught me how. He played board games in the kitchen with us for fun, not to decimate.

I dig down, trying to find the compassion to fill the silence. "I guess you're looking forward to the party?" I ask, right as he speaks too, saying, "How are those online studies going? That's what you're in town for?"

We both laugh awkwardly. He gestures with his club. "You go first."

Briefly, I contemplate dodging the topic of why I'm in town. But it's best I tell the truth. Once we put that home on the market, it won't be a secret. It'd be another rift between us if I don't mention it.

"Yes. I'm working on the online course." I clear my throat, then add, "But also a listener gifted us a house. Here in Darling Springs."

He stops his pace near a sand trap, sounding a little like a robot reprogramming its motherboard as he sputters, "What? How? Why?"

"It's a gift deed," I start to explain, but he cuts me off.

"I know what a gift deed is. You mean, a listener of the podcast just gave it to you? Heartbreakers and Matchmakers?"

I'm the surprised one now. "You know the name of the podcast?"

"Yes. I do, Monroe." It's said firmly, brooking no argument. "Why would someone give you a house?"

"She lost her first husband. She's off on a honeymoon with her new guy, and she said she wouldn't have had the courage to pursue this romance if not for us," I say, bracing myself for a snide comment. Or another backhanded compliment.

Instead, there's only the sound of the leaves rustling in the early evening, the birds chirping as they settle. Then a contemplative *huh* as his eyes look a little lost. Finally, he clears his throat, maybe clearing some unexpected emotion too as he says, "That's terrific."

I'm not sure if the terrific news is the widow finding love again or giving us a house.

We reach the hole, but the group ahead of us must not be finished since a put-together woman in khaki shorts and a mint green polo swings her club gracefully, then watches the ball soar. When it lands far, far away, she gives a fist pump. "Yes," she says, cheering herself on.

She spins around, then blinks, before she quickly smiles. "Hello, Doctor Blackstone," she says. She's about my dad's age, with mahogany skin and tight black curls under a golf visor. She has the poised demeanor of a fellow doctor, and I'm not at all surprised when my dad says, "Good to see you, Doctor Wesley. Retirement must be treating you well."

"I can't complain," she says, then nods up ahead. "I'm golfing with my daughter."

"Excellent," he says, then claps me on the shoulder. "This is my son. Doctor Monroe Blackstone."

Of course that's how he's introducing me. I can hear what's unsaid in the back clap too. *Don't tell her you're not practicing.*

I extend a hand. "Pleasure to meet you."

"And you," she says, warmly, then to my father she adds, "I see it runs in the family."

Yes, medicine does. As well as the inability to sustain a relationship.

"Yes, it does. I trust your daughter is keeping the practice going?"

"Of course she is," Doctor Wesley says with obvious pride.

"Wonderful," my father says, and it's a miracle he can get that one word out without coating it in the jealousy he must feel. He shifts gears quickly. "I'll see you this weekend though?"

"Wouldn't miss it for the world," she says, then her gaze lingers briefly on my father with a hint of appreciation—maybe attraction—in her eyes.

Save yourself. Find someone else. The Blackstone men are no good.

"I better go," she says. Then, smiles at him. Just him. "Jameson."

He smiles too. "Jada."

Is my father fucking flirting? Kill me now.

I'm going to pretend that never happened.

I hunt for topics to tackle next just in case he's thinking of telling me something about his romantic life, but he speaks first when she's out of earshot, saying, "I was just thinking. Would you be willing to give a speech at the party? Right after the cocktail hour."

Did I hear him right? He wants the son who disappointed him to extol his virtues? "You want *me* to give a speech for *you*?"

There's nothing but *yes* in his eyes. "Who better than my son?"

Anyone. Literally anyone. "What do you want me to say?" We're not close. We're not friends. Does he want me to lubricate the path for him to Jada? That's just weird. And it's not happening.

"Something appropriate for a retirement party. That sort of thing. You're good with words," he says, and I wait for the dig that's sure to follow.

But nothing more comes, so I set up the ball on the tee to keep busy. "So, something like *he's a great doctor and teacher*?"

Dad beams. "It's practically writing itself."

Not exactly.

"And maybe how you're glad everyone is here," he adds. "How nice it is to see everyone. Like all your friends."

Wait. What? He better not mean kids from high school. The last thing I want is a high school reunion vibe. There's a reason I don't do those things. The reason being high school sucked. "Who?"

It's a miracle I don't breathe fire when I ask.

His smile is gregarious. "Sawyer. Carter. Gage. Juliet. Axel. Those kind of friends. My assistant sent out invites this afternoon," he says, then points to the tee, *move it along* style.

But I can't move on. I drag a hand through my hair, brow pinched. "You invited *my* friends?"

"Yes. You're always mentioning them on the podcast. So I thought it'd make it more enjoyable for you," he says, and the therapist in me appreciates the effort, but the son is still struggling, especially when he just motions to the tee once more, moving on. "We're going to get all bunched up."

I turn to the tee. I'm not even sure what's happening anymore as I take a swing, feeling totally disconnected from my body.

I'm giving a speech, everyone is coming to my father's party, including his new crush, and he listens to my podcast.

22

JUST YOU

Monroe

There's still no dirty bathtub pic from Juliet, but that's no excuse for me to show up empty-handed when I return. I take a detour to Main Street on the way home, pulling over at The Slippery Dipper.

Grateful the store is still open at eight in the evening on a Wednesday, I hustle inside, scan the offerings, and grab a bath bomb. The scent is honey and cinnamon. Sounds good enough to eat and that describes Juliet, so I grab one. As I'm checking out, I spot a vanilla body spray.

When in Rome and all.

I snag that too, then set them down on the counter. The man at the register has a young dad vibe, tired but affable with red hair and fair skin. "How's your evening going?"

"Great," I say, choosing to answer how it will be rather than how it was. "And you?"

"Not so bad." He glances down at my purchases. "Good picks. My wife loves this bath bomb."

"Good to know."

He lifts a curious brow. "Want them wrapped?"

Dude is brilliant. "Sure. Good call."

He gives an easygoing smile. "Had a feeling."

I'm not usually this chatty with anyone but close friends. But I'm damn curious about something. "Do I give off buying a gift for a woman vibes?"

His smile widens and he nods knowingly. "Big time, man. Big time."

Yeah, I'm a little obvious, but I don't mind. When he's done, I take the wrapped gifts, and thank him.

"Hope your—" he stops, perhaps rethinking *girl-friend* or *wife*, understandably, then shifts to, "Hope she likes them."

Out of nowhere, my chest aches for a few seconds with the unsaid words. With a wish. But there's no time to linger. "Me too."

The bell chimes as I leave, and I'm about to hop back in the car, when I make a game day decision and rush into the bougie gourmet market next door. Juliet likes food, so I head to the deli counter and order a veggie grinder to go. With Gouda cheese of course. Then, a second for myself since it sounds good.

I don't call first and ask if she's hungry. If she cobbled together a meal while I was gone, this will keep till tomorrow. It's more of a gift this way.

At the self-checkout, the man in front of me is buying a pretty bouquet of flowers and a box of cereal. That's a good idea. I spin around, head to the floral section and grab some orange, peach and yellow roses that look like firecrackers. I grab one more thing for tomorrow's date with the brewer then I'm done and out of there.

But once I've returned to the house and punched in six-nine-six-nine, the home is eerily quiet.

Hmm. That's odd.

With the bags and bouquet in hand, I scan the living room. It's dark. The kitchen looks dark from here too. It's only eight-thirty. Maybe she conked out early? I toe off my shoes and pad quietly, just in case, but the hair on the back of my neck prickles with worry.

Fuck quiet.

"Juliet? Honey? Are you okay?"

I turn down the hall. No answer.

I pick up the pace, my heart skittering ridiculously with worry. Where is my Juliet and is everything okay? I turn into the bedroom, and my shoulders relax. She's here. But she's curled up on her side, hands tucked in prayer under her cheek. "Hey," she says, groggily.

My heart goes too soft. "I didn't mean to wake you up," I say, then close the distance and sit on the bed, snapping into practical mode. "Are you tired? What's wrong? What can I do for you?"

She winces, her hand coming to her forehead gingerly. "I think I have a migraine."

I set down the gifts on the bedroom floor, and take her hand, rubbing it. "Did you take Tylenol? Do you get migraines regularly? If so, do you have headache meds with you and where are they?"

She shakes her head. "I think it was the paint. The fumes got to me after a while."

"Paint is the devil. But I thought you were supposed to leave it for me," I say, sternly.

"I wanted to finish it. To surprise you."

My heart tries to fight its way out of my chest. "You didn't have to do that for me. You weren't supposed to."

"Bossy."

"Yes. Because I wanted to finish it. *For you.*"

"Don't worry. I won't fight you for the last wall. The paint tried to kill me. I had to lie down. I fell asleep for a couple hours."

I rub her hand more, unable to stop touching her. "Does it still hurt? It's good that you're lying down in the dark."

"It does still hurt."

Her small nod breaks my heart. "Let me get you some Tylenol."

She doesn't fight me on this either. "Thanks. I need it."

I reach for the sandwich in the bag, brandishing the brown paper. "If you're hungry, I got you a sandwich."

"I love sandwiches," she says.

I drop a kiss to her forehead, then whisper. "I know."

I take off on a mission to do whatever I can to make her feel better. Back in town, I rush into The Slippery Dipper, which is closing in five minutes. The man greets me with a curious smile. "Hey there..."

But there's no time for details. "I need a lavender eye mask."

"Gotcha," he says with a crisp nod, recognizing a spa emergency when he sees one.

Next, I'm back in the gourmet store, buying the world's most expensive Tylenol, then I'm zipping back to the house. The lights are still low, but this time, one shines dimly from the bathroom. The door's open, so I follow the soft glow, and...

Holy shit.

She is *in* the tub. She smiles at me. "Took the doctor's advice."

I drink in the sight of her in the claw-foot bathtub, draped in bubbles, with only the faintest lights on. It smells like warmth, of honey and cinnamon. Her hair's piled high in a bun, wet strands framing her face.

I'm strangely glad she never sent me a photo. Not that I'd wish a headache on her. But there's no picture that would compare to how it feels to see her here, like this, in the flesh.

I could stare all night, but I shake off the clutching feeling in my chest, filling a cup of water from the sink and offering her some Tylenol. She swallows them, then hands me the cup. I set it down on the vanity.

She gestures to the bubbly tub. "Hope you don't mind that I took the liberty of opening the gift."

"It was for you," I say, and I can't take my eyes off her.

"I had a feeling."

"I'm glad you opened it."

"Me too. I feel a tiny bit better." She nibbles on the

corner of her lips, giving me an apologetic look. "But not integrity-ruining better."

I roll my eyes. "Woman, there is no integrity being ruined tonight. I want you to feel better. I want you to feel good again."

She looks at me, her gaze holding mine. "I do now."

I close the toilet seat, sit down on it, and hang out with her as she relaxes in the hot water. When she's done, I get her a big, fluffy towel, and wrap her in it, pressing a chaste kiss to her neck. "Let's get you back in bed."

A few minutes later, she's in her jammies and settling into bed. "I put the sandwiches in the fridge. I'll have mine for breakfast," she says.

"Sandwiches for breakfast sound good."

"It's a date then."

I can't wait for it. I dart out to the kitchen, heat up the eye mask for twenty seconds in the microwave, so it's warm, then return to the bedroom and hand it to her. "Got you this just now. It should help."

She takes it and sets it on her eyes as she lies down. "You must be The Slippery Dipper's best customer tonight."

I sit on the bed with her. "I think I am." Then, impulsively, I add, "I thought of you when I was there."

I can't see her eyes twinkling, but her playful smile tells me they are as she asks, "Yeah? What did you think about?"

Maybe it's easier to say this when she can't look at me. When she can't disarm me with those bright green eyes. Or maybe she's already disarming me. I lie next to her. "The day I saw you there," I admit, my stomach fluttering annoyingly.

"Hmm. I don't remember that day," she says, her lips twitching.

"Evil woman."

"Is that where I ran into you?"

I dip my face, nip her shoulder. "You know you did."

She wiggles. "Maybe you should remind me."

I can see it so perfectly. I can feel it too. "You were reaching for a heart-shaped soap. I was grabbing the one next to it. Maybe, *possibly*, I let my hand slide so it touched yours."

"And here I thought you were good with your hands."

"I was. It wasn't accidental, Juliet."

A tremble moves through her body. It's beautiful to see. "Fine, tell me more about this un-accidental touch."

I close my eyes too. I can't look at myself in the mirror as I tell this story. "I recognized you. I hadn't seen you in a few years, but there you were. My good friend's sister. And none of that mattered. All I thought was, *I have to see her again.*"

"I'm starting to remember this," she says, but then tilts her head closer to me, tapping her chin. "Did we see each other? It's a little fuzzy with this headache."

I laugh softly. "We saw each other. At the arcade, at the movie theater, the beach. The tent."

"Ahh. It's coming back to me now."

But so's the ending too. That's the problem. We'd only spent a week together, but I wanted more. Only, it wasn't feasible. Hell, it's not feasible now. We have too much at stake. But more than that, I don't trust myself to be the man she needs. One failed marriage and a handful of short-term relationships that fizzled, too, are proof that my skills lie elsewhere. If I even tried, I'd probably turn out just like my dad, which means I'd be just as unworthy of her as the other guys she's met. I won't do that to her.

I can't have a future with her, but maybe I can rewrite the past. "I wanted to see you again, Juliet."

She inhales, exhales, like she needs more breath for this. "Yeah?" There's hope in her voice. Such a dangerous thing.

"I did," I say, with regret in mine. "But what could we do? I was moving across the country to New York."

"And I wasn't," she says, wistful.

I could stop this conversation, but maybe we need this—an admission that it ended too soon, before either of us wanted it to. Since we reconnected when I returned to San Francisco, we've been friends and co-workers, but we never truly acknowledged that week.

"I couldn't string you along," I add.

She says nothing. Just sort of hums thoughtfully.

"I wanted to though. Not string you along. But see you more. Again and again," I say into the reflection, forcing myself to face the truth of how I felt back then. I felt so much more than I told her. Than I told anyone.

"Me too. I wanted that too."

My heart thumps, missing what never happened. But at least that week no longer hangs unspoken between us. I squeeze her hand tighter. "How's your head?"

"A little better. You mobilized quickly to heal me."

"I hated to see you sick. I want to make it better."

She smiles. "The doctor in you."

I shake my head. "It's not the doctor in me," I say, firm and clear.

She takes off the mask, sets it on the pillow, turns her gaze to me. "No?"

My breath hitches. Her bright eyes on me are turning me inside out. "It's just you."

She sighs softly, then curls up in my arms. "How was it? Seeing your dad?"

I snort. Then scoff. "He wants me to give a speech at his retirement party this weekend."

"Will you?"

"I said yes," I say. "And he invited everyone. All our friends." Wait. She probably knows that. He said his assistant invited her. But what if I could do it first? "Have you checked your email?" I ask with some urgency.

"No."

"Good." I don't want him to be the one to invite her. That RSVP belongs to me and me alone. "He's going to invite you, but I want to instead."

"So you're beating him to the punch?"

"Yes. Will you go with me?"

She hums, then shoots me a quizzical look. "Will you be pretending to be one of my dates?"

I growl. Then knit my brow. Then breathe hard through my nostrils.

She laughs. "That's a no."

Damn straight. "Go with me. Just me."

"I'll go with you. *Just you.*"

I wrap my arm more tightly around her, tugging her against the crook of my neck. "I got you flowers too."

"I saw. I put them in a vase in the kitchen. That was sweet of you. They're fiery."

Like you. I saw them and thought of you. Everything makes me think of you. But I can't say any of that, or I'd be a dick who can't back up those words. Instead, I keep my reply simple. "The guy ahead of me in the store was getting flowers. That reminded me the market had them."

There. I'm not totally revealing I'm obsessed with her.

"I like them. And the body spray and the bath bomb. And I know I'll like the sandwich."

And that was a lot of gifts. Might as well slap a billboard on me that says *I'm too into you.* "Funny story. The guy who was buying the bouquet was also buying a box of cereal," I say, deflecting once more.

"Someone was optimistic," she says, amused.

"That's exactly what I thought when I saw it," I say, then kiss her forehead. Fuck it. "And I couldn't wait to tell you."

Soon, I undo my slacks and take off my shirt and stay the night with her.

In the morning, when she's off doing yoga, I finish painting. Then, I get ready to take her on a date as Dashiell.

That guy has no idea how lucky he is.

23

NEVER BEEN KISSED

Juliet

At the go-kart check-in counter that afternoon, I peer at the wooden sign listing the rules, then touch my wrist.

Shoot.

I turn to Monroe. Or Dashiell I should say. "I didn't bring a hair tie," I say with a wince. One of the rules is *Tie up long hair or tuck it into your collar.*

"No problem," he says, in a kind of hipster cool that matches the outfit. He's decked out in jeans and a plaid button-down, left open over a white T-shirt. The cuffs are rolled up on the button-down, showing off those forearms I can't ignore. With his ink, he definitely looks the part of the cool, laidback brewer. He reaches into the pocket of his jeans, fishing around. "Here you go," he says, handing me a black elastic hair tie.

My lips part in surprise. "You brought one?"

He gives a no-big-deal shrug. "Scanned the rules

last night when I found the place. Wanted to make sure we could do it."

Instant grin. "Thank you," I say, then loop it around my hair. With that done, and helmets in hand, we head to the outdoor track. "Thanks again for paint—"

But I stop myself. He's not Monroe, who finished the bedroom this morning while I was out. He's Dashiell, the ball-playing brewer who likes dogs and deep conversations, and I'm supposed to use this first date to practice my getting-to-know-him skills for a grade. I backpedal and try again. "So, are you a big fan of go-karting?"

Ugh. That's so basic. I need to talk better on this first date.

"I've gone a few times. But what about you? This is your first time?" he asks quickly—no, *smoothly*—shifting gears.

Sheepishly, I nod. "Yes. It is."

He stops in his tracks. "Shit. My bad. I should have asked you first."

Whoa. He's playing the sensitive brewer. Interesting. Kind of clever. "It's okay," I reassure. "I like trying new things."

He hooks a thumb toward the parking lot. "You positive? We can do something else. Mini golf, roller skating. There's a sweet roller rink a few towns over that plays retro tunes."

Like the kind you like?

But I can't say that since he's not being Monroe right now. "I swear I'm good with this."

He wipes his brow exaggeratedly. "Whew." We

reach the track. "Now, I don't want to be a mansplainer or anything, so just kick me in the shins if I get toxic. But here are a few good guidelines," he says, and I fight like hell to rein in a grin. He's nailing the emotionally aware side of this guy. I'm not even sure the real Dashiell is this thoughtful. Or that there were green flags in his bio to suggest he was. But it's endearing to see Monroe play this part, so I listen as he shares some tips.

Then I strap on my helmet and hop into the go-kart.

* * *

An hour later, I'm beaming as I rip off my helmet. "That was so fun," I say, pulse still racing as I offer Monroe/Dashiell a high-five.

"You did great. You're a natural," he says, smacking back. He gives a hopeful smile. "Burger and a brew?"

"Let's do it."

We head to the outdoor burger shack next to the go-karts, then grab a picnic table once we have our food—a veggie burger for me, and a chicken patty for him.

We shoot the breeze for a bit as we nosh, then he sets down the remains of his sandwich and asks, "So, you're a breakup party planner? That's fascinating. How'd you get into that?"

I reach for a napkin, then wipe the corner of my mouth. "I'd always loved celebrations growing up. Any kind of party was my jam. But I didn't know exactly what it would entail, so after I spent the summer working in a bookstore and sending out my resume, I landed a more typical job at a marketing firm."

The summer I met you again.

"Then I got kind of lucky with a client," I add.

"How so?"

"She was a party planner who wanted us to market her on social media. I worked with her closely and she took me under her wing and became a mentor of sorts when I was ready to make the jump to do it on my own. At first, I thought I would do the more typical events—award ceremonies, graduation parties, fancy birthday fiestas. But I did one divorce party, and I was hooked. All because of the guests. The women had the best time."

We're surrounded by other go-karters at picnic tables, but the way Monroe's eyes are locked on mine, it's as if we're the only ones here. "Was that the moment you knew it was what you wanted to do?" he asks.

I can still recall that party at a wine bar, the camaraderie, the sheer friendship and support palpable in the room. "Absolutely. It felt right," I say, enthused by the memory. "I started to plan more parties and then it just took off."

"What kinds of breakup parties do your clients want?"

"I've done so many kinds. I did a party where the guest of honor wanted to redecorate her home. We started by putting paper on her walls and her guests wrote their wishes for the next phase of her life. It was kind of beautiful," I say, emotion gripping my throat briefly as I picture that party and the women who came together to help their bestie move on to the next phase of her life. "Another was a makeover theme. We hired makeup artists and all the guests had super glam makeup done and then went out to sing karaoke in their best sparkly outfits."

His smile is as festive as that night was. "And did that help her move on?"

Proudly, I nod. "I actually had lunch with that client a few weeks ago. She met a new man and she's happily dating again."

Like me.

At least, I'm happily dating now. As in...this second.

Because this is the best date I've been on in a long time. So good in fact, that I call a timeout. "Jumanji."

Monroe dips his face, chuckling. When he raises it, he doesn't look any different though. But what did I expect? A transformation? "Yes, Juliet?"

Ah, there's that controlled, dry sense of humor I know so well. "I'm having a good time. Dashiell is so open and interested. Attentive and curious," I say, trying to figure out what's going on.

"And what's the problem?"

"I don't actually see this guy's flags?"

Monroe nods a few times, his expression hard to decipher. With a sigh, he shrugs. "I stopped acting half an hour ago."

"You...did?"

"I never heard the story of how you started your business, so I guess I got into it. Broke character."

Warmth floods my chest. Chased by something

deeper. An affection that feels big and boundless. "You were just enjoying my story?"

"Don't say that like it's such a surprise," he says.

I rewind to the beginning of the Dashiell date. "Were you role-playing at the start with the hair tie?"

His eyes blaze. They're almost hard. "No. That was me. I don't fucking know if this guy would remember to get you a hair tie. But I would, so I got it last night."

It comes out rough and intense like sandpaper, and yet it has the opposite effect on me. It feels like sweet heat, and it melts me. I can't resist him. I lean in for a kiss, then catch myself just seconds before my lips brush his. "I didn't mean to break the rules—"

"But I do," he says, curling a hand around my head.

Kissing me hard.

Passionately.

He grips my face, murmuring against my mouth, groaning.

God, the sound is so borderline feral that I surrender. I lean my head back, and he reads all my cues, dipping his face and kissing my throat right next to my ladybug necklace.

Before I know it, I'm moaning in a way that's quite inappropriate for an outdoor burger shack. I maneuver a hand between us, pressing it to his chest.

He stops the kiss with a hard shudder. A dark look in those blue eyes. "Let's get out of here," he says, and we race out to the parking lot.

Once we're in his car, he can't keep his hands off me. He's kissing me ravenously, like he'll go mad if he can't touch me.

I've never been kissed like this, and I don't want to be kissed any other way again. I can't keep my hands off him either. One palm slides down his firm chest. The other travels to the steel outline in his jeans.

Monroe lets out a heady breath as I stroke him. Then headier as I grip his hard length. I should wait till we're back at the house. But I'm so keyed up that I rub my hand harder, driven by his grunts, his groans.

And by this new desire gaining speed inside me. It's a desire I rarely feel, but it's consuming me now as I fondle his covered cock.

He breaks the kiss, grabs my chin. "What are you doing to me?"

I smile. Maybe a little wickedly. But also...boldly. "Well, I was definitely *hoping* to do something to you."

He lifts a brow in question. "What's that?"

I palm him some more, drawing out more of those needy grunts. "I have this thing..."

"Okay?"

"I haven't really loved giving blow jobs ever, but I'm definitely into your cock."

His eyes widen in surprise. I'm not sure if it's over the blow job admission or my avid interest in his dick, but I power on. "And I'd like to suck you. But..."

He swallows, then asks in a careful, controlled voice. "But what?"

There's no pressure in his tone, just the razor's edge of curiosity.

I flashback to Monday morning when he teased me about bike riding. "You said the other day you were good at teaching. And, fine, we were talking about riding bikes, but it got me to thinking, especially since this whole—" I stop before I say *experiment*. This thing feels like so much more, and yet it is just that. "Since this experiment is about teaching."

A dark cloud passes over his eyes, but quickly it fades, replaced by a flickering flame. "And...?"

Chin up. No shame. "I want you to teach me to give a blow job you'd really like, but one I'd like too. Would you be my blow-job coach?"

He guns the engine, while I seize the moment, plugging in my phone and calling up a tune.

In seconds, Akinyele's "Put It In Your Mouth" blasts through the air-conditioned car.

Monroe drives faster—maybe too fast. He whizzes past a sign for a road construction detour and then slams on the brakes as we hurdle toward the blockade.

24

LOLLIPOP TEACHER

Monroe

"Fuck me," I groan from the center of my law-abiding soul. Okay, *mostly* law-abiding. There were those months in college when I hosted an underground poker game. But the money I nabbed from the rich frat guys? Worth the risk.

In the rearview mirror, a big, bearded guy in a hard hat and orange vest trudges toward me, his expression stern as a school principal's behind aviator shades. Shit. "I should get my license and registration," I say.

Juliet ends the racy song but gives me a doubtful look. "They don't need license and registration at a construction site," Juliet whispers, gently rubbing my arm in apology.

"Right, right," I say, shaking my head then peering behind me. The guy looks pissed.

"But still, I'm sorry," she adds.

I wave a hand dismissively, exonerating her. "I'll take a thousand pissed-off dudes. Hell, I'll take a thousand speeding tickets for being your—"

I swallow *blow-job coach*, instead flashing a smile at the man frowning into my window.

"Did you miss the sign back there, buddy?" Doesn't sound like we're buddies.

"I must have," I say, contrite.

He flaps an arm toward said sign. "It did say *slow down*. We do work here."

And I am an asshole. "I know. I'm so sorry."

He peers through the open window again, all business. "No one was hurt, but maybe it's time for you to stop texting and driving, ya hear me?"

I wasn't texting. I was racing to have my dick sucked.

I give him an apologetic smile. "Yes, sir. I will."

Briefly, I weigh what to say next. Obviously, I deserve the reprimand, but I also need to know whether to turn around and go back the way we came or drive around those cones up ahead.

Then, my own voice fills the car.

"And this is your host Monroe Blackstone right along with Juliet Dumont on—"

What the heck? That's our last episode of the podcast. Juliet jumps to stab the end button on the display. "My bad, sorry!"

The construction worker whips off his shades, studies me, studies her. Then, in slow motion, his frown turns upside down. "Oh man! Seriously? *Seri-*

ously? It's Heartbreakers and Matchmakers in the flesh?" He taps his chest. "Big fan of the pod. And I'm telling you, I called it." He's punching the air triumphantly. "I can't wait to tell my woman."

I've never been recognized. Based on the way Juliet's jaw is hanging open—a good look—she hasn't either.

"That's great! We're so happy you like the show," she says, quickly recovering.

He points at her excitedly. "We placed bets, too, on the poet date last week." He curls his hands around the open window. "What happened with Mister Likes to Discuss Song Lyrics and Grapes? Was it a combo date? An extend-a-date? Gimme the tea."

A laugh bursts from Juliet. "He told me I was too old. Even though I'm only thirty and he was over forty."

The construction worker flubs his lips. "What a dick."

"I know, right," she says, so good with people. "But, tell the truth—did you bet against me?"

He sets his hand on his chest. "No way. Honestly, Dara and I both bet on you. You're the reason we're together," he adds, sweetly.

I tilt my head. "Is that so?"

His smile is endless, but he has no interest in me. His appreciation is for Juliet. "She is such a fangirl of your dating approach. She said your *future is bright* attitude is why she gave me a chance. So thank you. Seriously, thank you," he says with the kind of generosity that comes from the top and bottom of his heart.

"I'm so happy for you..." She pauses for his name.

"Dash," he supplies.

"As in short for Dashiell?" I sputter out.

He rolls his eyes. "Yeah, but pretend you don't know that. The only other Dashiell I know is this brewer dude in town. Real nice guy. I'm on his softball team."

Talk about a small town.

"Dash is a good name, then," Juliet offers.

Dash looks from the passenger to me. "Thanks, and I am so stoked to find you're a couple in real life. You've always had crazy chemistry on the pod."

Ah, hell. Do I tell him the truth now? If I lie and he finds out we fibbed, that'd be bad for our reputation. But we look like we're together.

"Actually," Juliet cuts in with the save, "Monroe is acting as my dating coach."

Dash knits his brow. "Didn't know you were a coach too, doc. But that tracks." His tone, though, is downtrodden. "But I definitely got a vibe from the two of you."

Well, shit. I do not want to lead a fan astray. "We went go-karting. We had a great time. We were sort of..."

I turn to Juliet, and her cheeks are still flush from the make-out session. "Practice dating," she adds cheerily.

"But, it's for an upcoming segment," I say, "so if you could keep it on the down-low..."

Dash mimes zipping his lips. "Thanks for the insider tip." There's a considering pause, then he drums his palms on the roof of the car. "All right. Now

listen, if you turn around and make a left onto Cedar
Lane, that should loop back around past the construction site. But I do not—hear me now—I do not want to
find out you were speeding again. Drive nice and slow.
Take your time. There's no rush."

I nod like a good boy. "That's excellent advice."

"And I can't wait for that segment."

He slips his shades back on, and his smile burns off.
"Drive safely. I mean it."

Then he's gone, and Juliet turns to me, lifting a
brow. "You are a bad boy."

"Just you wait."

Ten minutes later, I swing open the door to our
temporary home, and once it shuts, I meet her gaze and
say in a low rumble, "The coach is in the house. Now
tell me what you've disliked about blow jobs."

With zero hesitation, she answers. "I always feel like
I'm going to choke."

"That makes perfect sense. Dicks are like choking
sticks."

With a pinched look, she rubs her throat. "I don't
like my throat being jackhammered."

And I don't like the image of any other man doing
that to her. *Ever again.* But I've got to play the coach
now. "And that's what guys have done?" I bite out.

"Yup. It's no fun at all. But, I'm pretty into your
dick," she says, cupping my cock once again through
my jeans. "So, what's the game plan?"

God, her bravery is so arousing. But then again, so's her hand on me.

It fries my brain for a moment, but fortunately, I have the answer to her dilemma. I reach for her hand, removing it from the ridge of my erection. "It's all about the hands."

She lifts a skeptical brow. "But that's just a hand job, then, and who really wants that after the age of fifteen?"

I kiss her palm, murmuring into it. "Let me show you how it'll be good for both of us."

Thank the lord for Eleanor. I guide Juliet to the room full of mirrors. She gazes around, looking at multiples of us. "There are so many Monroes and Juliets."

I reach for her face. "That's the point. You can follow Dash's advice and take it nice and slow, and I can just enjoy the view."

"You want to watch me all over the room?"

"I do," I say, stroking her cheek, playing with her hair, then curling a palm over her shoulder. I adopt the stern tone she likes so much. "Now, get down on your knees and take my dick out."

"Bossy." But she drops down, gazes up, and unzips me. Eyes on me the whole time, she pushes my jeans and boxer briefs down. When my dick springs free, her breath hitches, and she licks her lips. "Mmm. Like I said, I like your dick."

The steel rod between my thighs likes her too. I thread my hands through her chestnut waves, unable to, uninterested in looking away. "And I like the view."

Her eager expression vanishes. "But how do you want me to do this?"

I take her hand from my hip, bring it to my cock. "Just wrap a hand around the base and then play with it however you want."

She narrows her eyes. "How is that going to be good enough for you if I don't suck all the way?"

She has no idea. I wrap my hand around hers, both of us covering the base of my aching cock. "Want to hear a secret?"

"I really do," she says.

"A good blow job isn't about me fucking your mouth."

She looks doubtful. "I don't know about that."

"It's about whether *you* enjoy giving it," I say, moving our hands slowly together. "If you're not having a good time, I'm not going to have one." I rub the head against her lips. "So have a good time with my dick, baby. And I guarantee I will."

She smiles, like *game on*. "Okay then."

She flicks her tongue against the head, and a jolt of pleasure flies down my spine. "Like I said."

"Really?" she asks, licking me like a lollipop, making me shudder.

"Yes, really."

I rope my fingers through her hair, but I'm careful not to yank or tug. I just want to touch her, that's all.

Darting her head forward, she draws more of me into her lush mouth asking for approval with her pretty green eyes. "I told you so," I groan, then I look away from her, watching in the mirror.

It's a view I haven't seen before—her cheek pops with my dick, and the spark inside me turns into a crackle.

She hums against my dick. Yes, she's getting into it now, taking my cock at her speed, at her pace. She doesn't swallow my dick. She plays and teases, licks and sucks. She rubs my shaft against her lips, sighing happily as she goes. "Is this working?" she asks as she rubs my dick over her top lip.

I curl my hand tight around the base, squeeze out a drop of liquid arousal, and offer it to her. "You tell me if I was right."

She sticks out her tongue, moaning wantonly as she swallows me. "You taste good," she murmurs.

That jolt of pleasure? It hits me again and again as she plays with me. My breath comes faster. My chest heats up as I stare savagely at my Juliet in the scalloped mirror, the gilded one, the full-length one offering an obscene view of an outrageously sexy woman hellbent on having fun with her man.

She looks eager. She looks like...like she's enjoying herself.

"The sight of you," I rasp out. She lifts her chin, eager for more praise as she sucks me. "You look like you're having a good time," I venture.

She drops me long enough to say, "I really will if you come in my mouth."

I shudder from those words. "Guarantee," I say, then I help her along. I grip my shaft tighter, stroking the base with a firm but short touch.

After a few seconds, though, she bats my hand away. "I've got this."

And holy hell does she ever. With her hand covering half my dick, she sucks me only as far as she wants me, spitting on her hand.

That, right there, lights me up. "Do that again," I urge, trembling.

She lets go, spits again, then curls her wet hand once more around the base. "Watch *me* now," she says, and that's a tall order. I'm so worked up that I want to shut my eyes and just give in to the sensations.

But I need to make this good for her, and it's no hardship to stare at her as she shows my dick a good time while I barely thrust.

I don't need to own her mouth. She already owns my body and soul. As she plays with my dick, my breathing turns ragged, my pulse spikes, and pleasure barrels down my spine, lighting up my cock.

Bright, hot bliss seizes me as I come in her mouth. She groans salaciously, like I'm the best thing she's tasted.

That's how she makes me feel, especially when she lets go and murmurs, "I have so much more to learn, coach."

I'm still shaking, still shuddering as I drop to my knees and kiss her, my jeans unzipped, my dick hanging out, and my heart slamming hard against my chest, wanting more from her.

I kiss her like I can tell her something meaningful that way. Maybe I'm just saying *I like the way you sucked my dick*. But I liked it because it was her.

I break the kiss and murmur, "You just do it for me." But before I get too caught up in the meaning behind those words, I stand, tuck myself back in and offer a hand. "Now, let me do something for you."

She's up in no time, and we head for the bunk bed, but before we make it, there's a knock on the door. Then a voice. "Dude. Let me in. It's Sawyer."

25

MY BROTHER IS A COCK-BLOCKER

Juliet

Three hours and a takeout dinner later, the cock-blocker is still here.

I love my brother, but right now, I hate him. Harnessing the fury of a thousand unfinished sex acts, I study the Scrabble letters on the kitchen table like I'm going to burn holes through them with my eyes.

"Now, c'mon. Don't tell me you're as intense as Monroe when it comes to this game," Sawyer chides, fiddling with his tiles, taunting as I wait my turn to pounce on the board.

Well, if you'd been seconds away from getting the good stuff, you'd be a jack in the box too.

Instead, I'm putting all my energy into this game, hoping to slaughter him, and sure, Monroe too. "Yes. I want to destroy you," I mutter.

But all I have are a couple of As, a couple of Ms, and one annoying C.

"And to think you were always the nice one growing up," he teases, then waggles a tile he might be considering playing. "But as I was saying, it was nice to kick around town today. Good thing I had to see a client in Duck Falls. Gave me a chance to check out Darling Springs again too. Scope out some things to do this weekend. I'm going to bring Katya to your dad's retirement party," he tells Monroe.

"That'll be nice," Monroe says evenly, and I can't read what he thinks of his dad inviting everyone to the party. I didn't think to ask more about it last night. I should do that.

If I ever get a second alone with him again.

Did that come out grumbly even in my head? Yes, yes it did. My inner monologue should learn to be nicer.

"Yeah, we all got rezzies for that night. Everyone is coming. Even Carter. He's not playing till Monday night."

"Oh!" I perk up. "Rachel's coming, then?"

I *really* didn't think about this weekend at all. My focus has been all dating experiment all the time.

"The whole gang. We got rooms at The Ladybug Inn this weekend," he says, then his brown eyes turn teasing as he drags his hand through his hair, a few shades lighter than mine. "*Your favorite.*"

Instinctively, I reach for my necklace, like I need to hide it from him. But maybe that's just because I'm hearing the echo of Monroe's *adorable* the other day.

How he *did* mean it sensually. "And I recall running naked through the front lawn was your favorite thing."

Monroe laughs, then claps my brother on the back. "Some things never change."

Sawyer tips his beer bottle my way. "Touché." He takes another drink.

"Are you going to stay through Saturday?" I ask. *Please say no.* If he's in town tomorrow, he might commandeer all of Monroe's time.

But thankfully, he shakes his head. "Just here for the day, then I'll be back. I have meetings in the city tomorrow."

"Business is good?" Monroe asks, inscrutable again. Is this really how he talks to his friend? With *business is goods* and *that's nice*?

Maybe I'm mad at Monroe too. Or maybe at myself. Should I be telling my brother the truth about the last few days?

I liked sucking dick for the first time ever!

Ugh. Maybe I just need an early bedtime.

"It's good, but it can always be better, right?"

"Truer words," Monroe says, lifting his beer bottle, too, and reminding me that work, understandably, is his true love.

"Ooh. I got one," Sawyer says and then sets down his tiles, spelling out J-A-S-M-I-N-E.

Monroe whistles. "Damn. Good one."

Sure it's a good word, but why doesn't Monroe just flip the table and tell Sawyer he needs to take me hard and ruthlessly up against the wall?

Because you're living in a make-believe world, honey.

Maybe that's why I'm annoyed with Monroe. Because he didn't flip the table and because he can't. We don't have a get-out-so-I-can-be-with-my-woman kind of relationship.

I heave the world's most annoyed sigh and stare blankly at my letters one more time. But hold on. Do I have the words to spell what I think I can spell?

Like I'm the devilish kid in a GIF, I select tile by tile, placing one at a victorious time into the board, attaching them to Sawyer's J as I spell C-L-A-M-J-A- M.

I drop the proverbial mic and say, "I'm outta here."

My brother peers at the board, then me. "But that's not a word."

"Oh, it's definitely a thing though." And I'm feeling the female equivalent of cock-blocked big time.

I push back in the chair as Monroe fights off a smile. "Well played," he says as I walk off, waving goodbye to the guys behind me.

But before I can turn down the hall, Sawyer calls out. "Hey, were you able to grab that citrus beach lotion from The Slippery Dipper?"

Oh right. He asked for that the day we drove up. I turn around. "No, but I can go tomorrow. You're taking off tonight, right?"

Please say yes.

"Definitely." But he waves a hand. "I'll get it on Saturday with Katya. All good. She loves that store."

"Yeah, me too," I say fondly, annoyance replaced by wistfulness as I glance at Monroe.

He meets my gaze straight on. "Same here," he says in a tone that's not at all unreadable. It's one hundred percent tinged with romance, so much it makes my chest ache.

I do leave this time, heading for the bedroom, where I shut the door and exhale heavily. Time is running out for us, and my irritation isn't truly about the sex I didn't have. I just wanted more time alone with Monroe.

But what's the point? We're not going to have alone time after this weekend, so I should get used to it.

After I wash my face and slip into jammies, I grab my phone, then text the girlies, asking if they want to get ready together for the party on Saturday.

That's only two days from now.

They say yes, then I turn to a self-improvement podcast, but it doesn't improve my mood about the clock winding down.

26

THE TRIPLE CHALLENGE

Monroe

Sawyer's a relentless competitor. He also adores his sister, so even if *clamjam* isn't a Merriam-Webster word, he leaves it on the board without protest.

"It's a challenge," Sawyer explains when she's gone. Ever the gamer, he attacks the board like a word warrior.

Me? I've got another challenge—getting to Juliet soon. Make that a double challenge since there's a curl of guilt in my gut. I'm sitting here drinking beer and playing a word game with my longtime college friend, all while lusting after his little sister.

It's more than lust, you dipshit.

The guilt tunnels deeper into me. If I were my client, how would I handle this?

As I pick up tiles, trying to assemble vexing words for the game, I keep turning over the issue. Guilt doesn't always need to be absolved. Sometimes, you have to live with it—like when a confession will only hurt the other person. But keeping this secret doesn't protect Sawyer. It protects me and keeps him unfairly in the dark. The kind of unfair that makes someone feel stupid or foolish if/when they learn the truth. I don't want that for my friend.

Guilt's not the only emotion taking up real estate in my ticker. There's something else jostling for space. It's the wish to *declare* this feeling. To name it. To acknowledge it to Sawyer.

Trouble is, it's not just my story to tell. I can't violate Juliet's privacy to ease my own mind.

So, I set the feeling aside, playing *apex*.

Sawyer sets down his beer, rubs his palms, and plays *ex*.

Damn. "Left my X open," I say, shaking my head at my gaffe.

"You did, and I appreciate it," he says.

I flip him the bird, and we play ferociously for twenty more minutes until I notice him yawning. Actually...has he been plagued by yawns for a while now?

He's only had one beer, so I'm not worried about him driving under the influence. I *am* worried about how tired he is even as he studies the board like an eagle.

Finally, he plays the word *my* off of clamjam, finishing the game. Getting to his feet, he unleashes another yawn as he says, "Pay up."

That's decided. "You need to stay here, buddy."

"Nah," he says, shaking his head.

"Yes. You do. It's not optional."

He sighs, then scratches his jaw, shrugging in admission. "I mean, it's a big house. And the furniture's all still here so..."

I gulp. Shit. I'm going to have to face up to some modicum of the truth. We don't have a spare bedroom in The Horny House. Only spare chaise lounges. I could offer him my bunk, but the last time I was in that bed, I fucked his sister. Soooo...

"There are a bunch of chaises," I offer.

His brow knits. "That's not weird."

I quickly explain, and he says gamely, "When in Rome." After we put the board away, he drops his beer bottle into the recycling bin, then stops with his hand still raised. "But where are you and Juliet sleeping?"

The kernel of guilt turns into a grapefruit as I pick up my half-full bottle, staring at it rather than him. "There's...a big bunk bed."

"You're sharing a bunk bed? Are you eight?"

The guilt expands to watermelon size. I wish I could tell him the truth. I wish I could say *I can't stop thinking about your sister, and how much more I want than this little experiment.*

"There wasn't anything else," I say.

With a nod, he accepts that, then cuts across the kitchen, but he stops again in the doorway, turning around. "And listen, I've been meaning to ask something all night."

I fiddle with the beer label then take a drink. "Yeah?"

"How long have you been into my sister?"

I didn't think spit takes were a real thing until just now.

Sawyer laughs at my expression. "I thought so."

"Fuck," I grumble, dragging my free hand through my hair. So much for taking the high road.

"Impressive that you're not denying it."

"There's no point. How did you..."

He scoffs as he returns to the table. "Not born yesterday. That whole dopey gaze when you talked about the store was a dead giveaway."

"Dammit." I'm so transparent.

He nods in agreement. "What are you going to do about it?"

"You're not going to tell me to stay the fuck away from her?"

He rolls his eyes. "What am I? Eight?"

Fair point. "I appreciate that." I lean back in the chair, sighing heavily. "I don't know, Sawyer. Your sister deserves the world."

"Yeah, she does. You can't give that to her?"

I want to. I desperately want to. "My track record is shit. I wasn't a good husband."

"You didn't cheat on Elizabeth, did you, man?"

"No. There are other ways to be a bad husband."

"And what were yours?"

"I was emotionally unavailable, Elizabeth said."

He snorts. "*She* was emotionally unavailable. Dude, you picked a woman who was obsessed with work."

I chew on that for a beat. He's not wrong. Elizabeth was a workaholic, but so was I. "I'd be the pot calling the kettle black."

"Maybe so, but she was also driven, ambitious, and single-minded."

"And it didn't work out," I add, then tap my chest. "Look at me now, I'm thirty-five, divorced and married to my job."

"That's your choice," he says, no ire, no judgment. Just an honest assessment.

"I want to be the best for my clients. They come to me for help and deserve someone who doesn't phone it in," I say, a little defensively.

He laughs, shaking his head. "If you're honest with them, you ought to be honest with yourself." He levels me with a hard stare, the kind that only a good friend can deliver. "You're afraid you're going to be like your dad."

Ouch. That stings. "That's the problem with friends who know you too well."

"Yup. They know you too well."

I scrub a hand across the back of my neck, letting his comments sink in. But really, this very reality has been sinking in for a few decades now. My father's been detached and dismissive since I was thirteen, probably before then too, so I taught myself to rely only on myself. That shit's hard to unlearn, harder to undo. Risky too. If I tried and failed, the collateral damage would be worse—Juliet. "You're not wrong. But the thing is I don't want to hurt her."

Sawyer leans forward, elbows on the table. "I get that. But you're the only one who knows what you're capable of," he says, ending his observation on a big, hearty yawn.

He stretches his arms, and quietly we leave the kitchen, gather blankets for the chaise. Once he flops down on it, he's out like a light.

I leave, and while I really should mull over his points, that's not what I do. My feet take me straight to the main bedroom. There's only one place I want to be.

She's asleep, though, so I'm quiet as I get ready for bed, stripping down to boxer briefs and brushing my teeth. When I'm done, I climb into bed, next to her, feeling a little unburdened, a little less guilty.

But still guilty in a whole new way.

How could I ever give her what she deserves? Maybe Sawyer's right. It would take a choice from me. What if I do it poorly? What if I don't have the skills to *do* love, like I have to teach it?

Sure, I could try to figure out my stuff better. Try to work on all these walls I erect. But is it fair to work on them with her? I don't think it is. It's not fair to ask her to wait for me to become a better partner either.

My heart twists painfully. I hate that feeling so instead I steal a sniff of her hair, that vanilla-honey scent going to my head.

Making me think *maybe someday*.

When her eyes flutter open, though, I'm thinking one thing. *Now.*

"Hey," she whispers.

I half want to tell her that Sawyer figured me out, but when she cups my cheek and strokes my jaw, I don't want to talk at all. I cover her warm body in one swift move, grabbing her wrists, pinning them above her head, and dropping my mouth onto hers.

She wraps her legs around me, hooking them over my ass. She's soft and pliant, arching up into me, asking for what we both desperately want.

I kiss her harder, and at times like this, words only get in the way. But there are a few I need to say. I wrench away and meet her gaze. "Sawyer is staying the night. Can you be quiet as I fuck you?"

"I can try."

I shake my head as I shift my body next to hers. "You have to, Juliet."

She smiles. "Then you'll have to make me be quiet."

Challenge accepted.

27

———

QUIET TIME

Juliet

It's hard to stay silent when Monroe's strong hand travels down my stomach, then inside my panties.

But I impress myself with my silence skills even as a shiver runs through my body. A shiver that makes me want to moan.

"How long have you been like this?" he whispers as he coasts a finger through my wetness.

"Well, I was asleep," I say quietly.

He dips his face to my neck, dusting kisses there while he explores my slickness. "Doesn't mean you aren't soaked."

"Are you asking if I was dreaming of you?"

"Or playing with yourself when you got into bed." It's less a question and more a statement. Or maybe a hope.

"You want that," I say.

"Want to see that. Want to watch that, Juliet," he says, his voice low, his throat going all rumbly, his eyes a little hazy as he, clearly, pictures me naked in bed, getting off to images of him.

"Maybe *you* need to be quiet," I challenge.

He tests me, though, two thick fingers traveling between my thighs, then returning to my aching clit with quick, strong strokes. His touch makes it hard for me to keep teasing him. Or to think at all.

My brain starts to go offline, my thoughts turning to colors, bright and hot. The way he touches me feels like more than foreplay. He touches me like he treasures me. I've never been touched like this, with such filthy reverence.

I lift my hips up, seeking more, then finally finding the words to answer his first question—how long have I been this aroused. "I didn't touch myself in bed. This is all from just now," I say.

A groan seems to come from the depths of his soul as he lifts his face. His blue eyes are flames. "Yeah? From kissing?"

"Is that so hard to believe?"

Like he can't help himself, he pushes his body against me, so I can feel the hard length of his cock nudging my hip. "No. But I fucking love it."

More strokes. More mesmerizing brushes of his talented fingers. More sensations overloading my mind.

"And maybe from earlier," I murmur, breath coming faster. "When I sucked your dick."

The fire in his eyes blazes. "You're such a good student, Juliet."

"Was I?" I know he liked it. But I want to hear that from him.

"Yes," he groans. "A perfect—" But he stops, catching himself, then smiling wickedly. "But you need more fieldwork."

I laugh softly as my hips tilt up. "That's your assessment?"

He nods, a glint in his eyes, a quirk in his lips. "Lots and lots of courses."

I hear what's underneath that too, and I love it. I love it too much.

Monroe spins away from me, grabbing a condom from the nightstand, then shoving off his boxer briefs.

In seconds, he's rolled it on, spread my legs and now he's notching the thick head against my entrance. My breath hitches, and a long murmur escapes my lips. "God," I mutter.

"Quiet," he whispers harshly.

I comply as he pushes in. My body welcomes him home. In seconds, he's filling me and I'm shaking with pleasure. It's twisting so quickly through my veins, it's like a flood of bliss inside me. I can't help it—I gasp, while I shudder.

His palm comes down on my mouth. His eyes are heated. He braces himself on one strong arm, then fucks me like that.

Strong, determined strokes. A firm grip on my mouth. Eyes locked on me.

Curling my hands around his shoulders, I slide a knee up higher against his hip. He sinks deeper, making sure I feel every inch of him as he eases out, then drives back in.

I feel it all so much. I'm helpless to the sensations whipping through my body, the tight coils of heat. The sharp, hot bursts of lust. Most of all, his hand covering my mouth with fierce determination. His palm drowns out all my sounds. The needy moans. The *oh god, oh fuck, oh yes.*

And others too. Like *I don't want to stop with you.*

The look in his eyes—something like ferocity chased by adoration—tells me something too. Something I can be sure of without words.

He doesn't want to stop either.

That tips me over, and I'm falling, *falling* deeper into him as my orgasm breaks me apart. Quietly with muffled cries, but loudly with this awareness inside me.

I grip him tighter, hold him closer as his body tenses, and he lets go of my mouth, grunting out the most desperate noises.

Before they bring the house down, I slap a hand over his mouth. Covering up his cries of pleasure till his breathing slows and his body stops trembling.

When I let go, he just whispers a heady *thank you.*

28

GREEN FLAGS

Juliet

On Friday morning, I pad through the house in jammies in search of coffee. Monroe's off for a run but Sawyer's standing at the sink in the hallway bathroom, door open, brushing his teeth with his finger.

"Gross," I say.

"Good hygiene is not gross," he retorts through a mouthful of paste.

"Maybe I meant you're gross," I say.

"Maybe I'll give you a noogie."

"Maybe I'm still faster and you can't catch me," I say, then wander into the kitchen desperately seeking caffeine.

There's so much to do today. The realtor is coming in two hours, and she said she can also put us in touch with someone who can handle all these goodies in an estate sale here in the home. It's weird to think of an estate sale with Eleanor still alive and well, but she definitely is. She posted a video of her cruise on her social feed, singing her Christmas song with her husband at karaoke on the ship. Something about her felt vaguely familiar, but I couldn't place it.

Mostly the image reminded me of how much I love karaoke. Does Monroe like it too? I bet that's a no, but I'll ask him. Mostly because I want to know if I'm right. A smile takes over my face as I picture him grumbling about karaoke and show tunes.

I yank open a cupboard searching for coffee when the heavenly scent drifts into my nostrils. Am I dreaming of coffee? I follow my nose, peering down the counter like a cartoon character tracking a scent to...a freshly brewed pot. There's also a pretty sky-blue ceramic mug with a Post-it note that has my name on it, along with a simple sketch of a ladybug.

At least, I think it's a ladybug. It's roundish and has spots. My heart gallops.

"Let me guess. He made you coffee and you're going all schmoopy."

Oh shit. I straighten my spine, rearrange my schmoopy features, and turn around to face my brother. "It's just coffee."

He rolls his eyes. "Save the innocent act for court. And no, he didn't tell me. I figured it out because I'm astute, and you two are also pathetically obvious."

Are you kidding me? My brother *guessed* right? That's it? "Um..."

"Yeah. *Um*, indeed. So, are you two a thing?"

"No, it's not like that. It's not like that at all. It's

like..." I sputter out because I don't know what this thing is like at all, other than an experiment with an end date.

He lifts a brow. "A hook-up? A fling? A one-night stand?"

"No!" I hate all of those terms for Monroe and me, and the frown on my face must tell my brother so because he closes the distance and sets a hand on my shoulder. "Be patient with him," Sawyer says, gently. "He's a work in progress."

My frown turns to a sigh, maybe a grateful one. "Aren't we all?"

A soft smile comes my way. "Truer words."

Then, Sawyer reaches around and snags my mug, fills it with coffee, and knocks back a big gulp.

"You sneak! You set me up!"

With a smug smile he puts down the mug and smacks his lips. "You don't want me to drive without caffeine, do you?"

"It's seven-thirty in the morning! You're wide awake!"

He sweeps out an arm toward the coffeepot. "And you have more coffee from a man who's too crazy about you to admit it."

Then he wheels around and takes off on a bigger mic drop than last night's *clamjam*.

*　*　*

I'm still a little buzzed from Sawyer's parting shot as I walk through town for my own exercise. As the summer air wraps around me, I turn over a slate of new questions in my head as I pass Downward Dog All Day.

Is Monroe crazy about me? He did draw me a ladybug. And brewed me coffee. And brought me a hair tie yesterday. And a lavender eye mask the other night. And rented me a limo before that. And joined me at breakfast with my mom one morning. And saved me from the cheese douche last week.

And called me a masterpiece.

On the one hand, he treats me like, well, like a man should treat a woman. On the other hand, he's gone on the record that he's not keen on relationships.

Why should I believe his actions more than his words? Just because I want to? That's foolish, even when his actions speak so loudly.

I want to believe them so badly it hurts. I rub my hand against my sternum as I near the lavender farm, drawn by the alluring scent and my new friend, who's outside setting up a big wooden sign listing the farm's hours.

"Hey, city girl," Ripley says, adjusting the placement of the white and lavender sign on the emerald-green grass. Her inked arms are strong.

"Nice guns," I say, admiring her.

"Thanks," she says, glancing at her toned biceps like she just noticed them. "I guess lugging signs and stuff for years has an effect. What's going on with you?"

That's the question, isn't it? But I think I know the answer. "Oh, you know, just stupidly falling for a guy who's not really available."

She gives me a sympathetic look as she dusts one hand against the other. "Really?"

I wince. "I think so."

"You think you're falling for him, or you think he's unavailable?"

I tackle the first question since it's easier. "I'm definitely falling for him. In just a few short days. Though, in my dumb heart's defense, I sort of fell for him eight years ago right here in this town."

An eyebrow lifts. "Details."

I check the time. I need to get back to see Luna Ferrara, the realtor, but I also need to process all my feels, so I give a condensed version of the past and the present.

Ripley listens attentively, nodding as I talk, then when I'm done, she asks, "So he got you a lavender eye mask when you had a headache? But was it one of mine? Because The Slippery Dipper carries mine. And if it was mine that means...extra points."

I laugh, flashing back to that night. "Come to think of it, it probably came from your lavender farm."

"Then, maybe talk to him about it."

Nerves fly through my body. "That sounds terrifying."

"Yup."

On that note, I turn to go, a plan coming together as I walk. Functional fitness indeed.

* * *

A couple of hours later, Monroe and I see Luna to the door and thank her for her time. "We appreciate you taking this on so quickly," Monroe says.

"And I appreciate your business." The realtor is a curvy woman with olive skin and a friendly smile. "This house will be so fun to list."

She takes off, and when the door closes, Monroe looks at his watch. "If memory serves, you have one more date. We should do that tonight."

He sounds businesslike, and I get it. We said three dates with three men at the start of this experiment. Monroe's simply sticking to the plan.

But what if we could have more than three dates? What if we could have dates that go beyond this week? Nights together in San Francisco? Perhaps, I'll use this last date to show my podcast co-host the sort of fun we can have together and then feel him out about all these pesky feelings. We've grown closer with each of our dates, stripping down our defenses, but we needed those *costumes* to get there. It'll be easier for me to broach the big, scary topic while we're still in experiment mode.

"Let's do it." We head to the back porch, where I open the Date Night app and thumb through prospects as if I'm simply hunting. But I quickly land on the guy I found during my walk back to the house. I take a quiet, steadying breath. With fingers metaphorically crossed, I swallow my nerves and ask, "How about this one?"

It's my choice, of course. I don't need his permission, but I do want this date tonight to go well, like the others have. Each date has brought us closer, and I want this one to do the same.

That's why I pre-selected Adam. He's a college professor who likes nineties tunes, tinkering on household projects, reading on cold days, and reading on hot days. Oh, he's also divorced. His smile is warm, his eyes kind behind those glasses, and his word choices in his profile are unadorned. He's thirty-eight. "No douche vibes here, right?"

Monroe studies his profile for flaws, then smiles like he's impressed. "No douche vibes," he echoes.

"Good." Another deep breath. "Then why don't we practice it as a third date?"

He gives me a quizzical stare. "A third date?" Like he's not sure he heard.

"Yes, that means the professor and I have gone out twice already."

"I know what third means."

"Do you though?"

His smile takes time to spread, then it turns naughty. "I do."

Fun *and* feelings. You can't do that on the first date. I close my eyes and soak in the sun, keeping my mind focused on Monroe's actions this week. *This morning*, especially. "Thanks for the coffee. And the ladybug drawing."

"You're welcome."

When I open my eyes, he's soaking in the rays, too, looking content, like he belongs here. "Do you like karaoke?"

He barks out a laugh. "That's random."

"Do you?"

He shoots me a challenging look. "What do you think?"

"No."

"You'd be right." He takes a beat, tilts his head. "But I'd go with you if you wanted to."

Maybe his words are starting to match his actions. I'm feeling all sorts of possibilities.

* * *

That evening, as I'm getting ready in the main bathroom, my phone buzzes with a text from my mom.

> Mom: Dating is so fun! I'm having the best time.

> Juliet: I'm so happy for you, Mom.

> Mom: And you? Are you having fun?

> Juliet: Definitely!

> Mom: I take it that means it's going well with the guy you met? Aren't the men better here?

> Juliet: You could say that. It's promising, if a little complicated.

> Mom: What happens next with him? Will you see him next week when you return to the city?

. . .

That's one question I don't have an answer for.

29

THE THIRD DATE

Monroe

At eight o'clock, Juliet knocks on the door. This date is dinner at the professor's house. She left a while ago, telling me to return to the house at seven-thirty and get ready, and then she'd arrive.

I've got a bottle of her favorite rosé, a takeout dinner from Clementine's, and the professor look. Eleanor's closet came through, and I found a pair of horn-rimmed glasses with no prescriptions for the lenses. I'm wearing a short-sleeved Henley. By now I've learned Juliet is into my ink.

Or the professor has learned it. Whatever. I don't care. She likes *my* arms, that's all that matters.

With Pearl Jam handling the vocals tonight—90s tunes were on the prof's profile—I head to the door and open it.

She didn't just understand the assignment. She nailed it. No, she elevated it. Juliet's wearing a short plaid skirt and a white button-down shirt, open just enough to tease me. Her chestnut locks are pulled back in a high ponytail. She clutches a notebook that she uses strategically to boost those beautiful breasts.

My gaze roams up and down the bold beauty in front of me, who kicked the role-play sky-high. So far, I've been the one who's been play-acting. Now she is, and I am motherfucking here for it.

"Hello, professor," she says demurely. "I have that paper for you. Can I show it to you tonight?"

I square my shoulders, school my expression, and adopt a stern tone. "Yes, but this is the third time we've worked on it. I expect serious improvement, Miss Dumont."

She bats her lashes. "I've applied myself, professor. Can I show you?"

So innocent. So committed to the role.

"Come in. But don't disappoint me." I shut the door behind her, then watch her walk across the hardwood in that sinfully short schoolgirl outfit that is frying my brain.

She stops at the living room couch, tilting her face up. "Do you have an office or a den we should go to?"

"I do, Miss Dumont. But I fully expect this paper to demonstrate everything you've learned."

She nods sweetly. "It will, sir. It will."

We head to the den, the pictures of old-time Hollywood stars watching over us as I walk behind the desk, taking the chair.

She doesn't sit. She comes right to the edge of the desk, leans over it, and slides the notebook right in front of me, giving me a perfect view of the swell of her tits.

I suppress a groan, but she catches it anyway, giving me a sweet, but seductive, smile. "You can find my very hard work on the first page."

She's flipped the script on me tonight. It's a little unnerving to give up control like this. But it's thrilling too.

I flip open the notebook. Then, the words that come out of my mouth aren't words. They're grunts and growls.

I shake my head, but not in a *no*.

More of a *holy fuck*. I swallow, clearing my head as best I can, then read her writing one more time.

Bend me over the desk. Spank me. Then take me. I'm yours.

I meet her gaze. Her eyes are wide and guileless. She can act. And she sure meant it when she said this was a third date.

"What do you think?" she asks innocently.

I *can't* think right now. I remove the glasses and stand, stalk around to her, and line up behind her. I slide a hand slowly, sensually up her beautiful back, pushing her down against the desk. As she flattens, she cranes her neck back to look at me. "I did it wrong, didn't I? I was supposed to write a paper." There's a quiver in her lips. Admission in her eyes.

"You were naughty, Miss Dumont."

"I was very bad. All I could think about in class was you fucking me."

My neck burns hot. My cock jumps, straining against my pants. "You've been so bad though. I'm going to have to spank you first."

She nods obediently. "I deserve it."

"You do." I lift up her skirt and freeze. She's got nothing on. A breath stutters past my lips. *My woman* is so daring. So bold.

I'm dying to drop the roles, but she seems intent on playing, so I draw a sharp breath, trying to keep my wits about me as I stare at her gorgeous ass, the creamy white flesh begging for pink handprints soon.

Then I lift a hand, bring it down, and smack her sweet flesh. She lets out a breathy *ohh.*

Desire seizes every cell in my body. It takes all my restraint not to fuck her senseless this second. But she wanted spanking.

I raise my hand again, then swat the other cheek. She flinches, letting out a high-pitched moan.

I spank her again, then one more time, then she says, "Why don't you see if I liked it?"

I am not in control. I am not in charge. She has me by the heart and the balls. I slide a hand over those gorgeous globes, then dip it between her thighs. My beautiful reward. "You're soaking wet," I whisper in a filthy voice.

Soaking is an understatement. She's slippery and hot and so aroused.

"Better fuck me now, then." She meets my gaze as I

unzip my pants, then adds, "But you should know, I'm a good girl, so I'm on birth control."

I stop, hands on my zipper. "Jumanji."

"Yes?" She's Juliet now.

"I need to know that means you want me to fuck you bare, baby."

"I do," she says, quickly adding she's been tested and she's negative.

"Same for me," I tell her, then I free my cock, grab her hips and line up at her sweet center. She raises her ass for me, inviting me to take her.

Well, that *is* the assignment. I tease her pussy with the head of my cock, eliciting groans and sighs and then wanton, needy pleas.

"You want this cock?"

"I do."

"Tell me how much," I demand.

"I'm dying for you to fuck me," she cries out.

"Then take it," I say, sinking into her and losing my fucking mind. She's so hot, so tight, so hungry for me.

I tremble everywhere with a wild kind of lust. Unchecked, fevered. A desire that takes root deep in my bones. I bend closer and push her hair away from her ear. "You feel so good," I whisper.

"So do you, Monroe," she says, staying out of character.

Thank fuck. "I needed to fuck you as me," I rasp out. "I needed you to be you. You know that, right?"

"I do," she says, her tone full of the emotion I feel too. Then I ease out, thrust back in. With her hips in my hands, I pull her back hard, slamming her onto my length. Pleasure rockets through me. An engine revved. A car humming.

Like that, I take her, pistoning my hips, thrusting in and out, sinking and reveling in the tight heat of her. Before I know it, her hand is between her thighs, and she's stroking herself, her breath coming in high, little gasps. "Oh god," she pants out. "I'm close."

"Same here," I say.

"Wait for me," she urges.

For a fleeting second, I want to say the same to her. *Wait for me.* To be ready, to fix myself, to be the man you want.

But the thoughts skitter away as lust grips me. I blurt, "Always," as I fuck her through her orgasm, which rattles the walls, the desk, and my goddamn heart.

Seconds later, I follow her into bliss, the world blurring away.

* * *

Later, after a shower, we lounge on the back deck. She's ditched the schoolgirl outfit, and she looks damn good in leggings and a comfy T-shirt. I'm in shorts. We've finished dinner, and once again I'm thinking of those words.

Wait for me.

Would she wait for me? Could I ask her to? Is that the next step after this third date? I've been weighing all day how to broach whatever *this thing* is between us, but I'm not sure I have a handle on it yet. I'm about to ask something safe like *how's your dinner*, when she says, "I need your advice, professor."

Oh. Okay. We're back to the roles. Fair enough. "Yes, Miss Dumont?"

She takes her phone from the pocket of her purple leggings, then clicks on her texts, swiveling it so I can see the screen and the last one from her Mom. **What happens next with him? Will you see him next week when you return to the city?**

My shoulders tense. Shit. She wants to do this now. She's readier than me.

"That's interesting," I say noncommittally. I don't want to screw this up.

"See, I don't want to lie to my mother, but the situation is kind of sensitive."

"How so?" I ask carefully, letting her lead.

She nibbles on the corner of her lips. "I don't know what's next. I work with this guy, so I don't know what to say to him about what happens...well, next week."

My pulse speeds. My instincts tell me to shut down this conversation, but I try to push past them. I fight against them, as I open my heart a bit, cracking the door a little. "I bet it's hard for him too."

There. That's a start. That's being open, right?

"Maybe he's thinking about next week too?" she asks, sounding so vulnerable as she finds a way to ask me what happens when we're back in the city, back in the studio, back in the real world. When we've left this make-believe land in the rearview mirror.

She's always been so much braver than I am. I try to

meet her with the same emotions. "He doesn't know what's next either."

Her lips flatten, and she dips her face. "Oh."

Shit. That wasn't the way to be brave at all. No more role-play. I reach across the table, lift her chin, make her meet my eyes as I try again. "I want to see you again, Juliet. So badly. You have to know that. Please know that." I sound desperate. I feel desperate. There's something else, too—something deep and powerful, something like forever—as she gazes at me with hope in her eyes. I want to run *to* that something else and run *from* it. "But I don't know how to be a good...partner."

Even saying the word scrapes my throat.

"Right. Because of..." She waits for me to finish the thought.

If I could tell Sawyer, I could tell her. At the very least, I need to be honest with her about my fears. "I wasn't there for Elizabeth. I'm not sure I know how to be there."

"I wasn't suggesting *that*," she says. It's prickly, but in the way an animal bristles its fur in self-defense.

"I know you didn't mean marriage," I say gently.

"I just meant next week." There's hurt in her voice, but she tries to keep it at the edges as she clears her throat and adds, "That's all, Monroe."

It's like she's saying: Can you do even a little? Can you see me next week?

But with her, there's no *just next week*. There's no halfway. My chest aches as I look at her. I can't test out a few more dates with someone I feel this much for already. What if it doesn't work out? "Relationships are like…" I cast about for an analogy. "The piano. I like the way it sounds. I want to play it. I can tap out Chopsticks. But you deserve *Ode to Joy*."

She's quiet for a long, painful spell. "I get it." She picks up the plates from the table, saying in a soft, sad voice, "Goodnight, Adam."

As she retreats inside, new awareness dawns. For this last date, she chose a man almost exactly like me.

30

A PIECE OF MY MIND

Juliet

Thank god for Eleanor's house. There's so much to do on Saturday that we don't need to interact much.

I handle packing up clothes in the Closet of Wonders, putting my blinders on as I sort through feather boas, sequined dresses, and fabulous corsets. Chin up. Move on. Just like Eleanor's moving on from this house into her bright and bold new romance.

Monroe's out of the home most of the morning, handling yard work, then finishing up minor handi-work in the poker room. Good thing because I don't think I could handle seeing much of him. It hurts too much now. It probably will for a while. But it's better I face these truths now, and I can't even be mad at him. He was honest with me from the start right up until...

As I stuff a sparkly sapphire boa into a box, I blanch

inside. I don't even want to finish the sentence in my head. The echo of the words, *the end,* is too painful.

Swallowing down all these feelings that have no place to go, I close the box, stuffing the costumes inside, then dust off my hands. I leave and head to the storage room down the hall full of mirrors.

I don't want to face that either. But I need to organize it, even if the images of the other day bombard me. Before I reach the room, my phone buzzes, so I grab it. It's probably one of the girls, letting me know they'll be picking me up soon. I packed a canvas bag with my dress and shoes for tonight, so I'll grab it when Rachel arrives. I booked a makeup artist for all of us at The Ladybug Inn, and I am definitely going to need both the girl time and some cover up for all these emotions before the party. I'm so glad my friends are here. But when I click on the text, it's not from Rachel, Elodie, Fable or Hazel. It's my mom.

> Mom: Are you okay? You didn't respond to my last text last night? Now I'm worried, and now I'm really wondering too if I need to give this guy a piece of my mind.

A sad smile tugs at my lips. She's so Mom.

Juliet: Sorry! But no, you don't need to do that.

Mom: Well…what's going on then? We're dating wingwomen after all. Tell me, tell me!

I slip into the room with the chaises, sinking down onto the rose-colored one, facing my mom's text in this house full of…costumes.

Full of reflections.

On a day where I'll be turning to makeup and pretty clothes to gird myself for a party with Monroe.

Am I just dressing up all my feelings and hiding them? Oh god. That's exactly what I've been doing. I've been *playing*. Playing at dating, playing at love, playing at feelings.

Not just with Monroe. But with everyone, especially myself. I scroll back up to my exchange with my mom from yesterday, I should be honest.

With her, yes. But also with myself. She said she wanted me to have sparks and butterflies. For the longest time, I thought the algorithm was against me. But I'm pretty sure I've never truly let myself be vulnerable. I thought I was putting myself out there. But I didn't even fully do that with the man I was stupidly falling in love with a second time.

With a shuddery breath, I answer Mom at last, practicing honesty with her.

Juliet: No, we won't see each other in the city and I'm sad about it.

Mom: Oh no! I'm sorry to hear that. Want me to call? You kids always like it when I text before I call. So I'm asking.

Juliet: Thanks, but I'd just cry if you called.

Mom: Oh, sweetheart. I'm sorry you're sad. But it sounds like Monroe was helping a bit? Sort of like a dating coach, which made me think…Why don't I hire you one in the city? I did a Google search, and there's this married couple who'd be great for you. I just know the one is out there for you.

Tears slip down my cheeks, my throat tightening, my chest squeezing. I swipe at them with the back of my hand, not wanting to ruin the chaise. I pop up to hunt for a tissue, flashing back to the moment in Monroe's car. He didn't even have any.

Really, that was the sign I needed. Not the photo of the tree house, but the lack of tissues. He doesn't need them because he doesn't let himself feel. But me? I feel too much all the time and I hardly even know what to do with this mess of emotions.

I've never known what to do with them. I've thought I've been chasing sparks and butterflies, but I've just been looking for the comfort of a relationship, like my parents had, rather than opening my heart to the magic of fully loving and letting myself be loved.

I race to the main bathroom, yank at the toilet paper and tear off a chunk, then dab at my watering eyes.

After a minute, the tears ebb enough for me to reply to Mom with a *no thanks*, when the sound of footsteps grows louder. "Juliet? Are you okay?"

Breathing through the empty ache inside me, I step out of the bathroom and face my fears. No costumes, no playing, no student-teacher game right now.

I lift my chin. "My mom wants to hire a dating coach for me in the city."

Monroe blinks. Swallows. Then after a long pause, says, "I've heard they're good."

"I turned it down," I say, meeting his gaze. His blue eyes are brimming with sadness too. I get it. It's hard when you can't be what the other person needs, even if you want to. But wanting something isn't enough. You have to do the work. I do more of it as I find the guts to add, "I'm picking myself as my next relationship. The thing I learned from all of this was that it was never going to matter who I chose. All my positivity hid the fact that I didn't know how to do vulnerability. Some self-sabotaging part of myself was picking all the wrong guys. And when I did find someone decent, I kept him at arm's length and then wondered why he didn't want to stick around."

"That's not true," he says, always my biggest fan. Funny, how he needled me for so long, but underneath it all, he was right behind me, believing in me.

Except, he's wrong.

"It *is* true. I want sparks and butterflies, but I settled because I was scared. I wanted the reassurance of a relationship without the risk of one. Then, with you, I was truly open. And that's what I need to do going forward. But it's going to take me longer to get over this week than it took me to get over Mister Cheese Douche, so I'm going to take my time."

He furrows his brow, then says, like the words are strangling him, "Like some time off from dating?"

I nod, resolute. "Yes. I need to work on myself. I need to get over...my wish for next week."

He steps closer, reaches for me, his lips parting, his voice flooding with genuine emotion as he whispers, "Juliet."

He sounds heartbroken. Maybe he is. I don't think I can handle his heartbreak right now. Not when I feel too much of my own. I hold up a stop sign hand. "I understand all your reasons, Monroe. I respect them." A car engine rumbles nearby, then cuts off. I glance toward the bedroom door as if I can see the front door and, likely, Rachel beyond. "But right now, I need to just...do my makeup and meet you at the party. And then my friends and I are going to do karaoke after." I flash him my best smile, meaning it this time. "I won't make you do karaoke," I say playfully.

"But I would," he says, reaching for my hand, trying to hold on. "I want to be the man for you. Know that."

It almost sounds like he's imploring me to stay. But his eyes brim with both hope and, I think, resignation too. He doesn't think he's capable. He doesn't think he ever will be.

At least, he's being vulnerable too. That's all I can ask. "I do know that. Thank you for being honest."

He's not asking me to wait for him though. He didn't then. He's not asking it now.

There are words, and there are actions. I need both. I deserve both. Monroe knows it, and the fact that he knows makes me fall a little bit harder.

But he's not able to catch me.

"I'll see you at the party," I say, and since Rachel's here, I leave.

31

PITY PARTY

Monroe

Supposedly, when one door closes, another opens. But I've never been a big believer in that adage. You have to open your own damn doors, and close them too.

But this time I literally believe it, since seconds after Juliet takes off with my heart in her hands, Carter strolls in. My football-playing friend jerks his gaze behind him as Rachel and Juliet drive off. Then snaps his focus back to me, assessing me with shrewd eyes. "Dude," Carter says, shaking his head as he strides across the living room.

And...that's all it takes for him to read the room.

Standing in the hallway, still shell-shocked, still hollow as a jack o' lantern, I shrug. Listlessly. "Yeah."

"Seriously?" he asks, quirking a brow as he confirms his take.

"Yes, seriously," I say, voice dead.

He stops a few feet in front of me. "You're just letting her go?"

I wave a hand. "It's complicated."

"Heart surgery is complicated. *This* is easy."

I stare at him like he didn't just say *that*. "Just because something isn't heart or brain surgery doesn't make it easy. Just because something is about emotions, or choices, doesn't mean it's simple."

He holds up his hands. "My bad. When it comes to analogies, that is. Point is, this is easy."

I check the time on my phone. I'm not due at my dad's party for a couple hours and it doesn't take me long to get ready. I'm itching to get away from the scent of her, the feel of her, the thoughts of her. "I need to get out of this house. *Stat.*"

"Let me buy you a shot? That is easy."

I give him a humorless smile. "Good analogy."

We take off in my car and head to Mister Fox, a pool hall on the edge of town. At the bar, we grab stools a few spots away from an inked, burly guy who's even bigger than Carter. Since my buddy's six-three, that's saying something. The dark-haired man gives us a chin nod.

There aren't many of us here at this earlyish hour, so the bartender heads over to us. The guy looks a little like, well, a fox, with his tawny hair and sharp eyes. "What can I get for you?"

"Two shots of Adictivo," I say.

"Coming right up," he says, then heads to the end of the counter to hunt for the tequila bottle.

Carter wastes no time, dealing me a hard stare. "So what's the deal? Did you two break up?"

"No." You'd have to have been together to split up. "Not really," I correct.

He shoots me a dubious look. "Which one is it?"

My chest twinges with self-loathing. I drag a hand down my face, muttering, "She wants to try. I want to try. But I don't want to hurt her if I can't be the guy she needs."

"Maybe let her make that decision," Carter says, like it's that easy.

But...

Damn him. That's good advice. I never gave her a choice. "Could I?" Except, reality hits me like an anvil dropped from a skyscraper. "*Fuck.*" I curse louder than I intended. "She's throwing herself a breakup party. Fuck, fuck, fuck."

The big guy looks my way. "Maybe you need to make it a double."

"Maybe that'll knock some sense into him," Carter says, while pointing his thumb at me.

"Does he need sense knocked into him? That's my specialty," the guy replies, with a glint of mischief in his eyes.

"Are you a linebacker? They're always trying to knock sense into someone," Carter asks.

"Linebacker of sorts," he says, then nods as the bartender returns our way. "Name is Banks. Close protection officer."

The bartender sets down the shots, offering a

helpful smile along with the liquor. "Translation: bodyguard."

Yeah, I knew that. But I don't say that. "I probably do need the sense knocked into me," I admit.

The bartender takes off to handle some new customers, but Banks is all in. Turning his big frame toward us, he says, "Let me guess. You messed up with your special someone?"

"He did," Carter offers, clapping my shoulder, happy to pile on. I deserve the piling on.

Banks arches a brow. "And now she's left you *and* she's celebrating? Did I hear that right?"

With an *oh shit* whistle Carter whips his gaze back to me. "Exactly. You've got your work cut out for you, man. She's moving on."

Again, the assessment is quick and cutting.

And wholly accurate.

After my dad's retirement party, Juliet's throwing what amounts to a breakup party—her *favorite* breakup party—for me. The one where she hired a makeup artist, and they went out for karaoke. She's doing it to move on from me.

Even if I asked her, there's no way she's going to wait for me.

Everyone is moving on in their lives but me. What am I doing with my life? "And I'm throwing myself a pity party," I say, turning the shot glass as aimlessly as I'm living my life.

Banks snorts. "No one wants to be invited to that."

That's the damn truth and so is this one. There is no waiting. There's only *now*.

I need to find a way to keep Juliet. Because what if I could be the man she needs? What if I could make a go of it? What if I could let *her* decide if I'm good enough instead of making the decision for her?

You don't ask a woman to wait for you. You treat her like the queen she is. I knock back my shot, pay for all our drinks, then take off with Carter, making a pit stop on the way.

32

PAPA BEAR

Monroe

There's just one little problem.

This party. Time *is* running out now after my errand, and I promised my dad I'd be there. Promised him I'd make a speech. Promised Juliet I'd take her as my date. She'll be meeting me soon. Even though I let her down, she'll still show up. I don't deserve her, but I'm going to try with everything in me.

I pull into a parking spot at the golf course in Duck Falls, arriving early. Wishing I could speed up time, I race walk into the clubhouse. Dad's chatting with a woman in chef whites. She gives a nod, then heads to the kitchen.

He turns around and scans the room, spotting me quickly. I head to him, tugging on the cuffs of my suit jacket, antsy to get this show on the road. Eager for the party to end, so I can take Juliet out. I hope.

When she arrives, I'll ask her on a proper date tonight.

I'm still working through what to say to her as my dad reaches me. "You're antsy."

It's that obvious? "I'm fine," I say, keeping up a wall.

His brow knits. "You sure?"

No, I'm in a total funk, and I'm this close to losing the love of my life, and maybe I already have, and I wish she were here, and I need to make sure she doesn't move on from me.

But fuck walls. I need to be more honest. I should start with him. "Not really," I admit.

Dad sets a hand on my shoulder, guides me down a quiet hallway. "What's going on with you, son?"

He hasn't asked me that in years. "Do you *actually* want to know?"

There's a long silence. He blows out a breath. Drags a hand through his thick gray hair. He's gearing up to say something important and the last time he said something important to me he taught me how to shave. It's been years since we talked for real. "I do. And here's why. I've been planning my retirement for a year now. And the first thing everyone asks is if I'm excited to spend more time with family. It's made me realize that I've done a terrible job of it. All that time fixing other people, and I never realized that our family is broken."

I freeze. Did he truly just say that? Something that observant? But then, he shocked me on the course when he admitted he listened to my podcast. I guess this is the week for surprising me.

"Why do you think I invited all of your friends to

this party?" He continues. "It's not because I don't have friends to invite."

I'm even more surprised, but a little confused too. On the golf course he said he invited them to make it more enjoyable for me. But I guess I didn't truly believe him. Perhaps I thought he'd just wanted adulation and admiration from colleagues. And that the addition of my friends was...well...to fill the room.

Maybe I should try listening more. "What do you mean?"

"I wanted you to be with your friends," he says, in an earnest tone I rarely hear. "They've become your family. I can tell that from your show. I get that. That's on me. But maybe when I stop working, we can..." He stops, clears his throat. He's not used to trying. It must all be so awkward, like learning to walk all over again. "Start...over?"

I definitely didn't have *put the past behind us* on my father-son bingo card tonight. But it sounds like a damn good idea. "As adults? Not as father and son? Not as someone who judges me?"

He takes that on the chin with a guilty as charged nod. "Yes. As adults."

I don't know if it's possible, but when someone offers you an olive branch, you should take it. After all, I'm willing to try. That's what my entire career is based on after all. *Trying.* That's what love is based on. *Trying.* "It might not be easy to fix this, Dad. A lot of things I'm realizing that are broken in *my* life tie back to you. But it's on me now to fix my own stuff."

"Maybe I can help?" He offers, and there's no judgment. No arrogance. Just a simple offer.

I take it. "I fell in love with Juliet, and I need to tell her before I lose her."

He slices a hand through the air, pointing to the exit. "Go get her."

A short laugh bursts from me. "Well, that's my goal."

He brooks no argument. "No. Do it now. Get her now."

"But it's your party," I insist.

His voice goes deeper, all papa bear. "But it's your life. And life is short. I should know that as well as anyone."

But the doors are opening, and guests are streaming in. Which gives me an idea. "What if," I begin.

I tell him and agreement flashes instantly in his eyes, then delightful deviousness. "And since it's my party, I'm going to change the schedule right now."

33

EXTRADATE

Juliet

With my simple sapphire blue dress, a French twist and classy evening makeup, I walk into the clubhouse. I look damn good. I need this look tonight to cover up the ache inside me.

"You've got this," Elodie says, squeezing my arm as we walk inside, her retro red polka dress swishing against her knees.

"We're going to be right there if it gets hard," Rachel reassures, looking equally gorgeous in a pretty fuchsia sheath dress.

"We've got you. Always," Fable chimes in, stunning in a black silk number.

Hazel's here too, but she had to take a call and said she'd join us soon.

My throat tightens, but that's been happening all day. "It's much harder to be the one having the breakup than it is to be the planner," I say to my sister and my friend.

"I know," Rachel says, since she's been there and done that. I hosted her breakup party when she moved back to San Francisco once upon a time.

People need more care and guidance for heartbreak than we give them. "Maybe I'll look into hosting retreats for the heartbroken once mine's put back together," I say, and the thought gives me new hope.

"Look at you. Always thinking of the future," Rachel says, cheery and bright.

"You can't stop being a futuristic optimist," Elodie says as her man Gage catches up to her and plants a kiss on her cheek.

"You telling everyone what to do?" He teases in his gruff tone.

"What? Me? Never."

"Yes. You. Always," he says. "Always making trouble."

She laughs, then shoos him away. "Go make yourself scarce. It's girl time."

"Say less," he says, knowing the sanctity of those words, then he smiles at me and heads off.

I smile back, grateful for the all-around support even though tonight I don't feel so optimistic, but soon I will. Thanks to my friends. "C'mon," Fable says, offering an arm. "Let's see our friends Veuve and Clicquot."

"My besties," I say.

"And they never let you down," she adds.

We head straight for the bar, grabbing champagne to toast to my new future.

Dating me.

"Here's to hot solo dates," I joke, lifting a flute then looking around at the clubhouse, with its fireplace, veranda beyond the dais and understated party decorations—silver streamers and gold and silver balloons floating up by the ceiling. The place is packed already, with easily one hundred guests. There's Agatha from the café at The Ladybug Inn chatting with a woman I spotted when I popped into Clementine's earlier in the week. Over in another corner, I'm pretty sure I recognize some men and women I saw streaming out of the Downward Dog All Day studio. But I don't see Monroe or the guest of honor. "I should find my date though. I promised I'd join him tonight."

"I'll track him down," Elodie says, but it comes out as a growl, like she'd like to throttle him.

She is the protective one.

"And I'll give him a piece of my mind," Fable adds.

They're both the protective ones, actually. I'm lucky like that.

We scan the guests in their party clothes, suits and cocktail dresses, barely a smidge of color, which seems on par for Monroe's dad. Then the clink of a fork against a glass interrupts my hunt.

I turn toward the front of the room, where floor-to-ceiling windows overlook the veranda and the rolling hills of the golf course beyond. Monroe's dad bounds up the steps onto the dais, a microphone in hand.

I lift a brow in curiosity. I know a thing or two about

parties, and usually there's more mingling before the guest of honor makes a speech.

"Thank you all for coming," he says, getting right to business. "It's great to see everyone. I've been excited about this party for a long time, but especially since my son is here and he wants to say a few words to kick this off. Without further ado, here's Monroe."

He didn't call him Doctor Blackstone. He called him by his first name. That's sort of sweet.

Monroe strides to the stage, and my breath catches. He's so handsome it hurts. I wish I'd had the chance to grab a moment with him so he knows I'm here, rooting for him, no matter what happens between us. It can't be easy for him tonight—coming here to praise the man who's complicated his life and twisted up his whole worldview.

His dad hands him the mic, then gives him a man hug with its familiar choreography. The clap on the back, the pull him in close, but never too close.

But his dad doesn't let go immediately. He whispers something. From a distance, I can tell there's a faint shift in Monroe's lips, a word shared quietly, maybe even a thanks.

That warms my heart.

Then, when his dad leaves, I gird myself. I made a promise to be here, so I give him all my focus, waving subtly.

His gaze holds mine, and there's that same look he gave me last night at the table, when he held my chin and said *I want to see you again*. I long for him, a pang that reaches down to the tips of my toes.

"When my father asked me to say a few words tonight my first thought was *no way*."

Nervous laughter skitters among the crowd. They aren't sure if this is going to be a roast.

That's not Monroe's style though. But there is something different about him tonight. A more intense determination. He's not talking in his podcast host voice. He sounds like...just a guy.

"I said *what do you want me to say*? I've never given a retirement speech. Do I say *he's a great doctor and teacher*? And my father said *It's practically writing itself*." He turns the other way. "And that's true. He is a great doctor and teacher." Monroe gestures to the crowd. "Many of you are here because you work with him. Or you were taught by him. You know that about him."

Monroe walks to the front of the stage, like he's gathering his thoughts for the next part. He's not holding note cards. There's no prompter. He memorized this. "What you might not know is he's always been my inspiration. He's why I went into medicine, before I switched. He always wanted to be the best, and I wanted to be the best in my field too. I still want that."

I smile, even in spite of my own heartbreak. The man tries so hard. He wants so deeply. He gives fully of himself.

Monroe stops, his eyes lasering in on me once more. My heart stutters, then thumps harder.

I hope that'll stop soon, this wild reaction to him. I hope it won't do that in the studio.

"But my dad had an inspiration of his own,"

Monroe continues, voice growing even stronger as he looks to the crowd, and to me. "Love."

He says it with such familiar reverence that I lift my hand, touch my chest, feeling his words.

"My mother allowed him to work the way he did and to be the best. Losing her affected him deeply. So deeply that it kept us from being the best father and son we could be," he says, voice catching, his emotions seeping through.

Damn you, Monroe. My eyes fill with tears. I purse my lips, trying to swallow them down, so I don't ruin my makeup. I never imagined he'd try to heal the rift with his father tonight. I rustle around in my clutch for a tissue, but Rachel hands me one, knowing me so well.

Monroe's gaze slides from mine, landing on his dad on the other side of the room. A solemn look passes between them, his dad nodding proudly. "We're going to make up for lost time now that he's got nothing to do but be the best golfer at the country club, right, Dad?"

Doctor Blackstone smiles. "Yes. Because life is short," he calls out.

Monroe nods sagely. "Because life is short. You never know how much time you have left. And I've made some mistakes with my time. I put being best above...relationships." His gaze hunts for mine, then locks, like he won't let go of me. It's intense and passionate like he was for me all week. "And this week, I put 'staying safe' above taking a chance on love. But someone very wise recently told me that the best decision you can ever make is to be open. That decision inspired me. *She* inspires me."

I gasp. The tears slide down my cheeks, and I swipe and swipe.

"In fact, she's been inspiring me for a long time. Since I first saw her again years ago in Darling Springs. I let her get away from me then. But I won't let her get away from me now."

I swallow past the knot of emotions in my throat, but the knot grows bigger, stronger. This feels so unreal. My stoic, cool, controlled man declaring himself for me, in front of his hometown, our friends, his father, and, most of all, himself. "Juliet, I can't stop thinking about you. I can't stop falling for you. I don't think I'll ever be at my best without you. And I want next week, and the week after, and all the weeks, all the time with you. I want to be the man for you always if you'll have me."

I'm a mess, tears streaming, heart soaring, skin tingling. A hand pushes on my back, urging me forward.

Right, yes. Walking. I can do that. As I put one foot in front of the other, the crowd parts, the partygoers cheer, and I run the rest of the way to the dais in heels. The man I fell in love with eight years ago, picks me up into his arms, and kisses me in front of the party.

A declaration.

A choice.

He kisses me more passionately than I'd expect in front of a crowd, but no one seems to mind. Least of all me. Especially when he dips me, bestowing one more soul-deep kiss, before he tugs me up, then whispers, "So you'll take a chance on me?"

I smile and I laugh, and I manage to say, "Was that not clear just now? I'll take all my chances with you."

"Good. Then this can be our fourth date tonight, and tomorrow we'll have the fifth, and then when we return the sixth..."

"So it's like an ExtraDate?"

"All the ExtraDates."

He kisses me once again, giving me sparks and butterflies.

34

LIKE FATHER, LIKE SON

Juliet

Monroe holds my hand as we circulate through the clubhouse. It's the best thing ever. Pretty sure I'm glowing. Though it might not be just from our interlocked fingers as we chat with his father's friends and colleagues.

This flush I feel inside and out is probably from the kisses Monroe keeps giving me. The soft brushes of his lips on my cheek. The curl of his hand around mine as we walk. The way he sweeps loose tendrils of hair off my neck and steals kisses.

After we peel away from a pack of doctors who high-five Monroe for "doing something tougher than heart surgery," he guides me outside, onto the veranda where he tugs me against him. The Gershwin tune grows fainter as we move into the corner, away from the windows.

"You're really mine." It's a statement, but it's full of wonder like he can't believe his luck.

I'm all tingles and starlight as I roam a hand up his chest, reassuring him. "Did you not read the assignment last night, professor?"

"Did you not remember what we *did* on the desk, Miss Dumont?"

I laugh, shaking my head as a summer breeze rustles a nearby tree. "You're not winning this one. I bet I told you already."

His brow knits. "I bet you didn't."

I swat him, but he grabs my hand, brings it to his mouth, kisses me again. "Mmm."

"I wrote out the assignment. Including the words— *Take me, I'm yours.*"

He stops kissing me. "Right. But I thought that was the student writing to the professor?"

"Your cluelessness is as adorable to me as my ladybug love is to you," I say, and his lips go all Cheshire cat for a second. "I picked Adam because he's just like you."

"Right. I *did* figure that out." But he ends the sentence with a curious stare. He's trying to put two and two together.

I *could* give him a hint, but nah. I think I'll wait this out. "You can do it," I urge play.

His eyes flicker as he assembles the clues. "Oh! Oh shit. You showed me a date...*with you.*"

I separate from him to slow-clap. "And he *can* learn. The teacher becomes the student."

Monroe rolls his eyes at himself. "Get ready for a whole lot of learning. Or un-learning."

"I'm here for it," I say genuinely, meaning it from the bottom of my soul. Then I rope my arms around his neck, bringing him close to me again, kissing his scar, before I say, "And yes, I was showing you a date with me. Fun and feelings."

He sighs. "I'm sorry I didn't quite get it."

I shake my head, exonerating him. "I think you did get it. You're here. Right now. It's all a process, right? That's what my brother said about you. That I should be patient because you're a work in progress."

Monroe huffs out a laugh. "Sawyer doesn't mince words, does he? He point-blank asked me Thursday night how long I'd been into you."

I'm eating up every word. "And what did you tell him?"

"I spit out my beer."

"That long, huh?"

He laughs, then gazes at the inky sky. Stars twinkle above us, brighter than in the city. "But I'll tell you," he says, gaze returning to mine, eyes bright and clear. "It started eight years ago. Then, I left for New York, and our lives changed."

I nod, understanding perfectly. "We went in different directions. Different lives. Different romances."

"Yes," he says, speaking frankly of the years apart. "Then when I returned to San Francisco after my divorce and we started working together on the podcast, I just thought of you as the co-host who drove me a little crazy."

Goosebumps spread down my bare arms as we tell the story of us. "I was your frenemy?"

"Maybe so. The woman who got under my skin. The woman whose dating life I was a little obsessed with. The woman I couldn't wait to see every week, but I couldn't put all those feelings into words," he says, then shakes his head, amused at himself. "Sawyer was definitely right. I'm a work in progress." He pauses, then takes my hand, curls his fingers through mine. "You don't mind?"

It's asked with such vulnerability that I fall in love with him a little more. My heart flips around in my chest and I'm so glad I can let myself get used to this fluttery feeling around him. "We can be works in progress together."

"Good. Now speaking of works in progress there's something I have to show you when we get home."

"Ohh. Is it reverse cowgirl? Because you forgot about that."

He squeezes my ass, then spins me around, drags me against him, my back to his chest, his lips on my neck. "Never say something so horrible again. I did not forget that. And just for that I will prove it to you tonight."

"You better," I say, rubbing my ass against him.

But after a few seconds, he gently pushes me away. "We should go back inside."

"We should."

"We should circulate at the party."

We don't make it inside for another twenty minutes.

When we do, I gasp. "Your dad's dancing with some-one," I say, nodding toward the guest of honor, dancing with an elegant woman about his age, who reminds me of Lady Danbury.

"That's Jada. She's a doctor too. Loves golf. Recently retired," Monroe says, warmth in his voice.

"Do I detect a theme? Like father, like son?"

He shoots me a doubtful look, then pulls me onto the dance floor, where he keeps me close as the music plays, and we sway together at last.

As I rest my cheek against his, I steal a glance at his father. I do detect a theme. Both men, trying to repair their relationship so they can start over.

My heart is full.

35

THE GANG'S ALL HERE

Monroe

It's about damn time.

Back at the house, I'm finally able to show her what I did earlier today. Been wanting to all night. After I toss my suit jacket onto the living room couch, I take her hand and bring her out to the back deck, the outdoor light on.

This deck feels like our special place. We've planned our dates here. Ate our meals here. Let down our guards. I sit in the Adirondack chair and bring her onto my lap.

"This is what I want to show you," I say.

She twists around, eyes on me as I undo the buttons on my cuffs. Anticipation flickers in her bright greens as she watches my every move. I feel the same way. I hope she likes this. When the cuffs are rolled up, she tilts her head, studying my left arm.

I don't say a word. Just hold my breath as she searches the red rose, the dahlia, then the calla lily. Her lips tilt, shifting up, up and into...astonishment.

"It's so tiny," she whispers.

"Yeah," I say, heart thudding harder, louder.

She lifts a hand, her finger tracing the air above my new ink. "You got a ladybug."

"I got a ladybug," I repeat.

"For me," she whispers.

"Always."

A little red ladybug sits in the lily. For her. On me. Juliet twists all the way, cups my cheeks, and holds my face. She doesn't kiss me yet. She presses her forehead to mine. "You're such a romantic."

I laugh and wrap my arms around her. "Maybe I am."

"You are."

"I love you," I tell her.

"You better if you're putting me on your skin."

"Go big or go home, they say."

She pulls back, her gaze immediately returning to my ink. "You got it today?"

I nod. "Blue Roses. The shop in town. I walked in there, and they did it."

"That was fast."

"It was necessary," I say, clearing my throat, needing her to know how much she means to me. "Hey."

"Yes?"

"You do deserve the best. I want to be that for you. Some days, I might not be. But just know I want to. I always want to."

Her smile radiates into my soul. "I do know that. And I love you too."

"Good. Now turn around, hike up that dress, and sit on my cock."

"Bossy." With a laugh and a purr at the same damn time, she obeys, tugging up her dress, skimming off her panties, then glancing back at me as I take out my dick, ready for her.

She sinks back onto me, surrounding me with her sweet heat in one sensual move. My chest heats up to furnace levels. I groan my appreciation for her. "You were ready for me, baby," I say as I curl my hands tight around her hips.

"You do it for me," she says, breathless already as she rises up and down on my length, taking me deep, seeking her pleasure, reaching her hands back to wrap around my head.

Like that, she rides me into the Darling Springs night.

* * *

In the morning, we're the last ones to arrive at the café at The Ladybug Inn. I only know that because Agatha, sporting her *I'm Pear-Shaped and Pears are Awesome* apron, has informed us as much.

"I'm guessing you two were quite busy last night after the party," she adds. "In fact, did you two sneak out for maybe twenty minutes in the middle of the party?"

Damn. She misses nothing. "I'll need to get you a

new apron that says *I'm a Hawk and Hawks are Awesome*."

Agatha bursts into laughter, then it disappears quickly. "You do that next time you're here, since that'll be real soon. Also, I told you so." She wags a finger at me. "Didn't I?"

Did she though? If I recall, she told me to come home more often. She didn't say *fix years of damage with your dad*. But I'm not here to split hairs. "You did," I say, giving her that little victory.

With a proud tip of her chin, Agatha says, "Good. It's nice to see family finding their way back to each other."

Juliet squeezes my arm. "It really is."

Agatha turns her attention to the woman by my side. "And I guess that means we'll be getting to know you here in town, Juliet?"

"I'll definitely come around from time to time," she says, and I like the sound of that.

"Good. Because I hear you're a breakup party planner. My sister Edith just split up with her longtime partner, and I want to throw her a party. I'm thinking motorcycles, bandanas, the whole nine yards. Can you do that?"

With a can-do smile, Juliet says, "We ride at dawn."

"I knew I could count on you. Let me show you to your table," Agatha says, then gestures to the biggest table in the joint.

Carter's left arm is draped around Rachel's shoulders, and she's shooting him a doubtful look as he recounts a football play based on the way he's demonstrating catching something with his right arm. By Rachel's side is Hazel, who's showing her husband Axel something on her phone. They're bent over, studying the screen, looking deep in debate. Bet they're debating some detail of their next co-written romance novel. Elodie's running her fingers through Gage's messy hair and the no-longer-single dad's relaxing and smiling, something he does a lot more of since she crashed into his life. Sawyer texted that he had to take off early with Katya, but I'll see him in the city this week. Fable's here too.

We arrive at the table, and Gage lifts a brow, gives an *I know what you've been up to* look. "Well, we didn't think you'd make it."

"I didn't either," Juliet offers innocently. "You have no idea what kind of stamina the Love Doctor has."

I was not expecting that. I jerk my gaze to her, but then go with it. "And her appetite is huge."

"That's what she said," Axel says, faux coughing.

Hazel rolls her eyes, chiding him with, "You can do better than that."

"I'm just warming up the banter muscle, sweetheart," he tells his wife.

"Ooh, I can't wait till it's hot," she says.

Carter pats the chair next to him. "Take a seat. I'm gonna take all the credit for this," he says, gesturing to the two of us.

"Why's that?" Juliet asks, sitting down first. I join her.

"I told him yesterday he was a dumbass who needed to go after his woman," Carter adds.

Hmm. Did he say that? "Not in those words," I correct.

Carter waves a hand dismissively. "Close enough."

"That's true," I concede. *Maybe let her make that decision* ought to be tattooed on my ass.

"Well, it did the trick," Juliet says, then pats Carter on the arm. "So thank you."

Rachel smiles, meeting my gaze. "Friends need friends who tell them they're dumbasses."

Elodie lifts her cup of coffee. "I will drink to that."

Fable nods appreciatively to Carter too, then to the rest of us. "And to friendship. Something we won't ever let go of, or get enough of."

Everyone seconds that with a hearty yes.

Juliet drops a kiss to my cheek, then turns to the table. "We should all drink to that."

And we do. After Agatha fills our mugs, the table toasts to friendship. And to friends who are just like family.

36

ALL THE DAYS

Juliet

"And welcome to another episode of Heartbreakers and Matchmakers," I say into the mic, dipping my face so I don't break into a giddy smile on air.

Sadie's at her laptop, shaking her head with amusement. She knows what we're going to tell listeners today. She's been having too much fun ribbing us since she learned we're now together. The *took you forever.* The *I saw it coming.* The *your flirting was endless.* I swear they're never going to stop from her.

Today's our first episode since we left Darling Springs and became not just co-hosts, but a couple. I'm giddy, yes, but also a little nervous about sharing that with our listeners.

But they made this possible in many ways, by listening to us, and giving us chances every week to spend time together. Time that brought us back together. After the intros, we slide into our first segment, where we address questions written in by listeners. When's the best time to share about your family, how to talk about sex-pectations, and when to end things.

After we tackle those topics, Monroe lifts a brow. "I have a dating question."

We planned that as the opener. But then Sadie surprises me by cutting in. Every now and then she joins us on air. I just wasn't expecting her to today. "Actually, I do," she says.

I blink, surprised. "Oh. Sure. The floor's yours."

With an impish grin, she says, "What took you two so long?"

Well, then. I smile at Monroe. "Valid question."

"And a very good point," he adds, then shrugs happily as he clarifies. "I guess now's as good a time as any to let all our listeners know that the Heartbreakers and Matchmakers are now...well, matched."

Sadie hoots. "Called it. Actually, the number of listeners who called it is probably about the same as the number of listeners."

I laugh. "Is that so? Has everyone been writing in and telling you we should go out?"

She nods vigorously. "Pretty much from the get-go." She leans back in her chair. "So, tell us. How did it happen?"

While we were in the thick of it, we agreed not to discuss our dating experiment on the show. We said we'd decide later if we'd ever discuss it on air. But on the drive back to the city, we made the decision and it was an easy one. We want to share our love, and our story. That's why we do this podcast—because we love love.

"I decided to give the apps another try while I was out of town. New town, new chance," I explain, then nod toward my guy. Monroe smiles slyly. "And I volunteered as her dating coach."

"You couldn't possibly have had an ulterior motive," Sadie deadpans.

Monroe acts aghast. "I just wanted to help."

It's my turn to smile slyly. Pretty sure he did have ulterior motives, but didn't know it. "And he was very helpful. So helpful he offered to be all my dates," I explain.

"How very generous," Sadie quips.

"Yes, I thought so too," Monroe retorts.

"You couldn't actually have offered so she wouldn't date anyone else," Sadie says, dry as the desert.

Monroe adopts a thoughtful look. "I mean, I *suppose* that was a benefit."

"Yes, just a little one," our intrepid producer says.

Monroe sneaks a peek at me. One that makes my heart flutter. And my lady parts too. "But at the time, I wanted to help." Then he laughs, self-deprecatingly. "At least that's what I told myself. I also couldn't stand the thought of her dating anyone else."

"And that wasn't a tip off to you?" Sadie asks him, incredulous. I'm having a blast watching her both tease him and grill him.

Maybe I'll get in on the action more. "Yeah, was it?"

"In retrospect," he grumbles.

"Fine, fine. So you taught her how to date," Sadie says, sketching air quotes, "By pretending to be other guys? So then, was she kissing you or some other guy?"

Ooh, good question.

"Me. Only me." His answer is instantaneous and possessive.

Sadie arches a skeptical brow his way. "You sure about that?"

"Positive," he says. It comes out as a growl.

"But how do you know?"

His eyes narrow, and he stares at me with heat and desire. "Because I do," he says, answering it in a defiant, but crystal clear way. Then, with his gaze locked on me, he adds, "Because I told her *I* wanted to. Because *I* said I wasn't pretending then. Because *we* talked and both admitted it was *us* kissing, *us* wanting, *us* connecting."

It's said with such passion that I can feel our practice dates all over again, in the form of flutters racing up and down my chest, settling in my core, heating me up.

"It was us," I say, caught up in the intensity of his admission. "Just us."

Sadie's waving a hand in front of her face. "Well, that clears it up, and I suspect we're going to need to sign off for now since Monroe and Juliet look like they're about to kick me out of the studio so they can break in this table."

That breaks us out of our lust tractor beam. I shake off the fog of hormones. Monroe drags a hand through his hair, like he's trying to clear off a cloud of lust too. "Sounds like we were practice dating as us, after all," he says.

Sadie smiles like *I told you so.* "That's what I was saying."

Monroe might have started each date pretending to be someone else, but with each one, we learned how to be together. We learned about each other. I'm not sure I saw it that way at the time, but looking back, we were dating each other all along.

"Let's keep practicing," I say.

"We will."

* * *

Thirty minutes later, we practice something else entirely in my bedroom. "Deeper," I urge.

My man drives into me, filling me so much, so fantastically that I arch my back. Pleasure ripples through me, stretching to the ends of me.

And, pleasure radiates in him too. I can tell from his sounds, his breath, and from the view. I'm gazing at the ceiling in my bedroom, where my very handy man indeed installed a mirror earlier this week.

That ass.

That back.

Those legs.

Those shoulders.

Monroe's body moves and pulses as he rocks into me, hips swiveling, then as he eases out, pauses, and...I moan a carnal, wild *yes.*

The sight of his ass muscles bunching as he thrusts into me are driving me wild. Sending me spinning. "Again," I cry out.

"Yeah? Like this?" he asks, a rhetorical question as he pumps into me, hitting that spot inside me again and again.

My toes curl.

My stomach clenches.

And my mind lights up. I'm watching him fucking me and it's the sexiest thing I've ever seen. This view of my guy. This view of him taking me, owning me, pleasing me.

I get it now—why mirrors are such a thing.

I've unlocked a new kink. "I love," I gasp out, my words bitten off by a wild cry ripped from deep inside me as my clit sings from the pleasure pressing down on me...

"You love what?" he prompts as he fucks me deep.

Words are hard. Thoughts are hard. My body is buzzing, my cells are pulsing. I'm close, so close. "I love watching us," I finally manage to say. "I just love... watching us."

This is my true new kink. My eyes wide open, enjoying the view of the man I love, taking me far into the night.

Another pump, another thrust, and my vision blurs and I spiral into the bliss of this love, this passion, this man.

In seconds, he's coming too, hard and loud, just the way I like it.

Later, we're lying in bed, cleaned up and sated, and he takes my hand. "Maybe we were practicing as us all along. I don't think I knew it for a while. Or that I wanted to admit it even when I did realize. But now I do, and you know what they say?"

He turns to face me, eyes expectant.

"Practice makes perfect?"

He nuzzles my neck. "Yep."

Someone else nuzzles my hair. Then purrs loudly, like an engine rumbling down the highway. I reach a hand up to scratch Mustache's chin. "I know you missed me."

My cat rubs his head against mine, answering yes in his own way.

Monroe scratches the feline's chin.

Yeah, I think I'll keep them both.

* * *

I have an hour before we hit the road a few weeks later, so I walk with Fable to Elodie's in Hayes Valley, catching up on her latest news along the way. Dating news.

"He's pretty fun," she says of a new guy she's started seeing. His name is Brady, and he's a stock broker. But there's some hesitation in her voice. I wonder if she can hear it too as she tells me more about him. "He's just one of those people who likes everyone," she adds but the report doesn't sound entirely great for some reason I can't quite put my finger on.

"I'm glad it's going well, but don't be afraid to listen to your gut," I say.

She gives me a friendly smile. "I hear you. I'll let you know if my gut says something interesting."

"You do that," I say, then flash back to a time at a football game when I saw her boss — the billionaire owner of the football team looking at her longingly when we were all in the suite. Something in his eyes made me feel like...he really saw her. Understood her even. "Maybe Brady is the right guy for you. Or maybe there's someone else."

"Can you send me this someone else right now?" She jokes, then waves when we reach the chocolate shop. "Have fun with your mom."

"I will. Can't wait to hear more about your guy," I say, then add, "Or your someone else."

She laughs. "Yes, me too."

As she leaves I head into Elodie's, scanning the shop for a familiar face. There she is. Mom's clutching a cup of hot chocolate and waving frantically to me from a table.

Like I could miss her in her pink sneakers, flare jeans and a sleek white top. But it's not even the fashion mom look that stands out. It's the glow on her cheeks.

"I seriously need your skin care tips," I say when I join her.

She wiggles a brow. "It's called...wait for it...a third date."

My eyebrows rise. "Is that so?"

"Yes. Tonight. Tell me everything I need to know about third dates these days," she says, then waves a hand. "Well everything you don't say on the podcast. Since I do listen."

It's sweet that she does. Though, that might also mean she knows Monroe gives it to me good every night. Hmm. Must rethink what I share. Not that I shared intimate details, but I don't exactly keep it a secret that he makes me grab the sheets every night. But I push those thoughts aside as I answer Mom. "Then, you pretty much know about the, ahem, sexpectations of the third date," I say.

She scoffs. "Please. That was the first date. Why do you think my skin looks so good?"

And I'm a little speechless. But I'm all ears as she asks me what to do if Josiah, the hardware store owner, wants to ask her to DTR tonight when they have dinner here in the city.

"I don't think you need to define the relationship tonight," I say.

"Oh good, because I just want to keep this little situationship we have for a bit longer," she says, then smiles.

It's the kind of carefree grin I never really saw growing up. I'm so glad it's there.

* * *

"I have the perfect tunes for our road trip," I declare as we cross the Golden Gate Bridge that afternoon.

"Is that so?" Monroe sounds highly suspicious.

"Trust me." With the Saturday afternoon sun bright and bold through the windows, I toggle through Spotify, hunting for the playlist I made, when Monroe reaches over to the console and hits a button.

News blasts through the car, something about politics and D.C. and it's all so screechy it sounds like a hyena sawing a trumpet. "Make it stop, make it stop," I whine, stabbing the off button.

"I sensed you were attempting to subject me to show tunes," he says.

"And you *did* subject me to news," I retort.

"All's fair in love and road trips."

"Don't make me play Rodgers and Hammerstein," I seethe playfully.

"Don't make me break out the top of the hour."

I flash him a scathing look as we wind through the Marin Headlands, on the start of our drive to Darling Springs.

"Fine," I concede. "How about a compromise?"

"What do you have in mind?"

"For every Pearl Jam, you give me one Tate McRae."

"I have no idea who that is," he says drolly.

"I know. But she's hot and makes me want to fuck you."

He hits the play button on my phone so fast.

I smile. I guess I won. He listens to my music the whole way, and when we get to our room at The Ladybug Inn he throws me down on the bed, hikes up my skirt and fucks me on all fours till I'm screaming his name.

Then we get dressed for a wedding.

* * *

With Monroe in slacks and a button-down—cuffs rolled up to show off the flowers and that ladybug ink I love madly—we leave the inn and walk down Main

Street. We're early for the wedding. Quite early. But Monroe was insistent we leave soon so we could walk to the farm even though it won't take too long.

We pass the arcade, Monroe tugging on my hand as the old Frogger machine winks at us from inside the window. "I have a confession," he says, using the same words he did that night of our first date.

Tingles rush through me as I anticipate him telling me he wants to kiss me, like he said that night too. "Tell me."

He pulls me close, tilts his head, then whispers, "I can't stop thinking about how bad we were at Frogger."

I swat his chest. "That's what you're thinking about?"

"I mean, we were terrible, Juliet. Awful."

I tiptoe my fingers up his shirt. "Probably because you couldn't stop thinking about kissing me."

"Ah, that explains everything." He tucks a strand of my hair behind my ear. "I've wanted to since the second I saw you in Darling Springs," he says, an echo of our first date at last.

The words thrum in my chest, making me more aware of every detail. The warm breeze, a summer afternoon, a heart that grows bigger. I kiss him, slow and tender and full of promises.

When we break the kiss, we resume our pace through town, passing the single-screen movie theater, its marquee advertising a Retro 2000s Night this week. "Hey, I wonder if they have a cheese and cracker night now?"

Monroe laughs fondly. "I'd almost forgotten you'd

made that suggestion. If they're smart, they took up *Anonymous* on it."

"And if they did, my snack snob legacy lives on," I say.

One night, we went there, but pre-planned our snacks. We'd lifted our noses in advance at the prospect of over-buttered popcorn and Junior Mints, opting instead to sneak crackers and cheese into the theater in my purse. Then we laughed and crunched our way through 1990s comedies on retro movie night, before we kissed as the credits rolled.

That week with him years ago was wonderful and poignant. We always knew it would end. Now, everything feels possible with Monroe. Now our days aren't winding down. They're unfurling in front of us, a red carpet into our future. "We should go tomorrow," I say, squeezing his hand, like I'm sealing this plan.

"It's a date. Since you did say practice makes perfect," he says, then comes to a halt. I startle, then follow his expression as his gaze drifts upward.

Oh. We're here.

We're under the awning with its logo of the woman in the claw-foot tub.

"Huh. Didn't realize we were here," he says, and it's cute. Truly it is how he tries to be all nonchalant about The Slippery Dipper.

"I had no idea either," I say, letting him have this moment. This stroll down the memory lane of our once upon a time summer romance.

He scratches his jaw. "Maybe we should go inside?"

What does he have up his sleeve? He's not proposing. It's way too soon. I'm sure of that. Maybe he just wants to buy me a bar of soap? Reenact that fateful day more than eight years ago? That's probably it since he seems in a romantic mood today.

"It's always a yes with you," I say.

We go inside, meandering only briefly before he says, "Let me get you something," he says, then heads for my favorite scents. The vanilla and honey. And I was right. He grabs a small candle, sniffs it, then hands it to me. I waft some into my nose.

Mmm. "Nice."

"Smells like you," he says, then before I can even return the favor and beeline for the rosemary and shea butter, he's at the counter, buying the candle from a red-headed man.

As Monroe asks how he's doing, how his kids are, how the wife is, I wander around the store, sniffing a strawberry body spray, then a coconut grapefruit body wash as Monroe chats more with the man.

Outside the store, he hands me the wrapped candle. "Here you go. Open it."

I already know what it is, but still I take it, undoing the purple twine, then the brown paper.

But there's no candle.

Inside there's a small box. From my sister's jewelry shop. I blink, confused but intrigued. "You got me..."

I know it's not a diamond. She doesn't sell those. Still, I'm so damn curious.

"Open it," he urges once more.

With a thumping heart and excited fingers, I tug off the top of the box. On a jewelry pillow, a silver chain sits, bright and shiny. Gently, I pull it out, and my breath catches.

It's a necklace with a charm on it of a little house, like the cottage Eleanor gave us, the home that brought us back together. "Oh Monroe," I say, a lump rising in my throat.

This man is so romantic. I don't know why I'm surprised. He's surrounded by it on our podcast, in his practice. But still, I'm thrilled and lucky that he is.

"It seemed...fitting," he says.

I unclasp it. "I want to wear it today."

"Yeah?" He sounds enchanted.

"I do."

"Let me help," he says, then moves behind me, as I brush my hair off my neck. Carefully, he drapes the chain around my throat, his fingertips dusting my skin as he hangs it just so, then as he links it together. "There. It's where I fell in love with you."

I shiver and smile all at once. "I know. I fell in love with you too."

A soft kiss from him makes my skin tingle. "Correction: fell in love with you *again*."

Correction: my skin doesn't just tingle. It sizzles.

I murmur as he kisses my neck on Main Street in the town where he grew up. The town where we fell in love again. Thanks to a house. "It's perfect."

When I spin around, I'm in his arms, where I belong. "Where's the candle?"

"I've got that too. It was just a cover up."

I laugh. "I figured as much once you gave me this. You had it all planned out?"

He nods toward the store. "That guy's big into giving gifts to his woman too. He helped me out with the switcheroo."

"You planned this to that degree?"

"I planned all our dates. Of course I planned this," he says.

Yes, of course. Since that's who he is.

We walk through town on this warm summer day till we reach Ripley's farm. There, Vikas and Bowen stand in front of their friends and family and pledge to love each other always.

"I now pronounce you together always," the officiant says, and I love that their vows are uniquely them. "You may now kiss your groom."

As they kiss, we all clap. I scan the guests, spotting Ripley in the back, her tattoos on display in her sleeveless dress. She looks relieved and happy, like she's glad she pulled off this wedding. A few rows away, a strapping man with the kind of watchful eyes that see everything is looking her way. "He looks like," I begin, whispering to Monroe as I nod to them.

"A bodyguard? Yeah, that's Banks," he says. "And he knocked some sense into me the day of my dad's party."

"Oh, I like him then. And I wonder if he likes Ripley? Or if he's watching out for her?"

"He's definitely watching her quite close," Monroe says. "And like he wants to know what she looks like naked." He swipes my hair off my neck. "It's a look I'm familiar with since it's how I look at you."

I love that look for me and as for Ripley and Banks, I'll have to ask her later.

For now, I turn all my focus back to the two handsome men walking down the makeshift aisle together. As they stop to say hi to all their guests including me.

Bowen looks me up and down with a knowing grin. "Looks like you're getting your happily ever after," he says. "Told you so, hun."

Then Vikas turns to Monroe, a stern look on his features. "Be good to her. She's one in a million."

I run my finger along the house charm, feeling the full weight of its meaning as Monroe drapes an arm around me and squeezes possessively. "I know and I will. I promise."

Vikas wiggles his eyebrows my way. "Like I said, yesss and please and sir."

That night as we dance under the Darling Springs stars, I can see our future clearly. It feels like today, and tomorrow, and the next day.

Monroe

A few weeks later, when we're back in the city, I get up early on a Sunday, the sun streaking through the bedroom window. Juliet's sound asleep, looking peaceful and happy. Even in her sleep. That's how she's appeared lately, and I'm damn glad I put that look on her beautiful face. Once I'm ready, I give her a soft kiss, then turn to leave.

She grabs my wrist and blinks her eyes open. "Hey."

"Didn't realize you were up," I say.

"I'm not but I need you to find out something when you play golf today with Wilder Blaine."

He's the owner of both a football team *and* the golf course in the city where I like to hit the links. Sometimes he's my golf partner, like this morning. "Okay. What are you angling for?"

She smiles. "I had this feeling he was into Fable."

I roll my eyes. "Juliet."

She sighs, like she's exasperated with me. "I'm a matchmaker. I can't help it."

"I promise nothing," I say.

But when I arrive I know I'll do everything I can to find out — for her. Love just has that effect on you.

And a funny thing happens when I play a round with the dark-haired, sarcastic, inked billionaire who owns the joint. I ask him a few questions about work, and before I know it, he's mentioned how brilliant the team's head designer is. How talented. "She's fantastic. I'm so lucky to have Fable Calloway working with me," he says.

The way he says her name makes me think Juliet is right.

When I return home I tell her everything, finishing with, "And I didn't even have to ask."

Her eyes pop and she throws her arms around me. "You're brilliant. And I just have a feeling."

I have a feeling too. As I nuzzle my face into her chestnut locks, I have a feeling I'm going to be happy for the rest of my life.

EPILOGUE: SOME KIND OF FULL CIRCLE

Juliet

Next Year

"Now, listen. You better have fun exploring the Galápagos," I tell Eleanor, who called into Heartbreakers and Matchmakers to celebrate the first anniversary of her honeymoon.

"Don't you worry. I am always having fun," our biggest fan tells us. "We have a snorkel lesson in an hour."

It's been almost a year since she gifted us that house. But really, she gifted us an opportunity to come together in ways I don't think either of us could have anticipated when we drove to Darling Springs that Sunday nearly twelve months ago.

We're in the studio for another episode of our show, which has grown tremendously since then. Sadie's in the booth with us today as always. She's become our full-time producer, and she's helped us as we've inked partnerships with dating coaches and experts, collaborated with Date Night, and interviewed romance experts from around the world on global dating trends. I even expanded into that line of champagne like I'd planned, thanks to my friend Aubrey. It's a fun tie-in to my breakup parties, which have grown too. Some of my clients want more *therapeutic* parties, so I've paired up with a shrink—not Monroe, but a woman I know—to offer those fetes to my party repertoire.

So much of the podcast's success, though, is due to Eleanor. She's a fairy godmother of sorts. "Before you go, I've always been meaning to ask you a question," I say.

"Of course darling," she says.

"It's something we've been debating over the last year," Monroe puts in.

"Is this going to be another bet?" Eleanor asks. "Because I do love your bets."

They've become a thing on our show in the last year. Little bets we tease the other with. We call them flirty bets and we nearly always report back on air. The consequences are romantic—plan a date night or give the other a massage. Some are downright naughty. Like, see who can edge the other the longest, or winner picks a sexy new position.

"I love our bets," Monroe says in a rumble that shimmies down my chest and goes straight to my panties. "Even when I lose I win."

"Flirty bets are the best bets," I say. "But this isn't exactly a flirty bet."

"Such a shame," Eleanor says, playfully pouty. "But fine, ask away."

I lean closer, eager to know the answer at last. "I have a feeling that you have a special connection to Darling Springs. Beyond just the house. When I saw your picture on social media, something about you felt familiar. I couldn't quite place it. I've never really been able to place it. But I've always been curious."

"Is that so?" She sounds highly amused.

"I say it's just coincidence," Monroe says, still the pragmatic one.

We don't always agree on everything. It makes for a good show.

"Monroe, don't you know Juliet is usually right," Eleanor says, chiding the man playfully.

I pump a fist. "Score. Alright. What's the connection?"

Without hesitation, Eleanor adds, "I own The Slippery Dipper. I was there the day you two met each other's eyes across a bar of soap. When I heard you were doing the podcast, I thought, *I remember that day. I had a feeling about the two of them.* I called in," she says.

You couldn't wipe the smile off my face if you tried. "No kidding?"

"Swear. Kind of funny, isn't it?"

Monroe's bright blue eyes sparkle. "That's some kind of full circle."

"I had no idea you owned the store or knew us," I say, amazed at Eleanor's astuteness and also her silence. "You never said a word."

"Some projects take longer to bake than others,"

she says. "And I didn't think you'd want to hear it at first."

"Why did you think we were finally ready to hear it when you gave us your house then?"

"Because I felt it every time I listened to the two of you. You kept flirting, teasing each other, provoking each other. Someone had to do something to get you to see it."

"Like make us spend a week in a house together," I say, fingering the house charm on the chain. It's warm against my skin. Monroe's eyes drift to it then sparkle with passion.

"It worked," she says proudly.

She was there when we met again. She called in because of it. We helped her with her romance, and she helped us with ours.

"I'm glad yours is still going strong, Eleanor. Oh, and thanks for the corset."

"They're magic," she muses.

"I couldn't agree more," Monroe says in a sensual rumble that makes me think of things we'll do tonight at his home. We live together there with Mustache, who proved he's the world's most unusual cat by being sweet to Monroe from the start, loving on him, like he loves on me.

We let Eleanor go, and Sadie, with a devilish grin, gives the signal it's time to wrap up. I'm a good girl, so I nod dutifully. "And it's time to say goodbye this week," I say, segueing into our sign-off.

Monroe cuts in. "Actually I'm not quite ready to sign off. There's something we never really closed the loop on. Talking about this whole full circle thing and all."

"And what's that?"

It can't be our dating experiment. We wound up talking about that on the podcast. I'm glad we waited until after we finished the practice dates to decide to share them on air. It made the experiment itself much more authentic. So I'm curious what he has in mind.

"About a year ago we made a bet on your date with the artist. Your first ExtraDate, as you called it."

"I do remember that. Now all my ExtraDates are with you." After a year, I haven't stopped being a little giddy about our love.

But we've already talked about the bet on air too. We discussed it a few weeks after we returned from Darling Springs. I'd even admitted to all our listeners that Monroe was right, and the date with the cheese guy hadn't lasted more than an hour. That meant Monroe could ask me anything on air, which he did. He asked if I'd go out with him that weekend. That makes me giddy, too, remembering all the moments we shared with listeners about our love story.

"But we did go full circle about that," I point out, glancing at Sadie as if her face will give me a clue about why Monroe's ticking past our regular hour.

She's just heads-down on her laptop though.

"Fine. Then let's go full circle again," Monroe says.

Unafraid, I wiggle my fingers. "Bring it on."

He looks me straight in the eyes, his expression immediately solemn and hopeful. "Will you marry me?"

I freeze. I wasn't expecting that. He stands, walks around the table, and drops onto one knee. "You're the one who got away, and I'm so thrilled I got you back. I never want to let you get away again, Juliet Dumont. You're the best part of my life, and I keep wanting to be the best for you every single day. Even when I fail, you're there for me, and I want to keep being there for you the rest of our lives."

He reaches into his pocket, takes out a velvet box, and opens it. The diamond solitaire is bright and beautiful, and I'm already crying with no tissues in sight, but I don't care.

"Yes! A million yeses."

Then I kiss him on air. I don't plan to let him get away again either.

EPILOGUE: THINGS I KNOW

Monroe

"Of course we don't agree on when this whole thing started," I say one fine afternoon in Darling Springs.

"The podcast bet," my wife calls out cheerfully.

"More than nine years ago," I add, then clear my throat, turning more serious as I look at the crowd gathered today in the backyard, wildflowers surrounding us, lavender scenting the breeze. "But if I'm going to tell the story of our accidental dating experiment, someone should pick a starting point."

I've told this story a few times already. I'll keep telling it for a long time. Today, I'm sharing it with a half-dozen new couples here at the house in Darling Springs, as my wife and I debate the start of our dating experiment. Whether it was the day I wore *that suit*, or the podcast bet, or if it was when we walked into the house we were given, or maybe way before that.

We never agree, but we always enjoy sharing the

story with the couples that come here to The Horny House, as we call it privately. Publicly, we call it The Heartbreakers and Matchmakers Home.

We didn't sell it after all. We couldn't part with the place that brought us back together with its sheer sex appeal. We turned it into a place for couples' retreats, and we host them together. Those retreats have gone so well that the proceeds funded the podcast expansion. Now, we can use our dating experiment to help bring others closer together.

This house has an excellent track record. Well, it's no surprise, really. Once you've slept in a mirrored bunk bed, you just can't go back.

"But really," I say, continuing my story. "What I learned most of all is that keeping the one you love is all about the work, and the heart and the soul you put into it. Let's get started."

* * *

Grab Rachel's and Carter's friends-to-lovers, fake dating, sports romance and meet one of my favorite heroes of mine! Plays Well With Others is FREE in KU!

I think you'll also love Hazel's and Axel's enemies-to-lovers, grumpy/sunshine, only one bed in the room romance! My So-Called Sex Life is FREE in KU!

And you'll fall hard for Gage in Elodie's fake engagement turned into marriage of convenience romance with the sexy single dad! The Almost Romantic is FREE in KU!

Don't forget that Fable and Wilder's fake dating the billionaire boss Christmas romance, My Favorite Holidate, is coming to your kindles in November!

Want a sneak peek of Juliet's and Monroe's wedding day? Scan this code or click here!

PS. Stay tuned for the Darling Springs small town series coming in 2025!

EXCERPT: MY SO-CALLED SEX LIFE

Hazel

It's weird how, in this city of nearly 1.7 million, you can run into the same people all the time. But Manhattan's more like a collection of small towns. Axel returned to New York a month ago, and I've bumped into him twice. First time was at the arcade three weeks ago when I was hanging out with my sister and her fiancé, Milo. The last person I wanted to see then was Axel. But he's friends with Milo so I didn't have a choice.

Some days, it's downright claustrophobic here.

I also think New York, with its twisted sense of humor, loves to play chicken. Well, Manhattan, I won't back down from this challenge you're throwing at me in the form of my once-upon-a-time writing partner sharing a table for two with me.

Oh, New York, you don't know who you're dealing with.

"So, your next book," I continue, crossing my arms,

gaze locked on the man I used to call a dear friend. "Is it? More scintillating? More suspenseful?"

Axel hums, marinating the question, taking his sweet time with it. "As a matter of fact, Hazel," he says, lingering on my name, overemphasizing it like he always does with names. I know why he does it, but I won't let that soften me. "Scintillating and suspenseful is exactly how the *New York Press* referred to *A Perfect Lie*."

Somehow, I manage not to roll my eyes as I give him an almost-real smile. "That's sweet," I say as if I mean it.

With a cocky glint in his eyes, Axel shrugs, accepting the comment at face value. "Thank you. That one meant a lot to me," he says.

I stifle a huge laugh. Of course he loves reviews from pompous news outlets.

"I'm sure it did." I lick my lips and go for the kill, "It's sweet that you're still as obsessed with reviews as ever."

His expression falters, blue eyes flickering with what might be embarrassment. I've hit a sore spot. Good. But then his face goes blank like he's rearranging his thoughts to hide them from me. "I'm not obsessed," he says, defensively.

"Don't you know by now? You can't make everyone happy with a story." I fight off a smile. Hell, it's hard not to grin when I can bust him on the thing he loses sleep over—what everyone else thinks of his words. I tried to help him with this, once upon a time. Look where that got me.

Axel nods slowly, like he's letting my comments

sink in. "True, Hazel. That's so true. And you'd know better than anyone. You can't please everyone even if you stuff all the quirky pets in the world into your rom-coms," he says, grabbing his own rusty knife and shoving it into me. I simmer as he taps the Lucite frame that holds the QR code. "Want to order, sweetheart? Or are you ready to walk out?"

I burn brighter, hotter. I stare hard at him. "No, Axel. That's your style."

Without acknowledging my comment, he asks, "So you're leaving then?" His gaze drifts toward the door. He looks so hopeful.

Boo-fucking-hoo. I lean forward. "As if I'd give you the satisfaction."

He laughs. "You're going to stay just to vex me? You'll willingly irritate yourself just to irritate me?"

I stare at him, *pot-kettle* style. "Sound like anyone you know?"

He shoots me a *well-played* nod. "Fair enough. Then, may the most irritating one win." He picks up the frame, then looks back at me, gaze shrewd. "Or do you have more arrows in that quiver of yours to shoot my way?" He sits up straighter, almost spreading out his stupidly firm chest. "Go ahead. Hit me with it. I can handle it. Get out all your anger, sweetheart."

I clench my jaw, inhaling sharply.

This man.

I can't believe he used to be my confidante. My close friend. My writing partner.

But I won't let him see my hurt. I have to do better.

It's only a meal and maybe it'll be good practice for the reader expo we're scheduled to helm this weekend.

"I'm all good," I say as lightly as I can. "And yes, let's order."

I grab my phone, scan the code, then check out the menu, grateful for something else to focus on besides him.

He does the same, scoffing a few seconds later. Haughtily scoffing.

I take the bait. "Don't see anything you like?"

His eyes dart around the restaurant, then he lasers in on me, lowering his voice. "No. I just wish I didn't have to use my phone to order," he grumbles. "I already have to use it for everything else."

I get that. I'm a little phone-weary at the end of the day too. "Why can't a menu just be a menu?" I ask, without any vitriol or irritation, just a little same page-ness that surprises me.

"Is it so much to ask to have my phone off during a meal? But nope. They make us use it."

"Evidently it's too much to ask," I say, agreeing as I read the dinner options. They're limited, but surprisingly...inventive. "I didn't think a place like Menu would have roasted beets with pistachios on a bed of pea shoots."

"Did you think it would be steak and potatoes?" he asks, a little derisively.

And...that detente didn't last long at all.

"No, obviously I wasn't expecting *that*, Axel," I say, overemphasizing his name, like he does to me. "I just thought it would be minimalist food too. And as stark as the decor."

"Or the company?" he asks, but it's not biting. He sounds truly curious.

I don't give in though. "Your words," I point out.

"They are indeed."

He flips his phone so the screen's facedown, pushing it to the side of the table. I tuck mine into my purse as a man in a tailored shirt and sports coat swings by, flashing a *barely there* smile.

"Welcome to Menu. I'm the restaurateur. We hope you enjoy the experience of dining here and making new friends just as much as we intend to enjoy serving you," he says, like a robot. "Can I start you out with some wine? We have a Shiraz from Uruguay. The grapes are harvested under a full moon."

I blink. Is he for real? Also, who says *restaurateur*?

"I'll have a beer, please," Axel says.

"A martini for me," I say. "Thanks."

The man's brow furrows. We've flummoxed him. "Are you sure? I mean, the full moon."

Axel smiles. "And what does the full moon do for the wine?"

I knew he wouldn't be able to resist asking. Truth be told, I was gearing up to inquire too.

"It's how the grapes are harvested," the owner answers, speaking in a circle. "And what about food?"

"Is it harvested under a full moon?" Axel asks, and I snort, wanting to kick him to shut him up but wanting him to keep going too.

"No. It's foraged. My chief forager does it himself."

"Ah, of course," Axel says, then looks to me. "Ladies first."

I wait for Axel to pull the rug of the comment out from under me with a barb about how I'm no lady. But he doesn't, so I give the owner my order—the beets and the mushroom risotto, while Axel opts for seared salmon with rosemary and asparagus.

"Thank you. And may I wish you the best interaction with the real world."

He turns and goes.

I cock my head, watching him, trying to get a read on the guy.

Axel stares too, then turns back to me. "Do you get the sense they're trying too hard?"

"Just a little bit. I mean, foraged food?"

"And *restaurateur*?" he asks with an eye roll.

"Not to mention full moon grapes."

"Also, does this restaurant not know what the other hand is doing?"

"Right?" I say, enthused he keyed in on that too. "On the one hand, it's all *let's be digital and read the menu online*, and on the other hand, it's *let's go forage and experience people.*"

"It wants you to love its quirks, even though they make no sense. I knew this was going to be a mistake." Axel leans back in his chair, huffing, but also giving me a view of his annoyingly handsome face.

Why are jerks so hot?

Seriously? Who decided that sexy jerks could ever

be good-looking? With freshly fucked hair, and undress-me eyes, and those goddamn black glasses that get me every time, Axel Huxley is the sexiest jerk of all.

The worst part? When I see hints of the man I used to know in his clever remarks, his sly observations.

The way we once got along.

But I won't be fooled again. Hurt me once, shame on you.

Hurt me twice, and I'm going to write my own damn name in Sharpie at the top of my whiteboard list of people who've pissed me off that week.

I've made my own shit list plenty of times.

I put my self-protection back on, so I'm not fooled by the banter. "So, what's the story with you kicking the tires here tonight, Huxley? Is this how the Nefarious Ned hires a hitman to take down Brooks Dean?"

The corner of his lips curves into a grin. "You know my new hero's name."

I roll my eyes. "Obviously I know who Brooks Dean is." Only the former-lawyer-turned-avenging-bounty-hunter-for-hire who traipses around Europe, solving heists and retrieving precious stolen goods as he falls in love. "You did mention twenty million times he'd be your next hero," I remind him.

"If you say so," he says.

"Oh my god, what do you think I do? Read your publisher's blurbs that far in advance before the book comes out?"

He smirks, then points at me. "Don't you? You can't resist keeping tabs on me."

I scoff. "You wish."

"But Nefarious Ned? C'mon, Hazel. Give me credit. My villains have better names than that."

I wiggle my fingers. "All right. Serve it up. Your next villain. What's his name?"

Axel's grin turns wicked. More wicked than I've ever seen from him. "Hazel. Her name is Hazel."

Damn it. I walked right into that one.

But I'm saved by the restaurateur. The man in the sports coat returns with our drinks, depositing the beer in front of Axel, and the martini in front of me. Then he frowns. "I'm so sorry, ma'am. We're all out of beets tonight. Pea shoots too."

Bummer. I do love a good pea shoot dish. "No big deal. I'll skip the apps. Just mushroom risotto then?"

He winces. "Apologies. Our chief forager canceled the dish. The mushrooms made him mad. We have chicken with kale picked from our rooftop garden though."

"She doesn't eat meat," Axel cuts in. "What do you have for vegetarians?"

The man's eyes pop. "Um...I could bring you the kale and some pistachios on the side?"

Gee, that sounds filling. But I can eat edamame at home later. "I'll just have the drink. Thanks."

Another cringe. "Sorry. We can't let you sit here with just a drink."

I blink. "Really?"

"Truly. It's a rule," he says, apologetic, even though he's likely the one who made that punitive rule.

But even though he and his chief forager ran out of beets and pea shoots, I'm not going to bolt. I won't let

Axel have the satisfaction. I'm about to ask the owner to bring me the kale when Axel says, "Can't you make her something with vegetables? You don't want to be one of those places that discriminates against someone for their beliefs, do you?"

The restaurateur gulps. "No, of course not, sir," he says, then scurries off.

I look at Axel, begrudgingly appreciative. "Beliefs? Are we allowed to do that?"

"Sweetheart, it's a fucking pretentious restaurant. And the lawyer in me could argue it's a belief with full conviction."

The lawyer in him could argue anything.

But is his vegetable defense an argument for an argument's sake? Or does he *want* me to sit here with him? That would make no sense. I study Axel, trying to figure him out. "All right. What's your deal, Huxley? Why are you trying to get me to stay? That was a perfect chance for you to let me walk away and have the table all to yourself."

"Ah, but what fun would that be? Especially when I have to see you on Sunday. This is like a little unexpected dress rehearsal."

Ah yes, I'm a game. Got it. "Thanks for the reminder. I'd tried to erase that from my head."

"Same here. But the more you shoot arrows at me, the tougher my villain will be."

This time I don't walk into the comment. I march straight through it. "And that'll make it more satisfying when your hero kills her."

He grins, slow and devilish. "He won't kill her. He'll just tie her up and turn her in to the authorities."

I lean back in the chair. Yup. I'm not leaving.

Read the rest of My So-Called Sex Life, a spicy, enemies to lovers, only one bed in the room rom com FREE IN KU!

BE A LOVELY

Want to be the first to know of sales, new releases, special deals and giveaways? Sign up for my newsletter today!

Want to be part of a fun, feel-good place to talk about books and romance, and get sneak peeks of covers and advance copies of my books? Be a Lovely!

MORE BOOKS BY LAUREN

I've written more than 100 books! **All of these titles below are FREE in Kindle Unlimited!**

Double Pucked

A sexy, outrageous MFM hockey romantic comedy!

Puck Yes

A fake marriage, spicy MFM hockey rom com!

Thoroughly Pucked!

A brother's best friends +runaway bride, spicy MFM hockey rom com!

Well and Truly Pucked

A friends-to-lovers forced proximity why-choose hockey rom com!

The Virgin Society Series

Meet the Virgin Society – great friends who'd do anything for each other. Indulge in these forbidden, emotionally-charged, and wildly sexy age-gap romances!

The RSVP

The Tryst

The Tease

The Dating Games Series

A fun, sexy romantic comedy series about friends in the city and their dating mishaps!

The Virgin Next Door

Two A Day

The Good Guy Challenge

How To Date Series (New and ongoing)

Friends who are like family. Chances to learn how to date again. Standalone romantic comedies full of love, sex and meet-cute shenanigans.

My So-Called Sex Life

Plays Well With Others

The Almost Romantic

The Accidental Dating Experiment

My Favorite Holidate

A romantic comedy adventure standalone

A Real Good Bad Thing

Boyfriend Material

Four fabulous heroines. Four outrageous proposals. Four chances at love in this sexy rom-com series!

Asking For a Friend

Sex and Other Shiny Objects

One Night Stand-In

Overnight Service

Big Rock Series

My #1 New York Times Bestselling sexy as sin, irreverent, male-POV romantic comedy!

Big Rock

Mister O

Well Hung

Full Package

Joy Ride

Hard Wood

Happy Endings Series

Romance starts with a bang in this series of standalones following a group of friends seeking and avoiding love!

Come Again

Shut Up and Kiss Me

Kismet

My Single-Versary

Ballers And Babes

Sexy sports romance standalones guaranteed to make you hot!

Most Valuable Playboy

Most Likely to Score

A Wild Card Kiss

Rules of Love Series

Athlete, virgins and weddings!

The Virgin Rule Book

The Virgin Game Plan

The Virgin Replay

The Virgin Scorecard

The Extravagant Series

Bodyguards, billionaires and hoteliers in this sexy, high-stakes series of standalones!

One Night Only

One Exquisite Touch

My One-Week Husband

The Guys Who Got Away Series

Friends in New York City and California fall in love in this fun and hot rom-com series!

Birthday Suit

Dear Sexy Ex-Boyfriend

The What If Guy

Thanks for Last Night

The Dream Guy Next Door

Always Satisfied Series

A group of friends in New York City find love and laughter in this series of sexy standalones!

Satisfaction Guaranteed

Never Have I Ever

Instant Gratification

PS It's Always Been You

The Gift Series

An after dark series of standalones! Explore your fantasies!

The Engagement Gift

The Virgin Gift

The Decadent Gift

The Heartbreakers Series

Three brothers. Three rockers. Three standalone sexy romantic comedies.

Once Upon a Real Good Time

Once Upon a Sure Thing

Once Upon a Wild Fling

Sinful Men

A high-stakes, high-octane, sexy-as-sin romantic suspense series!

My Sinful Nights

My Sinful Desire

My Sinful Longing

My Sinful Love

My Sinful Temptation

From Paris With Love

Swoony, sweeping romances set in Paris!

Wanderlust

Part-Time Lover

One Love Series

A group of friends in New York falls in love one by one in this sexy rom-com series!

The Sexy One

The Hot One

The Knocked Up Plan

Come As You Are

Lucky In Love Series

A small town romance full of heat and blue collar heroes and
sexy heroines!

Best Laid Plans

The Feel Good Factor

Nobody Does It Better

Unzipped

No Regrets

An angsty, sexy, emotional, new adult trilogy about one young
couple fighting to break free of their pasts!

The Start of Us

The Thrill of It

Every Second With You

The Caught Up in Love Series

A group of friends finds love!

The Pretending Plot

The Dating Proposal

The Second Chance Plan

The Private Rehearsal

Seductive Nights Series

A high heat series full of danger and spice!

Night After Night

After This Night

One More Night

A Wildly Seductive Night

Joy Delivered Duet

A high-heat, wickedly sexy series of standalones that will set your sheets on fire!

Nights With Him

Forbidden Nights

Unbreak My Heart

A standalone second chance emotional roller coaster of a romance

The Muse

A magical realism romance set in Paris

Good Love Series of sexy rom-coms co-written with Lili Valente!

I also write MM romance under the name L. Blakely!

Hopelessly Bromantic Duet (MM)

Roomies to lovers to enemies to fake boyfriends

Hopelessly Bromantic

Here Comes My Man

Men of Summer Series (MM)

Two baseball players on the same team fall in love in a forbidden romance spanning five epic years

Scoring With Him

Winning With Him

All In With Him

MM Standalone Novels

A Guy Walks Into My Bar

The Bromance Zone

One Time Only

The Best Men (Co-written with Sarina Bowen)

Winner Takes All Series (MM)

A series of emotionally-charged and irresistibly sexy standalone MM sports romances!

The Boyfriend Comeback

Turn Me On

A Very Filthy Game

Limited Edition Husband

Manhandled

If you want a personalized recommendation, email me at laurenblakelybooks@gmail.com!

CONTACT

I love hearing from readers! You can find me on TikTok at LaurenBlakelyBooks, Instagram at LaurenBlakely-Books, Facebook at LaurenBlakelyBooks, or online at LaurenBlakely.com. You can also email me at lauren blakelybooks@gmail.com

Printed in Great Britain
by Amazon

42806997R00195